ECHOES

STEPH MACCA

Triggers and Warnings   VI

Dedication   IX

Recap from Unhinged   XI

1. Chapter 1   1

2. Chapter 2   10

3. Chapter 3   20

4. Chapter 4   29

5. Chapter 5   39

6. Chapter 6   48

7. Chapter 7   57

8. Chapter 8   67

9. Chapter 9   77

10. Chapter 10   86

11. Chapter 11   95

12. Chapter 12   104

13. Chapter 13   113

14. Chapter 14 — 123

15. Chapter 15 — 133

16. Chapter 16 — 142

17. Chapter 17 — 151

18. Chapter 18 — 160

19. Chapter 19 — 168

20. Chapter 20 — 177

21. Chapter 21 — 187

22. Chapter 22 — 200

23. Chapter 23 — 210

24. Chapter 24 — 219

25. Chapter 25 — 231

26. Chapter 26 — 241

27. Chapter 27 — 253

28. Chapter 28 — 261

29. Chapter 29 — 272

30. Chapter 30 — 283

31. Chapter 31 — 293

32. Chapter 32 — 302

33. Chapter 33 — 313

Book Three - Ravage — 322

Stalk the Author — 323

Triggers and Warnings

- ASSAULT

- BLACKMAIL

- BLOOD AND GORE

- BLOOD PLAY (VARIOUS LEVELS)

- CANNIBALISM

- CHILD ABUSE/NEGLECT (BACK STORY)

- CHOKING

- COFFINS/CASKETS

- CUTTING

- DIVORCE BETWEEN PARENTS

- DRUGS

- DRUGGING

- GLORY HOLES

- GROUP SPICE

- INFERTILITY

- KIDNAPPING

- KNIFE/BLADE PLAY

- LETTER OPENERS

- MENTAL ILLNESS (INCLUDING cPTSD, PTSD, BPD, SCHIZOPHRENIA, ANGER MANAGEMENT, OCD, DEPRESSION, ANXIETY, SUICIDAL TENDENCIES, BIPOLAR DISORDER)

- MIND GAMES

- MORGUES

- MURDER

- ORGAN EATING (BACK STORY)

- PERMANENT MARKING/SCARRING

- REMOVAL OF BODY PARTS

- SCARS

- SEXUAL ASSAULT (OFF-PAGE MENTIONS)

- SPANKING

- STABBING

- SUICIDE

- SWEARING (INCLUDING THE WORD 'CUNT')

- TORTURE

- VIOLENCE

- WEAPONS

What an unhinged good fucking reader you are.

I knew you'd be gagging for the monsters under the bed...

Begging them to drag you down to hell and rearrange your insides.

Welcome home.

Recap from Unhinged

"Sam is dead," I breathe out in a panic when I reach him.

Theo nods. "Yep."

He's so blasé about the whole situation that it makes me feel uneasy. Suddenly, I find myself doubting everything. Theo even told me himself he killed someone and would do it again.

Mr. Whittingham steps back into the hall at the other end, police by his side. I guess they are investigating it after all.

I feel someone staring at me, burning holes into the side of my face, and I look over to my left, surprised to find Damon. He's hovering in the opposite corner and when he realizes he's got my attention, he gives me a little smirk, tilting his head. It's barely registerable, disappearing as quickly as it comes and I wonder if I imagined it.

The police talk to Mr. Whittingham, their faces serious as they ask questions. Mr. Whittingham nods, looking around the hall. He lingers on Damon for a brief second, eyes narrowing before continuing on. When he reaches me and Theo, he pauses, facial expression hardening.

"What's going on?" I mutter to Theo quietly, staring in horror as Mr. Whittingham points towards us. The police look in our direction before heading our way, patients scattering to make a path.

Theo puts his hand on my back. "Don't say or do anything," he whispers.

There's an edge to his voice that sets off alarm bells and feels like the room is going to start spinning at any point.

It's like time stands still, the police taking forever to reach us, when in reality, it's less than a minute.

"Step away," the first policeman says to Theo, glaring at him. His wrinkly face and aging appearance highlights the fact he's been doing this shit way too long. I can see his hand positioned on his belt, near his gun, ready to whip it out at any second.

Theo steps forward away from me, hand rubbing along my back as he does. The policeman looks him up and down briefly, before turning to me.

"Are you Avery White?" he asks sternly.

I stutter, looking at Theo. "Ye-yeah," I answer, trying to figure out what's going on. I focus on his badge, reading his name — Constable Lennon.

The second policeman steps forward towards Theo, pushing him further away from me into the wall. It takes everything in my willpower not to yell at them to get away from him, but I keep quiet, just like he said.

Everyone is watching us quietly, my eyes finding Grey's as he approaches Damon. He's staring back at me coldly, his walls back up. I swallow, forcing myself to look away and back to Theo.

Constable Lennon reaches to the other side of his belt, grabbing metal handcuffs. My heart sinks as reality sets in, my worst nightmare coming true.

Theo did kill Sam.

As he steps forward with the cuffs, I move towards Theo before I can stop myself, wanting to protect him.

Constable Lennon grabs me, slamming me into the wall. I let out a whine from the impact, hearing Theo yell out as well. There's so much happening but it's almost like I hear Grey's voice from across the room too, but I disregard the thoughts, letting myself go limp as I'm pressed chest first into the wall.

Suddenly my arms are pulled back, my shoulders yelling in pain as they are forced unnaturally to flex. I let out a small cry, hoping they realize they are hurting me and I'm not going to physically attack them. I feel him pat me down, something scraping against my shirt as he grabs it.

I turn my head to look over my shoulder, gazing in stunned disbelief at the staff access card in Constable Lennon's hand.

I feel the cold metal on my wrists, the clicking sound reaching my ears as my hands are cuffed. Constable Lennon presses his knee into the back of mine as he tightens the handcuffs.

"Avery Elizabeth White, you are under arrest for the murder of Samuel Joseph Hallman. You have the right to remain silent..."

Chapter 1
Avery

"Ring around the rosie. A pocket full of posies. Ashes... Ashes... We all fall down..."

Do I tremble in fear? Laugh hysterically? Cry and scream until my lungs are torn to pieces?

What's the appropriate reaction to being framed for murder? It's one thing to be rightfully accused but another to be framed. What type of sick, ironic joke is this?

My wrist is red raw from the handcuff, the metal pulling and rubbing against my delicate skin. I'm chained to a desk in a cold, pale-gray room; an obvious two-way mirror in front of me.

I look like shit.

As I stare at my own reflection, mesmerized by my pathetic appearance, I can't help but wonder what my viewers think of me too. I feel like a circus animal, chained and put out for show.

Come one, come all. Hear the echoes of my hauntings.

I'm innocent—for once. But who is going to believe me? I'm the woman who murdered her father after all.

I start laughing, slowly at first, before it gets maniacally louder. On the outside, they must think I'm insane. I guess I am. But the truth is I'm haunted by misery. The ghosts of my past hold on to me, pulling me down. I tried to fight because I didn't want to drown. But maybe it's my destiny.

I should have died *that* day. But for a brief moment in time, I had actually started to believe that I survived for a reason. Now, I realize it was hopeless, wishful thinking. Because people like me don't get second chances. We're designed to live through torture, built to be the fallen and forgotten.

Well, it was nice while it was short lived.

At least for a short period, I got to experience happiness again and to some extent, freedom. I'm grateful for that.

Sing-song voices echo in the distance outside the room, and I'm not sure if I'm imagining them or if people are locked in the cells down the hall. All I know is that I'm alone, being watched like I'm a science experiment.

Are they waiting for me to break? Confess my sins?

Or maybe, worse still, they have forgotten me. I spent my whole life as an afterthought—if I was even lucky to be that. The irony of being forgotten after being arrested on the accusation of murder is one for the ages.

Time stands frozen, the clock on the wall broken. But even the clock is still right twice a day. Everything in this room mocks me—the clock, the metal chain around my wrist, my own reflection.

Finally, an officer comes through the door. In his forties, his gray stubble is neatly trimmed, while his blue eyes scan my bound frame. He sits across from me, chair legs scraping along the ground, sounding like nails on a blackboard. I flinch, and again, when his beige folder hits the table with a smack.

"Ms. White," he starts, observing my face carefully. "Do you know why you were detained?"

I shrug. "Constable Lennon said I was under arrest for murder."

It crosses my mind that he used the word *detained* rather than arrested. But I don't read too much into it. There's no hope here, after all.

"I'm Detective Vernon," he says, sounding bored. "As you are aware, a body was found earlier today at Lilydale Foundation Center. I'm told you knew the deceased." He pauses, checking his notes. "Samuel Hallman."

Flashbacks come in waves from the day I was arrested for Dad's murder. I've been here before, I know this line of questioning.

I know how this ends.

"Yeah," I answer. I'm not sure what else to say. I obviously knew him, and for whatever reason, they suspect that I killed him. It's not looking good—witnesses saw us fighting. People know he was put into the hospital after a brutal attack. It's so easy to point it back to me that I can understand why they assume it.

But I can't understand how the staff access card got into my pocket.

"I'm told that you and the deceased had a volatile relationship at the center."

I can't stop the cringe appearing on my face as shutters rack my body. Volatile is correct, but defining us as having some type of relationship—that's crossing boundaries.

For whatever reason, Sam hated me. He made my existence at Lilydale a living nightmare. Worst of all, he tried to hurt me. Who knows how far he would have gone if Theo hadn't stepped in and saved me.

Theo.

My heart bleeds as obsidian eyes materialize in my head. If Theo really did do this, I need to protect him. Like he protected me.

It's not fair if he goes down for stopping a psychotic rapist. These people in this very building, they are the ones who are meant to protect us. But no one protects us at Lilydale. We're left to protect ourselves, written off from society as the villains. I'd have been long gone if it wasn't for Theo... and Grey. Fuck, even to a small extent, Damon too.

For the first time in my life, it's clear what I have to do. Theo is one of the only people who ever gave a shit about me—made me feel special and seen. If there's one good thing that I can do with my life, the one time I can save someone instead of needing saving, then this should be it. I don't know what my future holds, but at least Theo might still have one.

"Aren't I meant to have an attorney present?" I ask, reflecting from his question.

Detective Vernon glances up, still blasé with our interaction. "You haven't been charged with anything—*yet*. We're just asking questions."

"That can't be legal," I scoff. "I had my Miranda rights read. So, if you are going to be using anything said here to charge me, then I'm entitled to have someone present."

He slaps the folder shut, leaning back in his chair. His mouth opens but before he can say anything, a knock sounds on the fading, blue door. We both turn in unison to spot a female detective putting her head through the gap in the doorway.

"They've arrived," she tells him without glancing at me.

"Send them in," he replies.

I look at him, then the door, trying to figure out who would be here. Only a few seconds pass before the door opens again, my eyes widening slightly at the familiar figure.

Margaret walks in, dressed immaculately as always. She gives me a warm smile as she enters. A second figure follows her in, a male I don't recognize.

"Avery," she says in a friendly tone, like we're old friends. "How are you doing?"

"Splendid."

Detective Vernon stands, gathering up his folder. "Let me know when you are finished," he grunts, leaving the room.

As soon as the door closes behind him, Margaret takes his seat in front of me, eyes darting down to the handcuff. "You're hurt," she points out. "I can ask them to remove it."

"Don't bother," I grumble. "Didn't you hear? I'm the big, bad killer again."

There's sarcasm dripping in my tone, and I have no idea if we're being watched on the other side of the mirror. Maybe that's what this is—a secret ploy for a confession. At least Margie knows the truth. There's a small bit of comfort in that information.

"What happened?" she asks, ignoring my comment.

I shrug. "I don't know. One minute I was there, the next I was here. I told you that place was too much. I never should have gone there to begin with."

My eyes shift to the male still hovering near the door, uncomfortable with his unfamiliar presence while we talk about my past. Margaret follows my line of vision, softly nodding to him.

"Avery, I'd like you to meet Alexander."

Despite being the obvious elephant in the room, he makes no effort to move. His green eyes narrow over my frame, eyes lingering on the handcuff for a brief moment, before body-checking me with his gaze. It's as if he's trying to get a read on me, and I shift awkwardly, turning back to Margaret.

"What's going on?"

Margaret gives me a tight smile. "Alexander is here on behalf of the Foundation Center. He's one of the board members."

"Isn't that a conflict thing?" I ask, bewildered. "Or is he here to formally revoke my place?"

"Ordinarily, yes," comes a snarky reply from the doorway. He steps closer to the table, still observing me in a way that makes me want to rip my skin off my bones. It's not sexual—but it's certainly predatory. His salt and pepper hair is neatly styled back, his expensive Armani suit fitted to his tall frame.

Must be all those fees and donations they get...

"So, why are you here?" I question softly. I'm completely confused, exhausted. I had expected to be grilled for several hours by detectives until I broke, then thrown into a dark, cold cell. But this meeting was not something I could have anticipated. If Margaret wasn't here, I'd be really lost. Her familiar presence is grounding me slightly, stopping me from breaking.

Alexander doesn't answer me, instead looking at Margaret and giving her a curt nod. She sighs in relief, giving me a smile.

"Will someone please tell me what the fuck is going on?" I snap in frustration.

"The Lilydale board has agreed not to press charges and will also accept you back into the center. However, there will be some stipulations, of course," Margaret says, looking excited like she's delivering the best news of all time.

My stomach drops. "And if I don't want to go back?"

I don't know what I want. Of course I'd rather be there—a thought I never imagined myself thinking—but at what cost? Who knows what disrepair Lilydale is in now and what my future holds?

Who knows what will happen to me?

If this murder thing goes away, that's one thing. But I'll still have to face the wrath of the other patients. And Damon.

Oh, my fucking God.

Is this one of Damon's games? Getting me locked up after framing me, just to then bring me back to his kingdom to demonstrate his power?

At least I'd be with Theo. But something tells me, I wouldn't always be protected. And once again, that puts the people I care about in the firing line.

"Avery," Margaret stutters in disbelief. "Why don't you want to go back? You know the only other option is to serve out the remainder of your sentence in federal prison."

I pick a spot on the dark graphite wall to focus on. "Lilydale isn't all it's cracked up to be. No offense," I add, looking at Alexander. His demeanor is cold, ruthless, and I try not to flinch as his dead eyes narrow on me.

"You'll be going back," he mutters in a deep, warning tone. "The detectives are currently investigating this matter and speaking to patients. At this stage, the preliminary report is suicide."

Well, at least he calls us *patients*. Unlike Whitface who refers to us as students. This guy knows and sees it for what it actually is.

My eyebrows furrow at his words. "And do you believe that?"

"No," he answers without hesitation. "I'm well aware of the behavior of the patients and what they are capable of. But I doubt you did it. I'm not sure why you would masquerade around with a lie of that magnitude, but frankly, I don't care. Our reputation is on the line here. You *will* return to Lilydale. The Board has already decided on the matter."

"I was framed," I blurt out.

Pausing by the door, Alexander looks over at me, a hint of disgust on his features. "Obviously," he replies sarcastically. "Your social worker will discuss with you the stipulations of your return. I trust Arthur will also have some choice words as well."

He swings the door open, partially heading out before he looks over his shoulder. "And Ms. White?"

"Yeah?"

"Next time I will not be as generous."

I know the other option was prison, but there's something about his tone—a threat—that makes me believe he's not referring to my imprisonment.

He's referring to my life.

Chapter 2

Grey

Dainty trails of maroon drip down the walls.

Usually, the sight of blood calms me. There's something about the very essence of our being—the life that it gives and seeing it spill out—that pacifies me. It's a reminder that we can use it as a weapon, ending lives as well as saving them.

But not today.

Not fucking today.

I pull back my fist, ready to slam it into the concrete wall again, until a voice stops me.

"Will you just chill for five minutes?" Damon snaps under his breath. "I don't have time to clean your mess off my walls. We have bigger problems to sort out."

I whip around, eyes wild with every disgusting emotion humanly possible, finding Damon leaning against the wall on his bed.

We've been in his room for two hours, nearly three. And I'm losing my fucking mind.

I have half a mind to leave—*because I fucking can*—but he's the only thing anchoring me at the moment. From the moment that cunt Arthur ordered everyone to their rooms, I was on edge. Avery's cries still echo in my head, the image of her being shoved into the wall and handcuffed... touched by someone else. I need to hurt someone.

It took every fiber of my strength not to rip those constables apart limb from limb—and Damon's strength too. He had to physically hold me back as the entire gen pop watched her be dragged off. If I had my way, they'd all be with that pathetic excuse of a man called Samuel Hallman.

I know who I need to hurt, where I need to direct that anger.

Fucking Theo Ashwood.

He should have done more to protect her. The police held him back but he should have tried *harder*.

He should have destroyed them while he had the chance.

And now she's gone.

"If you're going to *sort things out*, I'd do it quickly. You have five more minutes before I leave this room and gut everyone who crosses my path."

Damon rolls his eyes, typing something on his laptop. "Sit down, Grey. I'm working on it. But I can't be babysitting you as well. Where do you want my focus to be?"

Begrudgingly, I jump up onto his desk, sitting on the edge. "I need answers. And I need them now."

I'm mad at him for holding me back. But as he said to me in the hall, there's no use spilling police blood because I'll be whisked away too, separated from everyone. And then there's no coming back from that.

"I know you do," he answers softly, a trait only reserved for those closest to him—at the briefest of times. "I'll get them."

"I'm serious, Deadman. Five minutes and I'm out of here. I don't care. I'll paint the hallways red and string Christmas lights up made of intestines."

He puts his laptop aside, standing up. Part of me hopes that he'll punch me, calm me down with the pain. But I know he won't. He's physically strong—enough to hold *me* back—but his mind is stronger.

"Free time is over so we won't be let back out today," he says casually, holding a hand up as my face turns violent at the mere idea of getting no answers until tomorrow. "But I'm going to go speak to Arthur. I've checked the camera feeds. The police have just left and Hallman's body has been removed."

"Downstairs?" I ask.

"No—city morgue. The police need to do their autopsy to finalize their investigation so that his family can make funeral preparations. They will have released him from Lilydale custody."

I fold my arms. "She's not going down for this, Damon. It's not fair."

Damon's eyes narrow darkly. "Who cares if she does? Don't you care about what she did to you?"

Gritty camera footage rolls through my mind, the sounds of her breathy moans and gasps in the morgue, and I see red again at the reminder. "She's been through enough," I spit out, much to the surprise of Damon.

"You love her," he laughs incredulously, shaking his head. "I should have known."

"I *did*," I correct him.

"No, you still love her," he points out, opening the door and peering out into the quiet hallway. "Don't mistake me for a fool, Grey. You're smarter than that."

I shake my head. "Love and forgiveness are two separate things."

Damon leans against the doorframe, looking at me with a bored expression. "I know you struggle with the line of forgiveness, but that subject aside, you still care for the girl."

"Avery," I say through clenched teeth. "Her name is Avery."

He raises an eyebrow. "Her name is as dead to me as Hallman is. Come on, you can come with me to see Arthur. I think putting the fear of the Devil in him would do some good. We all know he's going to have a field day dealing with this."

I take a final glimpse at Damon's walls covered in my blood, a sinister smirk tugging at my lips at the idea of unleashing some hell.

The two of us head down the deserted hallway until we reach the end where Connor is. He's by far my favorite guard—and best of all, we don't have to pay him a cent. If only Arthur knew just how much control we had now. He's making it too easy for us.

"Move," Damon orders, shooing him with his hand.

Connor steps aside, leaning against the wall. No matter how many guards they hire, they will never take control of them. Sure, a few try to stand up to us. But we promptly cut their legs out from underneath them, letting them crawl around at our feet. They learn quickly after that.

The access pad lights up as Damon's fingers punch in the code, before we find ourselves on the other side. Immediately, I spot Arthur's office door wide open, his grumbling figure behind his desk, barking down the phone. Our footsteps are quiet, but it's not them he hears. He senses us, eyes shooting up and finding our figures lurking in the darkness as we approach.

"I have to go," he says, slamming the phone down.

I smirk as he rises to his feet, just in time for us to enter his office.

"No security?" I mock. "Tsk. Didn't you hear? There's a killer on the loose."

Arthur scowls at me, but not before Damon holds his hand up, silencing both of us.

"Arthur," Damon lulls. "Always a pleasure. Stressful day?"

Damon rounds the desk, making the tight cunt scatter. I laugh, distracting him for a split second as Damon sits on the counterfeit throne. Whittingham might pretend he has reign over us, but we all know that's a lie. He should be afraid—*very afraid.*

Stuck between the two of us, he has no choice but to dig into those deep pockets to find his balls.

"What do you want?" he snaps at Damon. "I'm up to my eyeballs with police and board calls."

"So, you're aware of the situation then?" Damon replies.

I'm perplexed, because obviously, we're all aware of the situation. Unless there's another situation I'm not familiar with yet...

Arthur's face darkens. "Yes. I'm not happy about it."

"That sounds like a *you* problem, Arthur. Now, here's what's going to happen. My team is going to give your pathetic excuse for administration access to camera footage. If your IT people are worth a fraction of their money, you'll find what you're looking for. In the meantime, you *will not* be dishing out any punishments for this. Things will continue on as normal."

"I knew you had something to do with that," Whittingham hisses. "Do you have any idea how much money the facility has poured out to fix the cameras?"

Damon shrugs. "At the risk of sounding like a broken record, that's your problem. But what we are giving you will close the investigation. Hallman's death will be marked as a suicide. If you want to put on some show and dance about his death, make everyone mourn, be my guest. But that's the end of *that* matter."

"So, I hand the footage to the police and then what?"

I smirk as Damon tilts the chair back, kicking his feet up onto Arthur's desk. He makes a point of tipping over a mug of coffee with his foot, the liquid spilling all over scattered paperwork. "Then you do what you do best. Carry on with the recruitment process. I'm sure the board already has a candidate in mind to replace Hallman. A long list, no doubt."

Ahh, yes. The only topic that matters to Whittingham—money. The cog that keeps the wheels turning in this death hole.

"And the other thing?" Whittingham snipes.

I don't like his tone toward Damon so I take a casual step, smirking when he quickly scuffles back at my movement.

Damon looks at me, a small smile tugging at his lips. "I believe that should be resolving itself any minute now. Handle it delicately. Or else," he adds in a sinister tone.

"You're a real piece of shit."

It strikes a nerve in me, and I close the distance between myself and Arthur in two strides. I shove him against the wall hard, hand around his throat. Fearful eyes dart down to my hand, knuckles still coated in dried blood.

"Don't speak to him that way again," I murmur, tightening my fingers around his windpipe. "Or it will be the last thing you do."

I have to give it to the old cunt, he quickly swallows that fear, eyes narrowing on Damon.

"Had to bring your lapdog with you?" he snarls.

"Scary dog privilege," Damon corrects casually. "He needed some cheering up. But I'd take his advice and watch your tone. He's out for blood." He winks at me, and I squeeze Arthur's throat until he's a spluttering mess.

Finally, when his hands start clawing at mine, face a nice shade of purple, I release him. He slumps back against the wall, gasping for breath.

"I'm aware of your... *relationship*." It's directed at me, a murderous glint in his eye.

Oh, please try me. Please, please... push me over the edge. I'm begging you.

Damon sighs, disinterested. "We all know that you do not give a fuck about anyone's relationships here. Except, of course, yours and Dorothea's. Which I'm happy to meddle in if you can't control yourself and do as you're told."

Arthur snaps his head toward Damon. "Do not threaten us, boy. You will not touch her."

I watch as Damon gets to his feet quickly, strolling over to Arthur. He recoils as Damon peers down at him, hands in pockets.

"I'll fuck her and make her scream louder than your pathetic excuse of a dick ever could," he murmurs darkly. "Then I'll get Grey to rip her heart out so you can keep it on your half-a-million dollar desk for commemoration. But don't worry—I'm sure the board would appropriately replace her so you have a new fuck toy to wield power over. Especially since we know you don't have any here."

Arthur straightens up to full height, still having to gaze up at Damon. "Try to keep your minions in check. While you might have struck a deal this time, it won't last forever. You're on borrowed time, boy."

"Keep telling yourself that," Damon whispers darkly. "And you might believe it."

He turns slowly, giving me a nod. "Let's go. We have another visit to make."

I blow Arthur a kiss before trailing out of the office behind Damon. Kicking the door closed, I narrow my eyes at Damon suspiciously, dropping my playful façade.

"What is this deal you mentioned?"

Damon stops, pivoting his body to glance at me.

"I made a deal with the chairman so we had some leverage. And it's right on time, I see."

The entrance doors open, figures emerging from the darkness outside. My heart stops as I catch sight of Avery being led inside by two police officers, her hands cuffed in front of her abdomen.

Avery's gray eyes widen open in surprise as she halts her steps, spotting me instantly.

"Welcome back, Avery," Damon says loudly, his voice echoing around the chamber. "I'll be seeing you soon."

A flicker of fear appears in her eyes as she glances at Damon, but they quickly return to me. She's scanning me for a reaction—*anything*.

My walls shoot back up, my face cold as I turn away from her like she's a random person on the street not worthy of a second glance. Following Damon's pace to the guarded door, I hear her small, anxious breaths, her silence begging me to say something.

As we step through the door to the rooms, I give Connor a nod, relief flooding through me as he closes the door behind us, blocking her out.

Out of sight, out of mind they say. But that's just bullshit. Now that I know she's in the same building as me again, the tether between us pulls.

And I'm going to take that tether and wrap it around her soft body—whether that's to fuck her or kill her, I don't know yet.

Chapter 3

Avery

The sound of gravel crunches under my feet as I stare up at the Lilydale building. My wrists are numb, bloodied and bruised, but I feel displaced, knowing I'm returning to my own personal hell. It feels like déjà vu, my eyes hovering over the pristine white walls.

It's late, the sun long gone to sleep as shadows taunt me, imaginary laughter reminding me why I'm here.

The police officers keep a tight squeeze on me, their fingers digging into my elbows and arms as they practically drag me up the front steps. I'm relishing the thought of being in my room, alone, so I can catch my breath and process the past few hours.

I'm still confused about everything, but at least I'll be safe until morning.

One of the officers pushes the door open, and I'm surprised it's unlocked. I suppose that they are waiting for me, aware of my impending arrival.

Immediately, the familiar smell of roses hits me. But another sense cuts right through it like a knife, my eyes darting up on their own accord.

It's like I'm seeking him out in the dark, like my body just *knows*.

Grey and Damon are standing in the foyer, their eyes piercing into me. I stumble to a stop, stomach twisting in a violent grip as I stare at Grey.

For a brief second, a look of surprise flashes across his face, but it's gone in an instant—that cold, heartless expression peering back at me. My body feels heavy, like it's tied in knots as I hold his gaze.

"Welcome back, Avery. I'll be seeing you," Damon says in a dark voice, startling me.

The two of them quickly disappear out of sight, my heart racing as I watch the door slam closed behind them. A second later, Mr. Whittingham is standing in his office doorway, frowning.

"Bring her in here."

I yelp slightly as the officers grab me harshly, ripping me out of my thoughts as they drag me inside the office. My eyes notice the state of his desk, and I know that this is where Grey and Damon were minutes ago.

One of the officers shoves me into a chair, looking at Mr. Whittingham for instructions.

"Take them off," he says coldly, picking up soggy pieces of paper from his desk.

Hands roughly grab my wrists, not caring about my wounds, as they uncuff me. I silently rub them, ignoring the stinging pain as I wait for Mr. Whittingham to speak.

"You can go," he directs the officers, motioning to the door.

When it's just us, he throws himself onto his chair, eyes closed as he rubs his temples.

"You're far too much trouble than what you're worth, Ms. White."

"I'm sorry?" I blurt out, unsure if I'm apologizing or just bewildered by his comment.

Annoyed eyes open slowly. Anger, frustration, and a touch of something else I can't put my finger on, stare back at me.

"I trust you've been informed of the conditions of your return," he says, ignoring me and his previous comment.

I nod, remembering my brief chat with Margie before I was escorted out of the police building. They had all watched me leave, disgusted, as if a criminal was walking free. In a sense, they weren't wrong.

"Good," he snaps. "I'll escort you to your room. However, before you leave, I have some further stipulations of my own."

"Such as?" I ask, brows furrowed.

It's already bad enough that I have strict conditions, but now there's more?

Mr. Whittingham stands up, hands flat on the edge of his desk. He glowers at me with a hardened expression.

"You will receive a psychiatric assessment from Dr. Smith tomorrow. If you do not pass, you will be placed in solitary confinement for such time until you're deemed fit to be back among your peers."

I twitch at the word but keep quiet.

"And should you be involved in any further incidents, regardless of *innocence*, I will personally make sure you never step foot inside my facility again."

"Okay," I whisper. "Anything else?"

"Actually, yes. You can let me know if you hear of any disturbances within the facility from fellow students. And you can keep away from that *crowd* you seem to have grown attached to. Otherwise, I'll ensure they are promptly removed from Lilydale as well."

My neck stiffens as I observe his face, not entirely sure what I'm hoping to find. He wants me to stay away from who exactly? Grey and Damon? Theo? All of them?

There's only one-hundred patients here—well, ninety-nine now. It's not exactly easy to avoid everyone, even if I wanted to.

I have no idea if he has that much power. It's no secret that there's *another* ruler of this kingdom, but even kings can be lost in wars.

I'm exhausted—beaten down. I feel the fatigue in every part of my body. It's been a rollercoaster of emotion the past few days—from my personal information being leaked to everyone, to what happened with Theo and Grey, Sam's death, and my arrest. Reflecting on it, it seems likely that I might not pass this psychiatric assessment—now or ever. How does one come back from this?

I can't bring myself to speak, and thankfully, Mr. Whittingham doesn't seem to care. He rounds his desk, hastily motioning for me to follow. I quickly stand, tailing him as I'm escorted back to my room.

As our footsteps echo down the hallway, my mind can't help but wonder what tomorrow will look like. It's eerily quiet—the usual screams from people in their rooms appear to have dissipated, and it sends a chill down my body. With the chaos of today, I expected more. The silence is telling, and that alone scares me.

Standing outside of my door, my eyes gaze over the numbers before I'm pushed inside.

Everything looks the same, yet it feels different.

"Wait," I say, turning to look at Mr. Whittingham at the door. "Do I get my shower?"

The door slams shut in my face, answering the question. Sighing, I trudge over to my bed, laying down.

Despite the consuming weariness threatening my existence, I'm unable to sleep. My eyes watch the door, expecting someone to sneak in at my minute. But as the hours pass, I realize they aren't coming. I'm alone again, just like always.

I should be used to it. That was my entire life, my sole purpose. But now...

Now, it feels like a fate worse than death.

I've barely been asleep for three hours when the door is shoved open, banging loudly against the wall.

I jolt up in a panic, first morning light blinding me as drowsiness intoxicates me.

Through the haze, I spot a guard, hand on the weapon attached to his belt.

"Up," he shouts at me.

Frowning, I stumble up, swaying dangerously. "What's going on?"

We're never woken up *this* early. And judging by the quiet hallway outside, no one else is either.

"Let's go," he says, grabbing my arm roughly.

I whine under my breath as his fingers leave bruises on my skin, my legs barely mustering up the strength to carry my weight as I'm dragged into the hallway.

As we approach the communal bathroom, relief floods through my chest at the thought of taking a shower. I step into the tiled room, unable to focus on much, when the guard shoves me to the floor.

I manage to catch myself just in time, hands slapping against the dirty floor as my knees cry out in pain. I bite my tongue, sucking in a breath as I do what I do best—keep my pain to myself.

"Clean," the guard orders, throwing a rag down next to my hand.

"What?" I sit back on my calves, looking over my shoulder at him.

He shoves my shoulder with his foot, knocking me forward. "Start cleaning, murderer. Whittingham's orders."

In my sleep deprived state, it takes me a few seconds to process his order. Reluctantly, I grab the rag, digging into the grout on the tiles. The guard scoffs, knocking over a bucket next to me, the contents spilling over my hands and seeping into my shorts.

"With the bleach obviously. The amount of filth you lot bring in is disgusting."

A burning pain sears into my palm and I quickly sit up on my calves, hastily wiping my hands on the front of my shorts. "It's burning," I tell him.

"Too bad. Get moving."

I shuffle away from the pool of bleach, scrubbing the tiles as my eyes scan the bathroom. It's massive—there's no way it's possible for one person to clean the whole room without proper equipment. But I prove that wrong. It just takes an obscene amount of time.

By the time I'm told to stop several long hours later, my hands are red raw and stinging. The guard, who had finally grown bored of his phone, relented, dragging me up from the floor.

"Breakfast time," he grunts, pulling me toward the door.

"I need to wash my hands," I argue but he ignores me, heading straight to the hall.

When I step foot inside, I'm easily the last to arrive. Patients are sitting at tables, eating obliviously—death is normal at Lilydale, so life goes on.

A few people throw glances my way—some pitiful, some angry. It burns a hole in my stomach, my face flushing with panic. The pain of being exposed is still real, coupled now with my arrest. I've had a target on my back since day one, and despite it all, some people here would still love to watch me go down in flames.

"Can I just go back to my room?" I ask the guard quietly.

He huffs at me, shaking his head. Resigning, I slowly walk to the food, barely able to feel the hunger in my numb body. I grab a piece of unbuttered toast, taking a small bite.

My feet start to walk toward my usual table, but I halt, conflicted. I can feel multiple eyes on me, and I do my best to ignore the uncomfortable feeling. But in spite of my best efforts of control, I look up, finding Grey at a table with Damon and their usual crew.

I'm surprised to find him staring back at me, his face void of emotion. Damon looks at Grey to see what has his attention, before turning his head toward me.

I look away quickly. I can't deal with that right now.

Up ahead, I spot Theo at our table, and my heart misses a beat when I find him watching me too. He never normally looks up until I'm in my seat, and there's a small bit of confusion on his face—like he's waiting for me, puzzled as to why I've stopped walking over.

You have to keep away from them...

Whittingham's threat still hangs over my head. I want nothing more than to run to either of them. But I don't.

I take a place against the wall, staring unfocused at the floor as I nibble on toast for the sake of routine. Neither of them approach me—or anyone—and when we're finally ushered out of the hall at the end of breakfast, I'm manhandled again by the guard.

"What now?" I ask through clenched teeth as he squeezes a bruise.

"It's time for your psych assessment," he grunts, pulling me toward Dr. Smith's office.

Chapter 4
Avery

"Avery, it's so good to see you," Dr. Smith says happily as I'm shoved through his office door.

He seems absolutely unbothered by the fact I was just yeeted into his office like a ragdoll.

I shoot a glance at the guard, who slams the door closed in my face. Grumbling, I turn back to look at Dr. Smith, perched behind his desk, hands neatly folded together.

"Yeah, hi," I reply tonelessly.

"Take a seat," he directs warmly, motioning to the chairs.

I do so, but only because my legs are threatening to collapse underneath me. A huge sigh of relief slips out of me when my ass touches the seat, and I'm annoyed to find Dr. Smith already making notes.

"What are you writing now?" I grumble.

He looks up, pausing. "Just making some initial assessments and observations."

I fold my arms. "And what happens if I fail this wonderful psych assessment?"

"Do *you* think you'll fail?"

"Who knows with this place? You might botch the results."

Dr. Smith puts his pen down, a concerned frown on his face. "Why would I do that, Avery?"

I scoff. "You already proved that your ethics are fucked. I wouldn't put it past anyone in this place to do something for their own benefit."

He smiles gently. "I'm just going to ask you some standard questions. You don't have to answer if you don't want to but it would help."

I stay quiet, looking away, gaze stuck on the damn filing cabinet that started this mess.

Clearing his throat, Dr. Smith picks his pen back up. "Do you have any current mental health symptoms or concerns?"

"I'm concerned about my privacy and protection," I snap back.

"Have you had any thoughts of self-harm or suicidal ideation?"

"No," I say gingerly.

He nods. "Any thoughts about harming others?"

I scoff. "When have I ever been a threat to others?"

Dr. Smith glances up coolly. "It's just a standard question, Avery."

"I believe I answered it, *Dr. Smith*."

"Very well. As you recall you have borderline personality disorder. Often, events can trigger episodes. How are you feeling?"

I casually gaze back at him. "What the hell is an episode?"

"You may experience intense emotions that feel out of control. It can lead to outbursts of anger, harmful thoughts, becoming withdrawn or feeling paranoid."

My eyebrows furrow. "Given everything that has happened to me, wouldn't it be warranted if I was angry, paranoid or feeling withdrawn? I'm not exactly jumping for joy at being here. First, my personal information was stolen and leaked. Then I was framed for murder. This feels like a trap. No matter how I respond, there's no right answer."

"Of course your feelings are warranted. You have every right to be upset. These feelings would be beyond that—beyond a reasonable level of reaction to your circumstances."

"I'm not about to kill everyone, if that's what you mean."

Dr. Smith's lips twitch into a smile. "How do you feel about yourself?"

"I already answered that—" I start to argue, but he cuts me off.

"Not in respect to self-harm, but how do you feel about yourself? Let me put this in simple terms. Do you like yourself?"

I still. "I've never liked myself. Everyone I've ever crossed paths with made sure to remind me of how little I mean."

He makes some notes and I scold myself for being so honest. I should have stopped myself from rambling, but the words of self-hatred often just escape on their own.

"Have there been any situations in recent times where you felt differently?"

I stay quiet. I already have one foot in the grave and I'm not willing to bury myself alive at this point. Dr. Smith looks up, noticing my silence.

"There's no right or wrong answers here, Avery."

"The fuck there isn't."

He smiles again, leaning back in his chair. "You're not going to fail the psych assessment. But please try to find the courage to answer."

My eyes narrow suspiciously. I don't trust him—or anyone. He could just be saying all the right words to fool me. But he refuses to move on, waiting patiently until I finally relent.

"I started to feel better about myself when some people made me feel like I was worth it," I sigh. "But that's gone now."

Dr. Smith nods, pleased with my response. "One thing to understand about your condition is that self-worth is hugely affected. One of the key things to work on is finding a way to recognize that value without the need of external validation. But that being said, we're human. It's okay to feel good because of someone. That can often help us gain insight into rational things."

"Rational things?" I question wearily.

"Our brains can trick us into believing something that isn't real. Sometimes we need that support network to remind us and help us see the good."

Blinking slowly, I shake my head. "There is no good. It was a temporary, fleeting moment. That chance is gone."

"I disagree but I think you should try to consider other perspectives."

"Are we finished yet?" I snap back.

I hate how vulnerable I become in this room. I hate that there's a risk someone will see this information again. I don't feel safe, and I'm not sure I can handle that situation happening again.

Dr. Smith kicks his feet up on the desk casually, cupping his hands in his lap. His professional demeanor fades, like we're two old friends having a chit chat. "I'll pass on my assessment conclusion to Mr. Whittingham, but he won't be made aware of anything we have discussed today. However, I would just briefly like to discuss one more thing before we finish."

I sag in my seat. "What?"

He nods toward my hands. "Are you in pain?"

Looking down, I open my palms from their tightly squeezed balls, examining the red skin. "It's fine."

"I'm going to have the guard take you down to Dr. Markel to check for chemical burns. Bleach, I assume from the smell?"

I scoff. "Obviously."

Dr. Smith stands up, crossing his office to open his door. I hear him mumble a few words to the guard before he stands back, smiling at me again. "I'd like to see you again tomorrow, Avery. But if you need to chat beforehand, just let a member of staff know."

"I'll be fine," I mumble, stalking out of his office.

The guard barely looks at me as he escorts me further down the hallway until we arrive at Dr. Markel's room. He pushes the door open after a sharp knock, Dr. Markel's surprised wrinkled face glancing up from his table.

"I'll just be one moment," he says, tending to another patient.

I linger next to the guard, hugging my body until someone pushes past me. It jolts me out of my thoughts, eyes landing on Vivian.

Her eyes are red and puffy, cheeks still stained with fallen tears. Despite the pain across her face, she still manages to glare venomously at me.

White bandages catch my sight, and I frown at her injured wrist. It doesn't take a genius to put two-and-two together, her eyes even more pained and angry when she notices me watching.

"Get out of my way," she hisses, deliberately slamming her shoulder into me.

Another guard appears out of nowhere, quickly following after her, but before I can think too much about it, Dr. Markel calls out my name.

"Come in, Ms. White. I'm just quickly sanitizing the table but you can take a seat in a moment."

I hover awkwardly, eyes shifting between him and the guard, until I'm finally able to sit down on the examination table.

"What can I do for you?" he asks, humming to himself afterward.

I shrug. "Dr. Smith wanted you to give me a quick check over."

The mention of his colleague makes his eyes light up. He nods, pulling on some fresh gloves. "Could you direct me to where?"

I open my hands, palms facing up. He leans over, eyes scanning over the redness. "Slight chemical burn. Did you use water?"

"I was cleaning," I quickly interject before he can categorize me in the same way as Vivian. "And no, I haven't washed them yet."

Dr. Markel looks up, surprised. "Go to the tap in the corner and give them a wash with some lukewarm water. I'll grab some ointment."

The feel of the water on my hands has me longing for a shower, but at least I'm able to wash off my hands and knees at his basin. When I sit back on the table, Dr. Markel applies some ointment to my palms and legs, the cream taking away the burning sensation.

"I know we discussed some pain relief previously, so I'll give you a dose now."

"I don't want it," I say, but he ignores me to my surprise. I watch as his figure disappears through another door in the room, the sound of a cabinet opening and the rustling of plastic before he comes back. He holds a little white pill in front of my face, staring at my mouth.

"Say '*ahh*'," he mutters, like I'm a fucking child.

I just open my lips silently, begrudgingly letting him pop the pill in my mouth. He hands me a small bottle of water, and I quickly swallow, taking large gulps to hydrate my parched throat.

Making some notes on a file, he motions to my hands. "Come back this afternoon for another application. If the pain medication doesn't help, let me know."

"Right," I sigh. "Am I free to go now?"

"Yes, yes," he says, waving me off. "Wear gloves next time."

I stare at him bewildered for a second, wondering if he's having a senior moment. Has he forgotten where we are? Does he think I willingly have access to bleach and just randomly decided to wake up at the crack of dawn and start cleaning for the fucking thrill of it?

The guard grabs my elbow again as I step into the hallway, and this time, I jolt from his bruising touch.

"Can you stop that?" I hiss. "It hurts and I'm obviously not going to run. Even if I wanted to, I won't get anywhere."

He tightens his grip on me, coldly smirking like he's proud of himself. "Protocol. Suck it up."

I growl under my breath, knowing very well it's not protocol, but I don't bother to fight back.

As we approach the end of the hallway, I'm horrified to find Damon standing there alone. He looks as if he's waiting for me—arms folded, sneer on his face.

I wait for the guard to direct us toward the rooms or hall, but he stops in front of Damon, jerking me forward.

"This the one?" he asks.

Damon nods, not breaking eye contact with me. "She sure is."

My eyes widen in alarm. "What's going on?" I grill the guard. He ignores me again, turning and walking away. I'm left with the Devil, heart racing as panic starts to overwhelm me.

"This way," Damon orders, motioning toward the hall. He doesn't touch me, but there's a threat to his tone, warning me not to disobey or run.

Slowly, I follow in defeat. He leads us to the library doors, opening one side. His cold stare is telling me to enter, and against my better judgment screaming no, I do.

There's no winning here. If I refuse and stay outside, I'm at risk of being seen. If I enter inside, I'm alone with a predator—one who wants me dead.

But that's the thing about predators... They know how to hunt and chase.

My feet carry me to the tables at the back of the library, my eyes darting around. I know I'm looking for *him*, but as I suspected, he's not here.

"So, Avery. You've returned to grace us with your presence," Damon says coolly.

I spin around to face him, trying to keep my distance. "I guess so."

"Hm." He paces along the floor, casually weaving around tables. "You seem surprised."

"I am surprised," I answer quietly. "Especially since..." I trail off, quickly shutting down the words.

"Since, what?" he asks in a deadly, curious tone.

I shake my head. Damon pauses, resting his hand on a nearby table.

"I asked you a question, Avery."

Biting my tongue, I shake my head again. I won't let him bully me into finishing my unspoken sentence. The last thing I need is to cause more trouble for myself.

He laughs quietly, the sound sending a chill through my bones.

"Since what, Avery? Since I framed you for murder?"

Chapter 5
Damon

Her tiny, wringable neck bobs as she swallows hard. It's laughable, watching her feign confidence—trying to hide her fear.

Props to her. It's almost believable except her arms and legs are trembling ever so slightly as I tower above her. Still, she surprises me from time to time. Especially when she had the nerve to slap me across the face.

I see her eyes flash indignantly, her mind finally catching up to the situation. I wait, knowing something is coming.

"It doesn't matter," she says firmly. "I'll keep out of your way."

I survey her carefully, almost surprised at her resignation. It's as if she's accepted everything entirely, willing to over-look my so-called *betrayal*.

"Will you?" I ask casually.

Avery looks up, finding my face. "Yes."

"Hm." I pretend to think, fingers tapping on the table. "That doesn't work for me."

"What?" she sputters out. "Why not?"

I slowly walk toward her, noticing the way her legs fight the urge to scramble away. When I'm within reaching distance to her, I lift her chin with my pointer finger, tilting her face up.

"Because I'm not done with you yet."

Surprise and fear crosses her face, making my lips twitch in amusement. I love seeing the effect I have on people. Who needs violence to control people when you can control their minds and emotions? That's the thing about people here—Avery, especially—they are not in control of their emotions. They think that they are, but if that were the case, they never would have set foot inside Lilydale.

Emotions are useless.

Unless, of course, you have perfect control over them. If you can manipulate them, you can do anything. It's why I don't fear anything—why I don't feel sadness. It's weak, pathetic... some emotions do not deserve recognition. I don't care if we're supposed to be *human*—some make us vulnerable, and the second that happens, you give people the opportunity to control you.

Which is why I love to control.

Sure, I could lay hands on people. But eventually, we have the mental power to block out physical pain. Psychologically being in charge? That's much harder to fight. Plus, if we need to spill blood, I have Grey for that.

"Not done? What do you mean 'not done'?" Avery asks hesitantly.

I tilt my head to the side innocently, holding her gaze. "Despite everything, I still have use for you for now. But you'll only deal with me."

Her eyebrows crease together, my words processing through her fragile little mind. Yes—she won't be speaking with Grey. What I need her for is irrelevant to whatever sick little relationship they have. He can find new pussy to fuck with—preferably one that won't send him into a deadly spiral. I need him in control, focused.

"I really don't want to."

"I really don't give a fuck."

Avery's eyes gather tears, but she clenches her jaw, fighting back the urge to let them fall.

"And if I refuse? Are you just going to frame me again? Kill me? I don't care anymore, Damon. If you're going to do something, just do it."

I laugh, her small body jumping. "Oh, Avery. I wouldn't give you death. It's obvious you would welcome it. No, you'll work for me. You can refuse if you want, but it won't save you."

"Fuck you, Demon Boy," she suddenly spits out. My hand snaps down to her neck, my fingers wrapping around her skin.

"Don't test me," I warn her. "I'm not above getting my hands dirty. I'll subject you to a fate worse than death. Just consider this a courtesy call. I'll be in touch. Now, if you'll kindly leave the library, I think you'll find Connor waiting for you."

I release her neck with a shove. She stumbles slightly, regaining her footing. A quick glare is sent my way before she turns, storming out of the library. I watch her leave, the door swinging closed behind her, before it opens again less than a minute later.

"Grey," I greet coolly, watching as he walks toward me with his hands in his pockets. "I wasn't expecting to see you until this afternoon."

"What was that about?" he asks suspiciously.

I lean against the desk, folding my arms. "I was just welcoming Avery back. Aren't you meant to be in session with Christopher?"

Grey snorts. "I'd rather have my throat slashed again. So, are you going to tell me the real reason you dragged her in here?"

I smile at him, raising an eyebrow. "No. But when you need to know, I'll tell you."

His face hardens, all emotion leaving his eyes. Even without it present, I can still read his body language. I know he's surprised she's back, more so that I apparently brought her here. There's a part of him that's relieved, but an even bigger part that's fighting to destroy everything in his path. He's a walking paradox, a bomb ready to detonate into a bloodied mess of flowers and glass.

I have to handle this carefully. It's a delicate situation, and I know he wants answers.

I told him to wait last night—promising I'd fill him in later. I didn't give him a timeframe, but judging by the fact he's stalking the communal areas, he wants them now.

"Are you going to at least tell me what the fuck happened yesterday?" he asks in a low voice.

"What do you want to know?"

Grey leans against the end of a bookshelf. "You said you made a deal with the chairman."

"I did," I answer casually. "He wasn't too pleased but we have his balls in a vise for the time being."

He glares at me, unsatisfied with my answer. "Deadman. Spill it."

My face darkens. "Grey, you're my right-hand man, so you can get away with a lot. But you need to pull it back."

"This isn't just another move for you. This affects me too," he replies. "It's my life being dragged through it."

"Please," I scoff. "I warned you to keep away from her. You already knew the potential consequences. We don't need the same shit happening again. There's bigger things to focus on. Perhaps you should remember that instead of thinking with your dick."

Grey pushes off from the bookshelf, walking toward me. To anyone else, they would be worried—terrified even. But I know he won't lose control, he never does with me.

But he's mad... out for blood. I need to find a way for him to vent some of that frustration. Apparently, his last task wasn't enough, even if he did go partially rogue.

"It has nothing to do with my fucking cock."

"Don't insult me," I reply, paying no attention to the short distance between us. "Whether it's your dick or your emotions, you're too invested in this. You need to get control of it."

"I do have control," Grey answers, visibly relaxing. "I don't want to be kept in the dark."

I give him a tight smile. "You won't be. It will all become apparent soon enough. As for the board, they heard about the situation with Hallman and Arthur. It wasn't just for the society's benefit, but yours too. I need you to focus on your tasks. We're at a critical point now."

Grey lets out a long breath. "What do you need from me?"

"Make sure Jillian and Byrone are still on track. Security measurements are tightening here. The formal investigation is done, but despite our visit to Arthur, we can still expect some pushback."

He nods in agreement. "What do you think he has planned?"

Laughing, I shrug. "Probably the same bullshit as always. He won't do the obvious segregation tactics. With Hallman's death being a suicide, it would be fruitless punishing the collective. It would make him look like the bad guy. No, he'll want to try to control the situation from the inside."

"So, he'll be gathering intel, trying to get people on his side."

"Precisely. It's likely he'll have alerted the staff to keep tabs, but I suspect he'll also be trying to find some sheep as well—students that are stupid enough to side with him."

Grey's eyes widen slightly. "You think he's gotten to Avery?"

He always was a smart man. Grey reads people just as well as I do, if only he had complete control over his emotions. He did—until she came along. Which is why I need them separated for now.

"Definitely. Or at least, he will be trying," I confirm. "At the moment, she's the only one he'd have leverage with—not to mention *your relationship* with her. It's possible he'll have more people, but it's not likely they will have enough to give him the information that he wants."

Anger crosses Grey's face and I sigh. Here we go—those fucking emotions again.

"So, you're going to keep a handle on her?"

"I'm going to make sure she doesn't fucking speak," I correct. "Plus, like you said, she might have more useful benefits down the line. But at the moment, we need to keep everything off Arthur's radar. I have no doubt the board is scrambling to do damage control."

Grey nods sternly. "And you'll tell me more when it's relevant." It's not a question, but a demand.

"Yes," I answer, standing up straight. "So for now, I need you to prepare the society. Call for an emergency meeting tomorrow night. Have Leighton assist with preparations."

"Who needs to attend?" he asks.

"Everyone. I want all the members. It's important that we are all across this. We might need to review some of the operations and escalate them."

"Alright. Anything else?"

I scan his face carefully, knowing my next few words might tip him over the edge. "Yes. Avery will need to attend as well, but I'll pass the message along to her."

"Fine," he grunts, turning to head toward the door, but I'm not done.

"One more thing," I start, making him stop short. "You should know that Arthur has started punishing her."

Grey swings around, face blank. "Punishing how?" he says tonelessly, but underneath, I can see his blood start to boil.

I choose my words carefully, doing my best to weaponize—and subdue—my friend. "Connor has relayed the information that she's currently being subjected to chores."

His face twitches slightly in confusion and annoyance. "So, what? We all have designated jobs around here. It's nothing new."

"I'm aware," I snipe back. "But this will extend beyond that according to my information. You'll do well not to get involved."

"I'm not getting involved," he scoffs back in frustration. "Avery and I are done. We were done the moment she chose someone else."

"Good," I answer casually. "But if you see her scathed, remember that. Because we can't have you flying off the handle and ruining things. I'll find a way for you to vent your frustration, but you need to trust me and give me time."

Grey gives me a firm nod. "I do trust you."

I hear his words but I also see the way his fists have curled into a ball, the way his spine has straightened at the mention of her being hurt. This is going to be one hell of a task keeping him calm if he comes across her, but it's better he has some warning. I know how he processes things, how he makes plans to cover every single situation. At least now, he knows what to expect, so he won't be surprised. He loves control, needing to be in the know just like me. Knowledge is power, and I've given him that. It's up to him to respond to the situation accordingly.

It's just a matter of whether or not she's gotten her claws into him deep enough to disrupt that hard wiring that runs through his body and mind.

Chapter 6

Avery

I'm dragged back to my room for a short period.

I relish the chance to lay down on my bed, desperate for a nap. But it's short lived when the door swings open again a short time later.

"Get up. Time for class," the guard orders.

I groan, fighting back the urge to cry. It's amazing how much sleep can affect our functioning. It's no wonder that sleep deprivation used to be wielded as a torture method. I'm physically exhausted and hurting—mentally even more so. I'd give anything to just have a break for an hour, but everyone in this facility seems hellbent on breaking me.

Dragging my feet, I follow the guard to Charmaine's room, the burn in my hands starting to return. I'm tempted to request medical assistance, but I don't want to give anyone leverage against me. I don't want them to know that they are getting to me. It's bad enough the staff are trying to mess with me, but now I have Damon to worry about as well.

He's everywhere I go. And if it's not him, it's a proxy.

I slump into my usual seat, resting my chin on my palm while my elbow is propped up on the desk. We wait as the others arrive one by one, my heart malfunctioning as Grey enters last.

As he steps into the classroom, head up high, he briefly looks over at me. It only lasts a split second before he looks away, sitting down in his seat.

"Alright, everyone," Charmaine says loudly. "I know it's been a rough few days with the death of your fellow student, but we must continue. Today, we'll be diving into some history and geography. On your desks you'll find some reading to do. Please start there and familiarize yourself with the material. Afterwards, we'll have a discussion on the events and where they took place."

My fingers skim over the paper, eyes threatening to close at any second. I give myself a mental pep talk, telling myself I'll sleep in a few hours. I just have to get through class, free time, dinner... then I'll be on the home stretch. People do it all the time—parents, people studying, shift workers. How hard could it be?

As my eyes scan over the reading material, I have to keep going back, re-reading sentences because my brain can't comprehend anything. Eventually, I manage to finish, barely grasping the material but proud of myself for giving it my best effort.

"Okay, so by now, you should have realized that we're focusing on the Great Depression. I'm sure many of you have heard of it or have previously studied it to some extent," Charmaine says, pacing in front of her desk. "It started in

1929 and lasted until 1939. It was a severe global economic crisis which we know heavily affected the US stock market, leading to the Wall Street crash. As you would have read in your papers, it had a ricocheting effect. Not only did it start hardship in the US with unemployment rates, but multiple countries were also hit. Experts are also confident that this era contributed to World War II."

I slump further in my seat, not at all surprised that we are focusing on something as aptly titled as *The Great Depression*. The irony doesn't skip past me, and I shake my head to myself, watching Charmaine.

She continues talking about the flow on effects, the geographical scale, and statistics. But as she drones on, the urge to pass out gets stronger. I push through it, fingers gripping the side of my desk for support. If I can physically hold on to something, it might keep me alert. Maybe that's why the desks have scratch marks embedded in them.

My brain struggles to keep up when I get that niggling feeling back in my stomach. Turning my head, I find Grey watching me, his light eyes scanning my posture, lingering on my clenched hand.

Instantly, my hand relaxes—but not out of relief. I know he's studying me, reading me like a book. I give him a quick smile out of habit before forcing myself to look back at Charmaine.

Eventually, I feel his gaze shift away. I'm hit with a small wave of disappointment, but it's for the best. Knowing I need to keep away from them is hard, but if they tried to fight me on it, that would be harder. At least this way, if Grey avoids me too, it's half the battle fought.

By the time class finishes, I'm back with the personal pep talks as I count down the time until I'm back in my room. Guards escort us to the hall, and we crowd around as usual. Given everything that's happened, I'm surprised to see Damon standing on a table, ready to direct people.

It takes me a few seconds to remember my designated number, even though I still have no idea what the hell they even mean.

When *three* is motioned with his fingers, I head toward the hall doors, a sense of déjà vu hitting me as I go to the library. It feels like I'm the new patient all over again—nowhere to go, no one to see, trying to hide from prying eyes.

I can only hope that the library is deserted. My success rate of being alone in the library isn't great, but it's the best option I have right now.

The courtyard will be full of students, same with the hall. I could go to one of the empty rooms down the corridor, but it's likely that Theo will be lurking around there.

The scent of dust hits me when I enter and I'm happy to find that I'm the only person in here at the moment. Some groups had already filed out of the hall at Damon's command, but most seemed to be content with going outside to catch some sunshine.

Sitting at the end of an aisle, I lean against the wall, contemplating the option of taking a nap in here. If it stays vacant, I might be able to curl up and sleep for a little while. But I hate the fact I'll have to stay on guard. If someone chooses to come in, I'll be alone and unconscious.

Still, despite my best reasoning that I should stay awake, my eyelids start to feel heavy. I shuffle over so my back is half against the corner of a shelf, and half on the wall, pulling my legs up to my chest. Leaning my chin on my knees, I close my eyes, convincing myself that I'll stay awake with my eyes closed.

I listen out for sounds, on alert for the library door opening at any time, but it stays quiet. It's only when I realize it's too quiet that I jerk my head up. Somewhere in the back of my mind, I know I've drifted off—having one of those weird naps where you're not awake, but it feels like you are.

My heart nearly yeets itself out of my mouth when my eyes find Theo sitting in front of me, watching me closely.

I didn't even hear him come in.

"Fucking hell," I yelp, head connecting with the wall behind me as I violently jolt. "Ow."

"What the hell did you do that for?" he asks, concern on his face.

I rub the back of my head. "I didn't deliberately headbutt the wall. You scared the shit out of me."

"Are you alright?" he replies, and I know he's not just talking about my head.

Recovering, I take a breath, looking at him. "I'm fine. But I need to go," I tell him, standing up. My legs shake, a wave of drowsiness swimming in my vision. I must sway a little because Theo stands up, grabbing the tops of my arms.

"Sit back down."

"I can't," I mumble, focusing on a red book perched on the shelf to control my dizziness.

Theo squeezes my arms to guide me to the ground, a tiny whine escaping my mouth. He instantly lets me go, eyes honing in on my arms. Reaching forward, he lifts the sleeves of my gray shirt up, spotting the bruises.

"Who the fuck did this?" he asks, fingers skirting around the marks.

"Guards and police officers," I answer in a standoffish tone. "You know what they are like."

His eyes narrow on the bruises for a second before he lowers the material back down. "Point them out to me. I'll deal with them."

"No," I quickly say. "It's fine, really."

"It's not fucking fine," Theo growls. "And another thing—*why are you avoiding me?*"

My stomach drops. "I'm not avoiding you," I lie.

"Bullshit."

"I'm not," I argue weakly, still swaying.

Theo repositions his hands to my waist, picking me up slightly and sitting me back on the ground before I can protest. "*Sit. Down.*"

He takes a seat in front of me, blocking my path in case I try to stand again.

"Theo, I'm just tired. That's all."

"You're a terrible liar, Avery. What's going on? What happened with the police?"

I give him a sympathetic look, knowing he probably wants answers. Besides the awkward breakfast, the last time he saw me I was being ripped away from him in handcuffs. At the thought, guilt returns, but also, a little bit of suspicion.

I still don't know what happened to Sam. And Theo told me he had killed before and would do it again without hesitation. I was still willing to go down for him, but I had to know...

"Nothing happened with the police," I start. "They took me in for questioning and then I was released."

I purposely avoid mentioning Alexander, or the conversation I had with Margie. Some things are better left unsaid, especially if I need to protect him again. I've also been warned not to speak about things, to go with the flow. Apparently, Sam's death has been ruled as a suicide, but in my gut, I know that's not true. He was ruthless, an asshole—but despite everything, he wouldn't have killed himself.

Sam's apology still plays in my mind. It was so rehearsed, forced. But he didn't have a death wish—*did he?*

"They just released you?" Theo repeats, unconvinced. "Why would they arrest you for murder and then deem it a suicide? It's likely the autopsy hasn't even finished yet."

I shrug. "That's just what they told me." Pausing, I give him a non-judgmental, sad smile. "Theo, I need to know... what did you do to Sam?"

Theo raises an eyebrow at me. "I didn't do shit to him. I merely told him he had to apologize."

Staring at him in silence, I watch as his face changes—realization dawning.

"Do you think I killed him, Avery?"

"Did you?" I ask, barely above a whisper.

He breaks out in a laugh, the sinister sound almost confirming my suspicions.

"No, I didn't," he answers confidently. "Though, I wish I had."

"Oh..." I'm confused—and equally guilty for assuming it. "I thought—"

"You thought I killed him?"

I nod slowly. "It just seemed like it. He looked so terrified when he said sorry. Then when the police arrived, I thought they were coming for you."

Theo smiles, huffing into a laugh. "I would have killed him. I would have gutted him without hesitation. But that would have meant leaving you. And I'm not prepared to do that. Besides, if I was going to do that, I wouldn't be masquerading it as suicide. I would proudly wear his blood. I'd wear it like a medal."

"I don't think honorable killings are a thing," I mumble.

"There's nothing honorable about me," he replies coolly. "But no, I didn't kill him, Avery. But I'm flattered you thought so."

I stare at him bewildered, trying to decipher if he's being sarcastic. A genuine smile lingers on his face as he appears unfazed at my accusation.

That would have meant leaving you...

"If you didn't kill him, then who did?" I murmur, out loud.

Theo shrugs. "Beats me. The asshole had it coming though. I hope he suffered."

"Theo!" I scold. "Don't say that."

His eyes darken even more than usual. "I told you. I'm not a good guy, Avery. I don't give a shit about people like him. Frankly, the world is better off without him. After what he did to you, he deserved every single bit of misery. I'm just sad someone else took care of it."

"But you didn't want to leave me?" I repeat, changing the subject as my heart flutters nervously.

Theo looks away, smiling. "Don't get all mushy on me. Besides, you're avoiding the real question here. Why are you avoiding me?"

Chapter 7

Theo

Avery stills, her body tensing up. I flick my gaze back to her, watching the wave of emotions run over her face. She's trying to fight them, deliberately taking her time with an answer. Maybe she hopes I'll drop the subject, but there's no fucking chance of that.

"I'm not avoiding you," she says softly. "I'm just—"

"Tired, yes. You've said," I cut her off. "But you purposely avoided me at meals today. You also refuse to look at me whenever I ask."

Slowly, she locks eyes with mine, pain reflecting back at me. When she doesn't answer, I start putting the puzzle together myself.

"What are you afraid of?"

"Everything," she whispers, defeated. "Fucking everything."

My eyebrows furrow and I shift closer to her, grabbing her hand to calm her. "Listen to me. There's nothing you can say or do that will make me run."

Avery shakes her head sadly. "You will. Everyone always does."

"Is this about Hawthorne?" I ask her, watching as her face lights up in shock.

"Grey?" she murmurs. "What do you mean?"

Great. Now we're skirting around *that* issue too.

Of course I'm aware of their relationship. It wasn't like he was hiding anything—purposely always with her, dragging her into their mess. I don't know what their deal is, but I couldn't give a shit. Not my circus, not my monkeys. But, regardless, I know he has it bad for her. I also know that it's because of him and his little bitch boy that Avery has been dragged into their shit.

And judging by the look of despair on her face, he's a sore point. But I don't believe that's the whole story. Still, it's a start. The sooner I can break down those walls and get her to talk, the sooner we can move forward.

"You and him had something, didn't you?" I ask her casually.

More emotions cross her face, faster than last time. I can barely keep track as a war rages behind her eyes. Finally, she shrugs, getting glassy-eyed.

"Are you going to leave if I tell you?"

I growl quietly, semi-frustrated. Was she not just listening to me?

"I already told you the answer to that."

Avery looks surprised—caught off-guard. "Theo, there's a lot you don't understand."

"I understand well enough," I snarl. "But patience has never been my virtue."

"Yes," she says, confirming it with a broken voice. "But we had a fight. He found out... about you."

"Right," I draw out slowly. "And is he the reason you're avoiding me?"

She looks at me, baffled at my suggestion. Given the shit he's probably said to her about me, she's probably confused why I don't feel the same.

Truthfully, I don't care. Neither of them hid their interactions so it's not a surprise to me. At the end of the day, she's free to do as she likes. What I don't agree with is being blatantly ignored and avoided. Especially since she was just ripped away from me by police, and now she's back, withdrawn and secluded, on the verge of passing out.

Something happened and I won't rest until I know.

"No, he's not," she mutters. "But I assumed you'd be mad."

I laugh, startling her. "You're a grown woman. You can make your own choices. Why are you avoiding me?" I press again, watching her shift uncomfortably.

"I can't tell you," Avery answers. "But it's for the best."

My eyes narrow. The confirmation that she *is* avoiding me is one thing, but it's another to see her reaction. If *she* wanted to avoid me, she'd tell me. I know she hates confrontation, but people get defensive when they are in charge of their decisions and feel like they need to justify them. The fact that she's nervous about this conversation says a lot.

This isn't her choice.

A stray tear slips down her cheek, her hand quickly brushing it away. I reach forward and grasp her hand, pulling her forward. She's so weak that her body just falls forward, and I catch her, pulling her into my chest.

Stunned eyes gaze up at me, but before she can say anything, I lean forward, pressing my lips to hers.

I'm not above using this tactic again. The best way to get Avery out of her own mind is to distract her with something else. It worked in the morgue and I have no doubt it will work now.

Fuck. The morgue...

The feeling of her body against mine brings it all back, my mind remembering how it felt to fuck her.

Right on cue, her body slumps against me, the tension leaving as she kisses me back. We're nothing if not animals, driven by the primal urges buried deep in our DNA.

Her lips move against mine and my cock hardens under her touch. My arms wrap around her back, holding her tighter to me.

I nearly lost her when the police took her. I tried so hard to get to her, but the officers and guards had held me back, pinning me against the wall. It was one of the worst feelings in my life, watching her helpless figure disappear with them.

My hands thread through her hair, gliding my fingers as I deepen the kiss. She lets me, whimpering in my mouth as my tongue finds hers.

She tastes like Heaven. My fallen angel.

If God exists, he must be sick. Who would send a divine creature like her into the Devil's lair? And now she's stuck with me.

I don't care about anything else, as long as she's with me.

Avery's knees sit on either side of my waist as I hold us upright. When my torso starts to lose grip, I quickly flip her onto her back onto the ground. Straddling over her frame, I keep kissing her, hand sliding up her leg. She's in shorts today, but that doesn't deter me, my fingers sliding up under the fabric.

Her hips jerk into my touch as her hands grasp my head. I can sense her desperation and fear, afraid of letting me go.

I'm not going anywhere, Avery.

Sitting back, I grab the sides of her shorts, pulling them down her legs. She stares up at me, lips swollen and more pink than usual. As soon as she's bare, I shuffle back, spreading her legs open so I can see her properly.

My only regret about the morgue is I didn't get to see *her*. The darkness had stolen that from me, but now, I'm not losing that opportunity.

She's perfect. So fucking perfect.

Her pussy is already glistening with wetness, begging to be touched. And knowing I've done that to her? There's no greater feeling.

I can sense her trepidation as I just gaze at her most intimate parts in silence. But credit to her, she keeps her legs open. I can see them tremble slightly, and I know she's fighting the urge to hide.

My gaze flickers up to her face, a serious expression on my own.

"You're fucking perfect, Avery. Don't ever hide this from me. I want to see all of you."

Her eyes widen slightly at my words, but I look away, laying my stomach flat on the ground. I'm inches away from her, the smell of her sweet arousal hitting my senses. It's fucking intoxicating, ruthless. She could end me in a single minute if she wanted. I wasn't wrong when I said she's a fucking force of nature.

There's so much potential for her, locked up in a mind cage. She deserves better, she deserves to be free.

I take my time with her, my fingers prying her open as I examine every single inch of skin. I want to remember all of her, have her burned into my memories.

My hand runs along her thigh and pelvis, softly touching her soft skin. She shivers under my touch, drawing a smile to my face.

Slowly, I trail my thumb along her slit, teasing her. When I reach the top, I press inward, circling her clit with my digit.

I hear her suck in a breath, my stomach clenching at the sound. I can't wait any longer, my face leaning in so I can replace my finger with my tongue.

One swipe. Then two more.

Her legs buckle and shake so easily, my arms wrapping around her thighs so I can hold them in place. Then I bury my face into my new home, lips sealing around her clit.

"Theo," she gasps, surprised, hands clawing at the ground.

I smile against her, writing my name with my tongue. I've already marked her with my ink, and now, I'm marking her pussy with my mouth. I focus heavily on the last letter, drawing it over and over, until she's shaking against me.

Avery tenses up and I know she's close, so I slide two fin-gers inside her warmth, pleased when she clenches around me. She's squeezing me like she's holding on for dear life, and I'm fucking here for it.

I curl my fingers, finding her g-spot. Pressing up, I stroke it firmly, turning my attention to her clit. She whimpers my name again, voice breaking beautifully as she finds her re-lease. I refuse to let go, eating her until she's a fidgeting mess, impaled on my fingers.

As she slumps back on the ground, I remove my hand, crawling up her body.

"Look at me," I demand, watching as her eyes focus them-selves on me. When I have her full attention, I pop one finger into my mouth, sucking it clean. Her mouth falls open in awe, eyes sparkling with that light again. It's been dimmed the past few days, and I'm ecstatic to see the return.

When I'm finished removing every trace of her from my finger, I move my hand to her face, the other finger gently grazing down her lips. She opens them slowly, my cock twitching painfully. Our eyes remain locked together as she sucks my finger, tasting herself.

Fuck.

"You're so fucking beautiful," I tell her, reaching down to free myself from the gray slacks. My cock springs out, aching for the feel of her. She's so close, yet so far away, and it takes all of my control and restraint not to just slam into her.

"You are," she answers, making me pause.

No one has ever told me before in my life that I'm beautiful. And if you'd asked me before today how I'd feel about it, I'd be indifferent—repulsed even. But hearing her say it, sends a rush through me.

"Fuck, Avery," I growl, shuffling forward as I rub her clit with the head of my cock. "Do you have any idea what you do to me?"

She shakes her head, and it makes me want to kiss her. She's so naïve, so blind. It's no wonder she has people falling to their feet over her. In her mind, she's at rock bottom, watching as people hit the same level too. But in reality, she's far from that lie. She's a fucking powerhouse, bringing even the most broken, lost souls to salvation.

"I'll show you," I say to her, watching her eyes roll back as I stroke her clit with my cock. "I'll make you feel the same way you make me feel."

"Do it," she whispers, begging. "Please, Theo."

The sound of my name on her lips breaks the last tiny fragment of control, and I quickly adjust my position before slamming into her. Her back rockets up the carpet, cries spilling from her lips as I bury myself into her tight cunt.

I don't wait—*I can't*—as I smash our bodies together. Her walls tighten around me, locking us as one, and I grab the nape of her neck, bringing our faces together.

"I could die right now," I growl, looking into her gray orbs. "It would be the best death. I wouldn't want to be anywhere else except *in you*."

She moans, my mouth quickly covering hers as I swallow them. I don't care who hears. Let them. She's mine and right now, that's all that matters. I'll kill anyone who takes this from me. They will never touch her again. They'll never take her away.

If anyone lays a single finger on her, bruising her perfect skin, I'll soak them in gasoline and make a bonfire.

The sound of our skin hitting together echoes around the library, Avery's body sliding further and further up the carpet. My hand whips out and grabs hold of the bookshelf, while my other grips on to her. I kiss her heatedly—how could I not? She's the drug of my choice and I need this as much as she does.

I feel her start to spasm around me, so I let go of her neck, sitting up. My hand slips between our bodies, rubbing her clit fast. I'm fighting back my own orgasm, determined to get her there first. I won't rest until she's coming on my cock.

Her moans fall silent, her mouth opening wide as her eyes slam shut.

She's nearly there.

I wait, breathing heavily as the look of concentration on her face turns to relief, her pussy convulsing around my cock. The moment it does, I can't hold it back any longer, a growl ripping from my throat as I shoot my much needed release into her.

Our lips smash together again as we finish riding out our highs, and when we both stop moving, I pull back slightly to look into her eyes.

"You're not going to avoid me any longer, Avery. I don't care the reason why. Whatever it is, I promise that I'm the bigger threat."

Chapter 8

Avery

Bed never felt so good.

I had finally made it to the end of the day, showered, and was now curled up on my hard, kind-of-itchy mattress.

By the time Theo and I had finished in the library, it was nearly the end of free time. He stopped pushing for the real reason why I was trying to stay away, but his words still replayed in my mind.

"Whatever it is, I promise that I'm the bigger threat."

I don't know how I feel about it. Of course, I don't want to stay away from him. But I'm terrified of the consequences. I know he said he's the bigger threat, but we don't have the power here. Hell, we don't have anything.

It was a momentary lapse in judgment, but I needed him.

I can't do this alone.

Lilydale is already an isolated place. The only reason I've survived this long is because of the people I've met here—even if I do deserve the punishment for my actions.

Sleep starts to drift over me, every single muscle aching as I fade into black. I'm nearly out when a small click reaches my ears. It's so faint that for a split second, I convince myself

I was imagining it, until I hear the familiar creak of my door opening.

My eyes shoot open instantly. Peering through the dark, I spot a figure step into my room. My heart beats rapidly, with a small fraction of hope, as I try to pinpoint recognizable features.

There's only a few people who can do that...

"Avery," a voice draws out through the darkness.

I groan, shoving my face into my pillow. "Oh, God."

"Not God," he laughs. "The Devil."

"What do you want now, Damon?"

He laughs quietly to himself, his darkened frame leaning against the wall opposite me. "Are you trying to sleep?"

"It would be nice," I grumble, frustrated that I can't seem to catch a break.

"Too bad I'm not nice," Damon says. "Your attendance is required tomorrow."

I sit up in bed, crossing my legs under my body. Why?"

"Because I said so," he replies simply. "Despite your... *indiscretions*... the society still requires you to contribute for now. I'll send someone to collect you tomorrow."

"Grey?" I ask before I can stop myself.

Damon scoffs. "I don't think so. He wants nothing to do with you. Your contact with him will be minimal at most. Besides, no point being greedy. You're obviously still getting your *fill* from other sources."

The way he says it confidently, the knowingness behind his tone, I already know that he's referring to me and Theo today. He knows everything, after all.

"It's nothing to do with that," I mutter, trying to regain confidence. "I care greatly about Grey."

"How stupid of you."

"We might be done, but that won't change how I feel," I shoot back. "So, whatever sick comments you want to make, you can keep them to yourself. If he wants nothing to do with me, fine. But I still care about him."

Damon's footsteps echo around my room, and I swallow hard, knowing he's getting closer to the bed. "You dug your grave, Avery. Now you can be buried in it. I only say things once. I warned you not to fuck with him, and you didn't listen. So now you pay the price."

"And serve you?" I huff in disgust. "I'll pass, thanks."

"I only allow people of worth to serve me. You do not fit that criteria. However, do not mistake my mercy for weakness. I can end you—*and your little boyfriend*—whenever I like. But I'm more interested in your relationship with Arthur. Therefore, you're temporarily useful to the society."

I fall silent, shocked that he knows about my little conditions. But the real question is... how much does he know?

Damon continues. "If you try to cross me, I will make you regret it. I don't *need* you. You're being given mercy that most will never see. But make no mistake—this is for my benefit, not yours. If you're smart, you'll play along."

"And if I'm not?" I reply bluntly.

He laughs, a sinister threat lurking in his tone. "I'll nail your casket shut myself."

"Fine," I snap back. "But if it's for the greater good of the *society*, know that I'm doing this for Grey, not for you."

"Whatever helps you sleep at night."

"Clearly, it's not you. Now, if you'll please leave, I'd like to get a few hours rest."

Damon laughs under his breath, footsteps slowly heading toward the door. "I'll see you tomorrow, Avery."

Somehow, I manage to get a little rest. But like yesterday, I'm awoken by a guard, storming into my room.

As he grabs me from the bed, I'm still exhausted and drained, but thankfully, not as much as yesterday.

We bypass the bathrooms this time, and I say a silent prayer. But unfortunately I speak too soon, finding myself in the communal toilets, a brush being shoved into my hands.

I resist the urge to throw it in disgust, but reluctantly, do as I'm told and start scrubbing toilets. When we're finished there, I'm forced to clean the male urinals too, grumbling to myself at how putrid men are. You'd think after two decades they would know how to aim.

My hands are still red, but at least I can separate them from the bleach, giving them a good wash when I'm done before breakfast.

I won't let them break me.

If they think cleaning some bathrooms and toilets will make me snap, they are dead wrong.

At breakfast, I decide to defy them all, sending a big *fuck you* to the higher ups, sitting across from Theo. I can feel eyes on me, but it's just the other patients. It's normal—I'm used to the stares now.

The guards watch carefully too, and I know they are going to report back to Whittingham—but let them.

For the most part, we eat in silence, but I can see Theo's more relaxed today. He seems happy that I'm sitting there, and when the bell rings, I'm promptly escorted off to Dr. Smith's office.

The appointment goes slowly. I answer the bare minimum, but he doesn't seem surprised. Dr. Smith relays that he passed on my psych assessment results to Mr. Whittingham and I can only nod in response.

My head is elsewhere today.

A quick stop at Dr. Markel's for some ointment, followed by more history lessons, then free time. Theo and I hang out in the empty room where we tattooed each other, and make small talk. If he's suspicious of my behavior today, he doesn't call me out on it. And thankfully, he doesn't press for information again.

I spot Grey lurking around during free time, walking the halls, but he ignores me, sticking close to Damon. The latter gives me a knowing look when we head back to the hall after free time, and I keep myself calm and composed.

Fuck you, Demon Boy.

The rest of the afternoon passes by, and after dinner and showers I wait on my bed, cross-legged. I have no idea what time I'm going to be *summoned*, but I don't bother to try to sleep.

Finally, when everything falls quiet outside as people go to sleep, I hear footsteps stop in front of my door.

I stand up, watching as the door swings open. I glance at the familiar face, giving him a small nod. Byrone gestures for me to follow him with two fingers without muttering a single word, and I follow him to the library like old times. Except... I'm missing a crucial part of the routine.

As we enter, I'm greeted with the usual setup. The curtains drape over the ends of the aisles, closing off the book shelves. The smell of freshly prepared food hits my senses, and I can already see a bunch of people sitting at the tables which have been pushed together to make one long surface.

Damon is sitting at the head of the table on his throne of invisible thorns, casually talking to Grey as we approach. They both look up, giving me a hardened glance before I wait for instructions.

"Sit next to Jillian," Damon directs bored, waving me off with his hand.

My eyes find Jillian's and she gives me a tight smile, putting me slightly at ease. As I round the table, I have to pass Grey, and it's like a shock of electricity between us.

Sitting down, I do my best to ignore the burning desire to look over. I focus on the table of food in the corner, gazing over the fresh fruit, warm little finger foods, and various beverages.

More people arrive, filling the empty spaces at the table, until finally, we're a full house.

"Good Evening," Damon starts, leaning back into his chair. "I appreciate you all attending on such short notice. As you are aware, we have some pressing matters to discuss."

A handful of people nod casually, the room silent except for Damon's deep voice.

"While this evening is all about business, you will note that we've set up the private rooms for your enjoyment. Before we begin, Grey will fill you in on the information you have been waiting for."

I can't help it. My gaze snaps down the table to him at the mention of his name, heart palpitating when we lock eyes for a brief second. He looks away quickly, smiling sweetly at everyone.

"Samuel Hallman's membership has been permanently revoked due to his *unfortunate* death. While I'm sure some of you will miss the floppy fucker, rest assured that his death wasn't in vain."

A few quiet laughs echo around the table and I shift awkwardly. It's obvious that he wasn't well loved, but if he was a member of the society, he must have meant something to them.

Or, at least, had some *quality* contributions.

Everyone here is worth something to Damon. While I can't understand what Sam's appeal was, it's obvious he was needed for Damon's grand plans.

"Jillian was able to confirm that Operation Clown has been a success. We've gained control of the camera feeds in the facility and currently, the Lilydale staff have not been able to get it back. At present, we're feeding them what we want. This includes the footage from Hallman's room which featured the night of his demise."

Some people look surprised, which makes me feel a little better. At least I'm not the only one that this is news too.

"So, it's been ruled as suicide?" Byrone asks casually.

Damon nods. "Yes. And as you can see, Andy Jemison has taken Hallman's place in Cirque des Morts."

A few gazes land on a new figure at the end of the table. I look him over carefully, eyes lingering on the long scar down his left cheek. His dark brown eyes are on Damon, his pitch-black hair messy and unkempt. He nods, giving everyone a little wave.

"But this was already in motion before his death, correct?" someone asks. "Due to his indiscretions."

"Correct," Damon confirms. "And his girlfriend has been permanently banned. However, I don't suspect her to be a problem from here on out."

Vivian?

I feel eyes burning on me and I turn my head, finding Grey watching me carefully. Even though we aren't speaking, I know our minds are on the same track. I wonder if they know that Vivian tried to kill herself. They would have to—they know everything.

"We anticipate that the Lilydale board will replace Hallman shortly. Any opportunity to get more money in the door," Grey says, not looking away.

My eyes shift to Damon as he watches me carefully. I look away from both of them, staring at the table.

"Moving on to Operation Ringmaster," Damon continues. "Now that Jemison is on board, we will be pushing ahead. Phase one was successful, so now we are confident we are able to move to phase two."

A few people make notes on paper and I suddenly feel out of place again. I guess it's a 'you'll know if you know' situation, so I don't dare ask for information. I'm still not even quite sure why I'm here exactly, but something tells me it will become apparent soon.

"Jemison," Grey directs. "I will speak to you tomorrow about your tasks. Leighton will also be your contact."

"Rightio," Andy answers coolly. "And we established the issues with the files I was told about?"

Damon looks at me, leaning forward on his hands. A dark smile crosses his face, making me hold my breath.

"Yes. While we are aware that Christopher provided the society with the incorrect key, the files were nonetheless broken into. Upon review of Jillian's footage, we were able to ascertain that Capello leaked the file."

My eyes widen. "What?" I blurt out, causing everyone to look at me. "Vivian was the one who stole my file?"

Chapter 9

Avery

Grey stares at me, and for the first time, I don't look back. I'm stuck staring at Damon in disbelief.

"That's right," he answers casually. "She was the one who broke into the office and took your information. I believe it was Arthur's printer she used. Is that right?" he pauses, looking at Jillian.

Jillian nods. "Yes. With his staff access card."

I gawk at Damon. "When was this information going to be relayed to me? I thought we had a deal. I told you I had a right to have a say in how this was dealt with."

Tension rises in the room, a few people sucking in oxygen sharply as Damon stands from his seat.

"We *did not* have a deal, Avery. I told you I would consider having your input, however you broke that trust in the society. Everyone here is aware of your actions."

No one says anything, an uneasy silence filling the room. My eyes flicker to Grey, who has turned away from me once again. Anger washes over me, but I control it, keeping my voice low.

"Regardless of how you perceive me and my *actions*," I murmur. "This situation still involves me. I did nothing wrong. And if you would like my assistance, then the very least you can do is stick to your word. I figured that a man of your standing would at least honor that."

It's so quiet you can hear the pipes in the wall creak and groan. I'm doing my best to stay composed, strong. I deserve at least some information—and if they want to use me, then it can be on my terms.

Damon tilts his head up, eyes narrowing on me as he processes my words. "I would watch your tone with me. My mercy can only be stretched so far. You were advised that I would take your suggestions under consideration. Given you were detained by the police, we only had a short window to look into this and deal with it. We are giving you the courtesy of notifying you now of our findings. Be grateful that you are here at all."

"Here at all? I was arrested because of *you*."

He laughs, moving away from his chair as he heads toward me. I don't run though, straightening my posture. When he's behind my seat, I stiffen. Snickering again, he puts his hand on my shoulder, squeezing it harshly.

"Consider this a warning, Avery. Don't make allegations that you know nothing about. You know what they say about assuming things."

I resist the urge to tell him he's already an ass, staying quiet instead.

Pleased with my silence, he continues walking around the table, looking at the other members. "As you may have already guessed, the society dealt with the situation—at least with Capello and Hallman. Which brings us to our next point in the meeting."

He pauses when he reaches his seat again, but doesn't sit down. There's a smile lurking on the corner of his lips, and everyone waits for him to speak.

Damon looks at Grey, nodding.

Grey stands up, placing his hands in his pockets. "At present, we have reason to believe that those two have been aptly sorted. However, it is our understanding that Arthur is attempting to gain leverage from the patients. We believe that he has asked Avery to report back to him on inside information."

My eyes widen as everyone looks at me in surprise. I guess that answers my question about how much Damon knows.

Gray eyes meet mine, his face stone cold. "Avery, are you able to elaborate on that?"

I can only make a dumb '*uh*' sound as Grey waits for my answer, everyone's eyes on me. They have me cornered—they know it, I know it.

I could lie... but really, what would that achieve?

It's obvious that Damon and his society have more control over Lilydale than the staff do. If I'm smart, I'd pick sides. I'm more protected in this circle than I am banished on the outside.

It's a cold reminder that I *was* banished—only now *welcomed* back because of these stipulations from Arthur.

But maybe... just maybe... Mr. Whittingham handed me my 'get out of jail' card—excuse the pun.

Swallowing, I nod. "Yes, he had a conversation with me after I returned from the police station."

Damon nods, looking pleased. Grey, on the other hand, just appears downright mad.

"Well?" Damon asks impatiently.

It feels like my stomach is being clenched in tight knots. "He wants me to report back to him on things I hear around the facility."

A few people whisper among themselves, but judging by Damon's face, he already knows the extent of this. However, if I was a gambling woman, I'd wager that he doesn't know the rest of it.

"Also," I start, wondering if I'm about to sign my death sentence. "He had other stipulations too."

"Oh?" Damon answers, intrigued. "Such as?"

My eyes slowly flicker back to Grey. "I'm not allowed to socialize with any of you."

It's a broad mention, but I know Damon's smart. He knows I'm not referring to the society in general, but still, he nods slowly.

"Interesting. I wonder how he expects you to provide information then."

"It sounds like he's purposely setting me up for failure," I reply bluntly. "So that either way, he can get rid of me."

Damon sits down in his chair, tapping his chin. "I don't think you're the end goal. No—Arthur has something else up his sleeve. You're just collateral damage."

I roll my eyes. "I'm already collateral damage. Otherwise, I wouldn't have been framed for Sam's murder."

Before Damon can respond, Grey interjects angrily.

"What does that mean?" he snaps at me quietly.

I jolt slightly. "I think we know what I mean," I mutter. "You guys wanted me gone."

The table is still deathly silent, watching our interaction with bated breaths and wide eyes. Damon just laughs quietly, looking at Grey, amused.

"You don't know what the fuck you're talking about," Grey hisses through clenched teeth.

His harsh tone is a somber reminder of his new feelings toward me, the hurt returning in my chest. I look at him sadly, shrugging.

"It's okay. I don't blame you," I answer softly.

It's not how I wanted to have this conversation. I didn't want an audience to witness my confession or guilty feelings. But, I may not get another opportunity.

Damon puts his hand on Grey's shoulder, calming down the inferno building in his eyes. "Leave it," he orders Grey.

"No," he growls. "She's spitting out bullshit."

I cringe. "I'm just saying that I understand. And that I'm sorry."

It's an apology to him, even though I still maintain I haven't done anything wrong. I know I hurt him, and at the end of the day, that's what matters. His feelings are valid, and while everything we had is gone, I still want him to know that.

Damon squeezes his hold on Grey, looking around the room. "We'll adjourn the meeting temporarily. Please enjoy the food and use of the private rooms while we deal with this. Avery, keep your ass seated."

No one needs to be told twice, everyone quickly pushing off from their chairs as they grab food or head to the isolated aisles. I stay in my chair, watching as some people give me pitying looks, while others ignore me completely.

I look over at Damon and Grey, the two of them whispering heatedly to each other. Finally, Grey relaxes, letting out a sigh. I'm amazed that someone like Damon has the power to calm him, and for a weird second, I'm actually appreciative of that fact.

When everyone disappears from this end of the library, I expect to be alone with Damon, but he turns and vanishes out of sight behind a curtain.

I gape at Grey's lone figure, trying to process what is happening.

Grey takes a few seconds to compose himself, breathing deeply. I don't dare move or say anything, heart racing.

Maybe he'll speak to me?

Finally, he opens his eyes, looking at me coldly. "Come with me," he demands, stalking off toward the library doors.

I quickly push my chair back, rounding the table to catch up with him. We head past the closed off aisles, the sounds of people talking and fucking inside.

As we head outside the library doors, I'm astonished that Grey motions for me to go into the dark, quiet hall with him.

The doors close behind us and I take a quick glance around, making sure we're truly alone. There's not a soul in sight—probably not in us either—and finally, I turn to face Grey.

"Hey..." I start, unsure of what to say.

He stands tall, arms folded. "What the hell is your problem?" he asks angrily. "We did you a favor inviting you back and you just start badmouthing Damon."

"I didn't plan to do it," I say weakly. "Besides, isn't it the truth?"

Grey glares at me. "You think we framed you?"

"Yeah, kind of..." I trail off.

He shakes his head, laughing in disbelief. "Wow, Avery. After everything I did for you... that's how you perceive me."

My eyebrows furrow. "Wait... are you saying it wasn't you?"

"Why the fuck would we frame you for murder?"

"I..." Unsure of how to answer, I just fall silent.

Grey paces in front of me, face finally cracking. He looks hurt—again. "I don't believe you."

"It wasn't you or Damon?" I ask, bewildered. "You didn't put that card in my pocket?"

He stops, glaring at me. "Of course not! I'm mad at you. So *fucking* mad at you. But I'm still trying to protect you for some stupid reason. The fact that you would ever think that. Fuck! I obviously didn't know you at all."

Panic.

Just pure panic in my blood.

"Grey," I say, moving toward him. "Just let me explain things."

"You already did," he replies angrily. "And I don't want to hear it again. You're free to do what you want, Avery."

I hate the way my name sounds on his lips now. It sounds like poison—choking him from the inside out. I'm a walking suffocation, but I take the chance, knowing I might not get the opportunity again.

I cross the distance between us, putting my hands on his arms. He stiffens, but surprisingly, doesn't shove me off.

"Grey," I murmur softly. "You mean everything to me. Since day one, you saw something in me. It was the first time in my life that someone really cared enough to fight for me. And that means so much to me. With Theo... it was the same." The mention of his name makes Grey's eyes flash, and I tread carefully, continuing. "You both treated me like I meant something. I'm not used to that. And with us, you and me, it's—*was*—so special. But I didn't know it was just meant to be us. This is all new to me. And I'm learning to survive here. I fucked up, I know I did. And I can't forgive myself for hurting you. But I'm willing to help you if it means finding a way to fix the hurt."

Grey stares at me silently, eyes scanning my face.

"I'm sorry," I say sincerely. "I know what we had is over. But I just want you to know that I'm not going to tell Whittingham anything. And I'll do what Damon needs if it's what you want. You can ignore me if that's what you need. Now that I know the truth, I'll deal with it and leave you alone."

It feels like a tiny weight has been lifted from my shoulders. I don't even know what I've rambled, but at least I've finally said my peace.

I believe him entirely when he says that they didn't do it. I can hear it in his voice, in his pain. Despite Damon taunting it, I now realize it wouldn't have made sense. They were nowhere near me when it happened.

He just continues to stare at me in complete silence, but slowly, a part of me notices his hardened face fading. Not fully though—just enough that I don't fear for my life. Though, if I'm being honest, I don't think I ever would—even now.

Finally, he just nods, turning around and heading out of the hall with a silent command to return to the library.

I follow behind him, unsure how to feel. But somehow... it feels like a step in the right direction.

Chapter 10

Grey

I don't know how to take any of her words.

Each one is like a stabbing to my chest, a wound that burns and refuses to close. But still, somehow, I believe her.

It's still not quite enough though. But the anger I felt has dissipated slightly.

I still need a release though.

As I head back inside the library, I sense Avery behind me, her quiet footsteps ringing loudly in my ears. I'm so consciously aware of her movements.

I immediately find Damon lingering by the meeting table, watching me with a collected gaze as we enter. I give him a stern nod before disappearing behind a curtain to give myself a minute to calm down before we get back to business.

No one is in this aisle thankfully, and even without seeing her, I know she's hovering outside, wondering if she should follow.

Right on cue, I hear Damon summon her over, thankful for his intervention.

In the next aisle over, I hear muffled groans and sounds of pleasure, the stark reminder making me mad. I want to fuck her so hard that it hurts. I want to slam into her with such force that we defy the laws of physics and become one person. It seems fitting anyway, since she already has my heart. She might as well take my body and soul too. At least then I'd find some type of peace. Sure, it would probably be hell too, but if she sends me there, I would have a nice family reunion no doubt.

I stay hidden for a few minutes until Damon's voice booms out around the library, calling everyone back.

Swinging back the curtain, I resume my place next to him, ignoring burning eyes on me.

"Let's get on with it," Damon says firmly, hands planted on the table in front of him. "My patience is starting to wear thin. Now, if there's no further interruptions," he hisses, looking at Avery daringly.

A smirk tugs on my lips. In my peripheral vision, I notice her slouch in her seat, cheeks red. Even with the embarrass-ment I know she feels, there's a more relaxed vibe to her. I wonder how many times she said those sentences to herself over and over, how many times she imagined saying them to me.

I'm surprised at myself. I really thought I'd lose it. While she had probably imagined apologizing a million times, I had envisioned pinning her against the wall, squeezing the air out of her body while my cock was buried deep inside her.

I've never experienced the amount of love and hate simul-taneously as she brings out in me right now.

And worst of all—I know she's right. We were never officially together. But despite that, I thought it was obvious she was mine.

I told her that.

I hate sharing—ever since I was little. Any time I was made to share things, they got broken. They were taken from me. Not to mention what happened with my parents.

I'm fucking possessive. I'm dangerous. I'll fucking kill for what's mine.

And that extends to *her*.

We can't go back now. I can't move forward on the path I had laid out, so I guess it's time for Plan B.

Damon is right. We have too much at stake. I need to focus on the plan. We've worked too hard to be distracted now.

I just need to figure out how that includes dealing with *her*.

Arthur's little game has thrown a wrench in the mix, and although I am not surprised, it's a whirlwind of issues I have to deal with now. If I had my way, we would banish her. If she's out of sight and out of mind, I can almost breathe. But she's here. And we have to keep a tight leash on things.

If that old cunt gets his way, we'll lose everything.

I can't lose it again.

"We will be moving to weekly meetings until further notice," Damon tells everyone. "I require regular updates on the operations and you can be sure your tasks will increase. We're at a critical point, so keep all eyes on things. We'll also need to re-evaluate the groupings. Grey and I will create an alternate system over the next week and report back. In the meantime, the guards will continue to notify us of any plans from Lilydale staff."

I look over at Damon, wondering if he's going to tell everyone about his little deal. I doubt it—it's a secret that he's kept forever. And while the two worlds have never collided before, it's not the right time.

I'm still bewildered that he stepped in and did it. I trust he will give me answers soon. But upon reflection, I think I already know the reason partly. But it's never a case of what meets the eye with Damon. Sure, I probably know one of the reasons—but I bet there's at least three more.

"Will Whittingham issue any punishments?" Byrone asks.

I laugh, jumping into the conversation. "No. We've spoken to the old bat. He's not in a position to exercise that poor excuse for power. Punishing the patients for a suicide would reflect badly on them."

Damon nods. "I suspect that Hallman's death has probably brought some attention to the facility. While it's not uncommon for untimely deaths to occur, two suicides in close proximity will have hurt their precious mission statement. They will be doing damage control."

Avery's eyebrows shoot up in surprise. Sometimes, I forget how new she is. It feels like she's been here forever, but in retrospect, she's still just a newbie.

It was a different time back then. The last suicide rocked the facility—staff and patients—and I don't think anyone is going to forget it any time soon.

Especially not me.

"Do we think it will trigger anything else?" Jillian asks carefully.

Damon shoots her a warning glance, even though she's chosen her words well. "Not at this time, no. However, I'm keeping a close eye on things. I certainly think the board is trying to shake things up though. At this stage, we're not sure what their next plan is."

She nods quickly, putting her head down. Typing away on her laptop, my eyes narrow suspiciously. I know Damon trusts her somewhat, but you never know with Lilydale.

"What do you need us to do?" Jemison speaks up. "Will you approach us individually?"

"Yes," I answer casually, answering for Damon. "I'll be paying a few of you visits tomorrow."

Damon throws me a smile which I return before lazily glancing off around the room.

"That's all for tonight. I'll have more to report tomorrow. You'll be escorted back to your rooms in an hour, so make use of everything before then." Damon pauses, nodding toward the red curtain. "I believe Grey was able to line someone up tonight."

A few people murmur excitedly, standing as the meeting finishes. I spot Jemison eagerly strolling to the exhibition entrance, followed by a couple of others. Laughing to myself, I walk over to the alcohol I sourced, grabbing a bottle of whiskey to myself.

Swigging a quick mouthful, I head over to Damon, ignoring the fact that Avery is still sitting at the table awkwardly, like she doesn't know what to do.

"Good call on this," I tell him.

"Not quite what I had in mind in terms of venting your frustration, but whatever your poison," he replies coolly. "Maybe take a trip behind the red curtain."

He says it loud enough that Avery looks up at us in surprise, a brief flash of hurt crossing her face. It has the exact reaction he hoped for, small tears pooling in her eyes. But she doesn't cry though, only shoving back her chair to head over to the food.

I give him a knowing look, but he just shrugs, unfazed.

"Don't play with fire," he warns, and I know it's aimed at me.

"But the pain feels so good," I taunt back.

Damon rolls his eyes. "I'm serious. I let you have your little one-on-one. Hopefully that has cleared your head now. But stay focused. You know what you need to do tomorrow."

I nod. "I'll send Christopher your best. Or worst. Whatever you feel."

"You can send him to the grave for all I give a shit," he retorts. "Don't forget to pay a little visit to Markel. The docile fuck can barely practise these days but I wouldn't put it past Arthur to go to the least obvious."

Handing Damon the whiskey bottle, I laugh. "Give it a few more years and he'll have dementia. That's if he doesn't fuck himself into a heart attack."

He takes a sip, deep in thought. "Grab Capello's file while you are there. I have a few things that need to be confirmed."

"No worries," I mutter, turning around and heading over to the food.

The kitchen staff have to prepare the usual daily food in the most cost-effective way possible, but with a little bit of *persuasion,* I was able to convince them to provide us with something a bit more edible. I've been waiting all day to get my hands on the brisket, and apparently, that's what has Avery's attention too.

Reaching past her, I grab a handful of the tender meat, watching as she looks up surprised. I bet she didn't expect I'd be in close range again so soon, but seeing her reaction makes me want to taunt her even more.

If I can't have her, then maybe I'll just torture her. Just like she tortures me.

"Moist, isn't it?" I murmur. "Slow-cooked at the perfect temperature."

Avery glances at the meat, nodding slowly. "I guess so."

Popping a piece into my mouth, I lock eyes with her, annoyed that she's still yet to eat.

I shouldn't care.

But I do.

It's fucking annoying.

Picking up another piece, I hold it up to her lips, pressing it against the soft curve of her mouth. Juice trickles over her lips and suddenly Damon's words hit me. I am playing with fire—I want to burn.

When Avery's involved, I want everything.

Life.

Death.

Torture.

Pleasure.

Pain.

Every-*fucking*-thing she can offer me.

She looks at me, stunned, but opens her mouth so I can push the meat inside. Tipping her chin with my finger, I close her mouth, turning away. "Eat."

It's as if she's on auto-pilot, following instructions perfectly. A range of expressions cross her face—surprise, bewilderment, confusion, appreciation.

"It's good," she mutters after swallowing. "Really good."

"I know," I reply back in a snarky tone, reaching for a baked potato. "You should eat. Stop wasting my efforts."

Before she can respond, I walk away from the table, heading to the red curtain. I have no intention of involving myself with anyone, but as I disappear behind it, I hear a soft gasp from the food table. It hurts knowing that I'm hurting her, but at the same time, the pain is all I have to hold on to.

Jemison is balls-deep in the glory hole, while a few others are making out against the shelves. I lean against the shelf myself, watching curiously. These fuckers have no idea just how good we treat them. We're not all that scary. Fear is a powerful tool to wield, but at the end of the day, we reward everyone just as hard. Respect us and do as you're told, and you'll reap the benefits.

It just comes with a price first.

Chapter 11

Avery

I'm dragged out of bed with the first sign of morning light, feet barely getting a chance to touch the floor.

As the guard pulls me down the hall, I'm happy to find we're heading in the opposite direction of the bathrooms and toilets. Given my lack of sleep last night, I don't trust myself with chemicals. Hell, I don't trust myself enough not to fall asleep with my head in the toilet like my father used to do after a night of heavy drinking.

When we reach the door at the end of the rooms, I find myself in the main entrance of Lilydale. Despite being early, I spot Mr. Whittingham in his office, the door wide open.

I'm shoved inside by the guard, stumbling three steps before Mr. Whittingham even bothers to look up.

"Good Morning, Ms. White," he says in an annoyed tone.

"Hello," I mumble back, peeking over my shoulder to see the guard slam the door shut behind him as he exits.

"Take a seat."

Frowning, I sit down on the other side of Mr. Whittingham's desk, watching as he takes a sip of hot coffee.

"I trust your return has gone well," he asks, tone indicating that he doesn't give a shit either way.

I nod, unsure how to answer. "It's been fine."

"Your psych assessment was done by Dr. Smith. No concerns apparently," he trails off sarcastically. "And I'm sure you are aware I've been allocating special tasks for you."

Clenching my jaw, I just nod again. I'm fairly confident my nose hairs are now permanently singed from bleach.

Mr. Whittingham leans back in his chair, eyes falling to my hands resting in my lap. It takes me a moment to pick up on his curiosity, before frustration awakens me. Obviously he's been made aware of the burns, but judging by his glance, I wasn't scorched enough.

"How long do you need me to do the *special tasks* for?" I ask a little too bluntly.

It's way too early for interrogation. After the events of the *Cirque des Morts* meeting and the little sleep I managed, my filter ability is somewhat lacking today.

"As long as I please," he snarls back. "Now, do you have anything to report back to me?"

My eyes narrow. Does he know that Damon held a meeting last night?

I assume that he knows about the society, but I have no idea how much exactly.

I shake my head. "Nope."

Mr. Whittingham glares at me. "Are you sure?"

"Positive."

We enter into a stare-off for a few seconds, the frustration evident on his morning face. Slowly, he looks away, grabbing a bunch of paperwork.

"I need these sorted alphabetically."

I'm caught off-guard, jerking slightly like I've been hit with a rubber band. "Oh, alright."

There's not too many in the pile—it should be relatively easy.

He pauses, pointing to the corner of his office behind me. "Those as well."

Turning my head, I glance over my shoulder, eyes widening at the seven enormous stacks of paper.

Mr. Whittingham stands up, walking over to the corner. I rise to my feet as well, watching in horror as he kicks over the first pile with his foot. The pile scatters all over the ground, in turn, knocking over the next one.

It's a sea of white, my body sagging in disbelief.

"And I need them done this morning," he muses, folding his arms.

There's no way it's possible. I know it, he knows it.

Before I can speak again, he raises an eyebrow. "Unless, of course, there's something else we need to discuss first. Anything at all."

Our eyes meet, the glint in his challenging me. He definitely knows something went down—he's testing me.

That's his mistake though. He might flaunt whatever title he has, but there's bigger, scarier people here.

"Nothing at all," I remark defiantly, dropping to my knees in front of the stacks.

I can feel his anger next to me, a tense silence filling the room.

Giving a little huff under his breath, he walks back to his desk, slamming a few things in the process.

I never thought I'd see the day where I'd be loyal to Damon, but I guess even Hell can freeze over.

Scanning the first piece of paper, I find the corresponding letter, making smaller, separate piles to stack them.

And then I repeat it, over and over, until I have lots of tiny paper cuts on the tips of my fingers.

Sometime later, I hear the bell signaling for breakfast, but I already know that I won't be allowed to eat. Thankfully, the food from last night has given me the energy to be a stubborn little shit, holding Mr. Whittingham to his challenge.

A couple of times I scan over the contents of the paperwork, noticing it relates to patients. I'm not surprised though—the staff have already made it clear that ethical boundaries mean nothing in a place like Lilydale.

Some names I recognize, others I don't. And as I take note of dates, it dawns on me that this paperwork probably doesn't even need to be sorted. Multiple pages have 'copy' stamped across them, and judging by all the modern technology around the place, I'd be willing to bet that most things are electronically saved.

This is just another torture method since scrubbing floors and shit stains hasn't done the job.

Eventually, halfway through the mountain of sorting, a guard pops his head in the door, motioning for Mr. Whittingham.

"White is due for her appointments with Dr. Smith and Dr. Markel."

I'm not sure whether to feel relieved or annoyed. Another day in a row where I'm forced to interact with those two idiots, but a blessing in disguise to get away from this task.

"Fine," Mr. Whittingham snaps, glancing down at me. "We will continue later. Get her out of here."

The guard harshly pulls me up from the ground, making me yell out. "I can walk you know!"

Ignoring me, I'm shoved through the doorway, eyes landing on Teddy at the reception desk. She turns up her nose at me, muttering something under her breath. I don't catch it though, already pushed through the other doors, back into the secured area.

"You can let her go, thank you," Dr. Smith snarls at the guard when we reach the doorway. "She's more than capable of using her own limbs."

"That's what I'm saying," I growl, ripping my arm out of his grip.

My appreciation for Dr. Smith is short-lived when I enter his office, noticing a board game set up on the floor.

"What the hell is this?" I ask.

He smiles from his desk, standing up. "Have you played chess before?"

I raise an eyebrow. "Not really."

"It's quite simple once you get the hang of it," he muses, kneeling in front of the board. "I'll explain it to you."

I don't move, standing by the door as I glare at him incredulously. Dr. Smith sighs softly, tilting his head to the side.

"Sit down, Avery. Isn't it exhausting always being *on*?"

"It's exhausting being here," I tell him. "And having to deal with your weird tactics. What psycho bullshit are we doing today?"

He smiles knowingly, only motioning again for me to sit.

Begrudgingly, I walk over, dropping to the ground. I've seen chess boards before at school. Lake St. Louis High was pretty proud of their extra-curricular clubs. Unfortunately, I wasn't allowed to join any, but I was forced to watch a school championship chess match in my junior year. It was the single most boring thing to watch—more deafening than a Wimbledon tennis match.

"It's a strategy game," Dr. Smith starts, fixing up a few pieces. "We have sixteen pieces each. The aim is to capture the king."

I take a wild guess at which one is the king, lifting it up with my fingers. "Got it."

He laughs. "The *opponent's* king. Essentially, you have to trap it. I believe Wikipedia refers to it as *threatening the king with inescapable capture*."

"Kings are meant to be powerful though," I mumble back. "A good king would never allow himself to be caught."

"Exactly. But in chess, you control the pieces. While the king might be powerful, he means nothing without the control and protection of the board."

My eyebrows furrow. "Interesting theory you have there, Dr. Smith."

He smiles. "In fact, the most powerful piece on the chess board is the queen."

My head snaps up as I glance at him suspiciously. What the hell is he talking about? There's a slight shift in tone to his voice, making me think we're no longer talking about chess.

In theory we're talking about it, but with Dr. Smith, there's always a hidden motive. I have no doubt that today's session is more than meets the eye. I might not know much about chess, but I know it's a psychological game of strategy. We're doing this for a reason... and for once, I can't help but suspect it's nothing to do with my mental state.

"Right," I answer nonchalantly. "And these?" I point to a few pieces.

"Pawns."

"How fitting," I mumble sarcastically. "We're really just going to play chess?"

Dr. Smith laughs, getting comfortable in a sitting position. "We could talk about your feelings if you like."

"Chess, it is."

After giving me a brief rundown of the pieces and available moves, we start our game. I'm so confused—he should have just given me a Rubik's Cube to solve. But as we progress, I start to get the hang of things. Clearly, I'm no match for him though. He easily beats me with a smug look.

"We'll play again tomorrow," he says, gesturing to a clock on the wall.

I'm surprised to find the hour session has already passed. Right on schedule, the door opens as the guard looks inside, frowning in confusion at us on the ground. He stays quiet though, stepping forward to reach for me before Dr. Smith snaps at him firmly.

"She can walk. I'm sure she's more than capable of walking down the hallway to Dr. Markel's office."

I give him a rare smile of appreciation, heading out the door. It's nice not being manhandled for five minutes, even though I want to choke him with a rook.

The trip to the doctor is quick—some more ointment, general questions about my health, and a goodbye.

Afterwards, I'm taken back to Whittingham's office, stomach growling. When I enter, he's not alone.

Familiar salt and pepper hair, dressed in a suit worth more than my existence. The two men look at me as I enter, and it's easy to feel the difference in power between them. While Whitface pretends to hold power, the older man exudes it.

"Ms. White. Welcome back," Mr. Whittingham says. "Before you continue, I believe you've met already."

A hostile glance comes my way, and I give a brief nod. "Yes."

"I'll be in touch, Arthur," Alexander murmurs. "Keep me updated."

I swallow nervously, not wanting to deal with Alexander, but thankfully, he just gives me a cold glare before disappearing out of the room.

It takes a few seconds for my nervous system to calm back down, and I awkwardly point to the pile of paperwork. "Shall I continue?"

Mr. Whittingham nods. "You've been excused from class today. I imagine you won't be done by free time either," he taunts, sitting down in his chair. "Once you've sorted the piles alphabetically, I also expect each individual letter to be in alphabetical order based on surname."

My eyes scan over the paperwork. I should have seen this coming, to be fair.

Holding back a sigh, I perch myself on the ground and get to work.

It's going to be a long day.

Chapter 12
Avery

By the time I finish sorting everything, it's late.

Free time and dinner are long done. In fact, I think people have already been taken back to their rooms for the evening and are fast asleep.

My stomach can't stop growling from hunger. Dizziness threatens my vision, little black dots floating in orbit, but I finish it.

I fucking finish it.

Mr. Whittingham looks up from his desk, a mouth-watering steak in front of him that Teddy had dropped off before she left for the evening. His lips curl in disappointment, and that alone is reward enough for missing out on food. The smell of his extravagant dinner is torture, but I'm hopeful that this means I won't have to come back tomorrow.

"Done?" he asks, annoyed.

I nod. "Can I leave now?"

He chews the inside of his lip, contemplating the answer. He probably wants me to stay, wondering if he can dish out another shitty task.

Finally, he grunts to himself, pressing a button on his desk. A few seconds later, a guard enters, looking at him expected-ly.

"Escort Ms. White back to her room, please," he orders without glancing at me.

I breathe a sigh of relief, quickly getting to my feet. I realize it's the same guard as earlier and I give him a glare, daring him to lay hands on me.

Rolling his eyes slightly, he stands aside so I can exit, hand poised on his taser.

The two of us walk side by side to the secure part of the facility, a wave of nausea and exhaustion creeping over me. I ignore the burning feeling in my stomach as my body rips itself apart from hunger. Maybe I can just sleep it off.

My door slams closed behind me as I enter my room, feet heading straight for the bed. I lay down on my side, curling up as I try to dismiss the overwhelming thoughts of food. Never did I expect to crave the moldy-ass food they serve here. I guess when we are desperate, we do stupid things.

Laying in the darkness, I wait for sleep to take me away.

I remember when I was younger, my father used to with-hold food too. Even when he didn't, it would be rare to find items in the fridge that weren't alcohol. Sleep was always my comfort, because when you are away from your thoughts, life seems easier. You could tell yourself that the nightmares are irrational. Your body will switch off and you stop feeling the tearing sensation. And best of all, for a brief few hours, you can pretend you have a different life.

A creaking noise stirs me from my thoughts, my head lifting weakly from the pillow. Oddly enough, I feel like I'm used to late night visitors now—even if it is Damon.

"What can I do for you?" I ask quietly to the shadowed figure, unfazed.

Before a reply can come, I'm hit with the smell of food. I stiffen, wondering if I'm dreaming. Perhaps I'm just hallucinating now, like parched men in the desert seeing a mirage.

"Apparently you haven't eaten today."

My spine straightens rapidly as I shoot up in bed. But it's not the confirmation of food that has my attention—*it's the voice.*

"Grey?" I murmur wearily.

The door softly closes before footsteps head over to the bed. I'm still in disbelief, fighting back the urge to reach out and touch him. My fingers want to check that it's truly him—I'd know instantly.

Something is placed down next to me, and I reach over, my hand finding a plate.

"It's leftovers from yesterday," Grey answers, sending emotions crashing over me.

It's him. It's definitely him.

"Thank you," I breathe out, not reaching for the food.

I wish I could see him, but the dark makes it impossible. Seconds tick by in complete silence, and I'm surprised he doesn't just leave now that he's fulfilled his reason for the visit.

"You should eat," he grumbles. "I can hear your stomach growling."

My restraint snaps and I extend my hand through the shadows, finding his torso. He tenses up underneath me, his own hand grabbing my wrist gently.

"Don't, Avery."

It's not aggressive or angry—just a pained plea.

Slowly, I move my hand back, wanting to respect his wishes despite every single nerve in my body screaming for him. Grey keeps hold of my wrist for a second, before finally letting me go.

"You brought me food?" I ask gently.

"Yes," he answers. "Your absence was noticed today. I assume you were kept busy by the old cunt."

I nod, even though he can't see it. "Yeah."

I'm terrified of saying or doing the wrong thing, wanting him to stay for as long as possible. But as I fall into silence, it causes me to panic more. What if *that* drives him away? Should I say something else? Will he leave if I start eating?

Will he leave if I don't?

"Just eat, little killer," he sighs, exasperated.

"Will you stay for a few minutes?" I ask.

I hate how desperate I sound, but there's hope fluttering in my stomach at the mention of my old nickname. Maybe my words had more of an impact than I thought.

"I shouldn't."

"I know," I murmur. "I just really want you to."

Desperation turns to pity. But somehow... *it works.*

Grey sits down next to me on the bed, pushing the plate toward me. "It's the beef brisket," he says casually in a quiet voice. "It's not much, but it's something at least."

I reach down, plucking a piece in my fingers. It tastes just as good as yesterday, even if it's not fresh and hot.

He doesn't make an effort to leave so I take it as a good sign, eating happily. My body no longer feels like molten lava is flowing through it, and slowly, the stomach growls fade away.

Deciding to take a leap of faith, I choose my side officially. "Mr. Whittingham was asking a bunch of questions today. I think he knew that the society held a meeting last night."

"Hm. I'm not surprised. He generally likes to keep tabs. What did he ask?"

"Just if I had anything to report to him. He didn't mention you guys specifically, but I think he was trying to use chores and food as leverage."

"Cunt," Grey snaps under his breath. "He's a miserable power-tripping bastard."

I plop more meat into my mouth, nodding as I chew. "I didn't tell him anything," I admit. "I wouldn't ever. I just want you to know that."

The tension between us relaxes slightly. "I know," he responds. "Otherwise you would have been with the gen pop."

"You noticed I was missing?" I ask wearily.

He's already confirmed as much, but there's a part of me that needs to hear it directly. I know it would have been obvious from my absence in Charmaine's class, but I need this. I need something to hold on to.

"We all did."

I can't help but wonder who everyone is. Does he mean Damon too? I know he tracks everyone and everything, but my presence is the last thing that *demon* would give a shit about.

"Especially Ashwood."

My whole body freezes, unsure if I heard him correctly.

"What?" I mumble stupidly.

Grey laughs quietly, making me nervous. "He came and saw us at dinner—asked if we had seen you."

"Wait," I stop him. "He approached you?"

I've never seen Theo approach, well, *anyone*—let alone Grey and Damon.

"Yep," he confirms. "Said you'd been missing all day. Once I confirmed you were missing from class too, we realized where you were."

"What do you mean?" I ask, confused.

Grey shuffles backwards on the bed, resting his back against the wall. "I sent Damon to check it out. Connor told us you were in Arthur's office."

"Who the hell is Connor?"

"One of the guards," he replies casually. "Anyway, Ash-wood expressed... *concern* that you likely hadn't been provided with food."

I have no idea how to take any of this. Grey and Theo interacting, worried about me starving, and now this late night encounter.

Pushing the empty plate away, I reposition myself against the wall next to Grey. "So, you brought me food?"

"Everyone needs to eat," he says quietly, but I know it's a deflection.

"Thank you. It means a lot."

"I should leave now," Grey mutters, starting to move.

I quickly grab his hand through the dark. "Wait."

He stills, fist curling under my palm. "Please, don't. I already know what you are going to say."

"You don't," I quickly reply. "I'm not going to stop you from leaving. I just wanted to say thank you again. And maybe," I pause. "Maybe we can be friends. Or at least be civil. We don't have to make things awkward."

Grey stays soundless, and it's that familiar silence before the inevitable heartbreak that I once again recognize.

"I can't be friends with you."

I know what he's going to say, but I want to fight him. No—I need to fight him on this.

My other hand reaches out, finding his face. I cup his cheek, envisioning his face in my mind.

"Don't just be friends with me then. Don't stay away from me. Please—I need you."

He moves so quickly, so stealthily, that by the time I've processed it, I'm already on my back. Grey leans over the top of me, face inches away from mine.

"I can't watch you be with someone else, little killer. It makes me want to kill him."

He should scare me. Everything about this should set off alarm bells, but they don't. I know him—I trust him.

"Grey—"

"The *only* reason I haven't killed him is because of you."

His lips brush over mine for the smallest fraction of time. Not a kiss, but not accidental either. There's something pulling us together, and I can feel him fighting it.

"I still love you," I whisper.

"I know you do."

My chest aches, but deep down, there's that niggling feeling. I'm not sure if it's hope or delusion, but surely, he still loves me too.

"Do you love Damon?" I ask suddenly, throwing him off-guard.

"What?"

"In any way, shape or form."

He pauses, unsure where this is going. "Of course I do. He's like a brother to me."

I nod, our foreheads grazing against each other. "Say for argument's sake, you love me too. We're all messed up here, right? We're the unhinged... the lost souls. But despite all that, you love more than one person. Because we're not bad people. Love isn't an emotion that bad people can process. We've been fucked over. Don't we deserve love?"

I'm rambling, already forgetting my main point. I think I'm trying to make it clear that I'm so beyond fucked up that I don't know how to love properly. Years and years of neglect in a loveless life have left me craving it. It makes sense I'm trying to overcompensate now—like how men with tiny dicks buy really expensive, massive cars.

"You deserve love, Avery," he answers. "Which is why I allowed him to live."

"But I want you too," I breathe out, grabbing his face in my hands. "You might not be mine, but I'm still yours."

Grey pushes off from the bed quickly, leaving me to scramble up.

"I have to go," he says, heading to the door. "If Arthur gives you any more trouble, let Damon know."

"Wait—"

It's too late. He's already gone, the door locking shut behind him. I run over, tugging on it with all my strength, but nothing happens.

I was so close. I know it in my soul.

The invisible string tightened again for the briefest moment, and I'm positive he felt it too.

I'm going to chase you, Grey. I'm not letting you go that easily.

Chapter 13

Damon

"Well?" I ask, looking up as Grey enters my room. "How did it go?"

I know where he's been. He didn't ask for permission—though even if he had and I said no, I know he still would have done it anyway.

"Arthur was sniffing around," he grunts.

My eyes narrow at his worked-up physique. She's gotten to him—*again*.

"Don't make me regret this," I warn him, folding my arms. "I told you it was best not to be involved directly."

Grey straightens up, looking at me with a blank expression. "It's under control."

"Is it?" I ask, amused. "Because every time you speak to her, you're a fucking mess."

Anger flashes across his face but you know what they say—when you find where it hurts, you keep pushing.

I lift an eyebrow, noticing his silence. "I told her that she would have no contact with you. Still, I let you both speak privately because I knew it was what you wanted. I trusted that you would remain in control. However, I'm starting to see I've made a mistake."

He shakes his head. "Right now, she is a direct link to Arthur. As a pivotal member of *Cirque des Morts*, I need to be able to interact with everyone."

I laugh. "Grey, be real for a second. This has nothing to do with the society. You just don't want *me* to be Avery's point of contact."

"And why would that bother me?"

"Because you think I'll break your fragile, little toy."

We enter into a stare-off, until Grey finally relents, shrugging. "She's not mine, Damon."

"But do you want her to be?"

I see his jaw harden. "Are you asking me that as my leader... or as my best friend?"

"Does the answer change depending on the question?" I ask.

Grey doesn't respond straight away, but I already know it does. And therein lies the problem.

"As your leader," I start. "You know how I feel. She is an imposition and a fucking liability." He opens his mouth to speak, but I hold up my hand, silencing him. "But as your best friend, your brother... it pains me to see you like this."

"But your answer is still the same," he says knowingly. "You don't like her. You've made that clear."

"I don't like anyone. I hate everyone equally," I shrug. "However, all I can do is advise you to really think about what you are doing. If you make dumb decisions, that's on you."

Grey snorts. "But only from the best friend perspective."

"This is where it is a little... murky. Because while I *could* overlook things, it still raises the issue of her compliance. She's unstable, Grey. And with our situation, our worlds are one. If she fucks up your personal life, it directly affects my business. Therefore, I will be forced to take action."

"It doesn't matter anyway," he sighs. "I'm not getting involved."

I scoff in disgust. "Because of Ashwood? Do you honestly think you can't take him?"

He looks at me with a small smirk, fire returning to his eyes. "You know I fucking could."

"But you don't want to because it will *hurt* her," I taunt. "Well, I'm not sure what else to tell you, Grey. You have a decision to make."

"Are you ready to tell me about the deal?" he asks.

A laugh escapes my throat. "Deflecting? Soon," I confirm. "At the moment, I have a matter to deal with tomorrow. And you and I have pressing issues to discuss."

Grey pounces on my bed, spreading out. "Such as?"

"I've been told the Lilydale board has made a decision. The guards anticipate the new arrival within the next day or two."

"Fun," he drawls out, bored. "Want me to welcome them?"

"I think I might do it personally this time. I need to determine how to place him."

It's time to rearrange the grouping system, but I won't be able to finish it until I meet the new patient. It's obvious that the staff do everything for a reason—so, whomever has been chosen to take Hallman's place will have some significance about them. I just need to figure out what makes them special.

"And Capello?" Grey asks.

"She will need to be dealt with in due course. Once she's stabilized we can continue our investigation."

He nods. "Do you think she'll tell us how she got the staff card?"

"Possibly. But I'm more interested in knowing whether or not she had anything to do with the second staff card being placed on Avery."

Grey pauses. "Do you think she did? Capello was quite upset at the time. Unless she's one hell of an actress, I'd say she was too busy with the news of Hallman's death. There was only a short window where someone could have gotten to Avery in the chaos."

"Surprisingly, no. I don't think Capello had anything to do with it. But perhaps she knows something about it."

"Does she know that Hallman was murdered? Or does she still think he—?" He drags his thumb across his neck.

I shrug, not giving a shit. "You're welcome to find out. I did promise you a venting system. Just try not to push her too far."

Grey snorts. "That's not fair."

"Did you speak to Christopher and Markel today?" I ask, ignoring him.

He nods, reaching into his pocket to retrieve a few pieces of scribbled notes. "Good luck deciphering Markel's handwriting. It's a disaster. As for Christopher—he promptly locked me out of his office."

"Of course he did," I roll my eyes. "Dramatic flare is his style. I'll speak to him myself. I'd love to see him try to lock me out."

Grey laughs warmly. "As powerful as you are, Deadman, I don't think Christopher will open up to you."

"He'll have no choice," I respond casually. "Besides, I'm better at mind games than he is. All that money and education still can't beat me."

"I believe it."

While Christopher is slightly older than me, he didn't pursue the art of mind control early on. He spent too many years flaunting his wealth and getting his dick sucked. Myself on the other hand, my family used to joke that I came out of the womb arguing. By the time I was in elementary school, I'd already learned to switch my emotions off. I knew how to read people—teachers included.

Christopher might think he's intelligent, and while he is, he had to learn the skills from somewhere. And it sure wasn't that so-called prestigious university. No—I know he was obsessed with monitoring me. It's probably why he got into psychiatry in the first place—I was his first ever test subject.

It's just a punch to the gut that he chose to come here of all places. Any chance to try to have one up on me. Still... I don't care if he has *staff* power. That means absolutely nothing. In the real world, power is demanded, just like respect is earned. I've done both. No matter what he says or does, he will never have power over me. He will never control me.

And that extends to *Cirque des Morts*.

My Circus of the Dead.

That's what we are here—dead.

Dead to society, dead inside. And sometimes, like Hallman, *actually* dead.

I'm their fucking leader. And the best thing about us?

You can't fight death. It's inevitable.

Now, I just need to figure out what to do with Grey. I may have been wrong with my initial observation. This whole mess with Avery is rocking the boat. I thought if I kept them apart, it would be easier for him. Apparently, I was wrong.

Every time he has anything to do with her, he's a loose cannon—destroying everything in his path. But with her... he's a nuclear weapon.

Except, she had to go and fuck everything up. We could have made this work, but she dragged Ashwood into the mix.

Now, I'm stuck trying to control a rogue missile while dealing with Arthur's bullshit.

But, all that aside, Grey is one of the only people I genuinely tolerate. I care about him, which is more than I can say about most other people.

I know there's a fine line here. We cross it all the time. But now, I have to decide whether or not I can allow such calamity into my business. Not just for the sake of keeping things calm, but also for the sake of Grey. He's never doubted me—never crossed me. And despite *my feelings* about Avery, I perhaps owe it to him to pull back on the reins.

For some clusterfuck of a reason, he cares about her.

It's bad—I know it, he knows it. But still, he wants her. And I can't have him distracted, stalking after her just to catch a glimpse or start a fight.

Maybe I need to kill Ashwood. Or at the very least, remove him from the equation.

Something tells me that would also backfire. It would create a ripple effect—anything I do to Avery, will in turn set Grey off... which leads right back to my original problem.

There's only one real solution here.

And I fucking hate it.

"Christopher," I greet coldly. "So generous of you to make time for me."

He looks up from his desk, a bored expression on his face. He hides his surprise well, but I can see it in his eyes.

Connor had taken the liability of providing me with the good doctor's schedule for the day—a small window of no sessions providing the perfect opportunity for a quick visit.

After sleeping on it, I decided it was time for a little family reunion. Especially since he had declined my gift of Grey yesterday.

"Damon," he responds. "Always a displeasure. Are you here for your first session perhaps?"

I laugh darkly, giving Connor a small nod. He shuts the door behind me, giving us privacy. "Sure—we can call it that. Bill it however you like. I'm sure you would love to finally understand how my mind works. Sadly, I don't think you'll achieve that in today's session."

He tilts his chair back, folding his arms. "Why don't we skip the bullshit? I assume your little lap dog reported back to you yesterday."

"He was quite disheartened that someone in your profession would *turn* him away. Isn't it your job here to support *all* the patients?" I shoot back, sitting down across from him.

Christopher raises an eyebrow. "Your friend is quite special. His file almost needs its own cabinet, yet, we all know the information in there is largely fabricated. Mr. Hawthorne is very good at portraying whatever he needs to be."

"You sound disappointed. Tell me—have you actually managed to cure anyone? Or is that not your prerogative?"

"Some people don't want to be cured, Damon. You're the prime example of that."

I laugh under my breath. "And what exactly do I need curing from, Christopher? Please enlighten me."

He stands up from his chair, walking over to the filing cabinet. I watch carefully as he unlocks it with his key, rummaging around until he pulls out a file. My own name on the top of the manila folder brings a smirk to my face.

Christopher throws the file into my lap before heading back to his chair. "You tell me. You seem to know everything."

I casually place my file on the ground without opening it. I already know what's in there—including Christopher's notes and the old psychiatrist's dribble.

These so-called professionals are great at making observations, but at the end of the day, they are just that. People perceive the world in different shades of color. Psychiatrists are instructed to look at the black and grays, picking them apart until something comes undone. I've never given any of them the luxury of that. So at best, their observations are just personal opinions.

Meaning... *absolute bullshit.*

"I just wanted you to know that I'm aware of what you are doing behind the scenes," I say coolly to him. "And I think you'll be surprised to find that there are repercussions."

He laughs, finally breaking character. "Is this about Ms. White's file again? The staff are already aware of your involvement and poor attempt to steal personal information."

I throw him a smirk, standing up. I step onto my file, showing him just how much regard I have for his pathetic excuse of a job.

"It's not, actually. But I do believe you'll understand what I mean soon. Any minute now, in fact."

His eyebrows furrow in confusion, but I turn around, heading to the door without elaborating. I swing it open, pleased that Connor is nowhere to be seen just like I had ordered. Glancing over my shoulder at Christopher, I give him a final parting gift.

"If you need a shoulder to cry on when it happens... perhaps call a real psychiatrist."

Chapter 14

Avery

It's around two in the afternoon.

Or... at least I think it is?

I expected to be woken early by some daunting task from Mr. Whittingham. But there was nothing.

In fact... nothing at all.

The bell has rang several times throughout the day, signaling the usual routine. But I've been locked in my room without a single guard or visitor.

No breakfast. No lunch.

Not even any professional appointments.

I've just been purely forgotten.

Nothing is accidental though. I know the staff keep tabs on all of us—they have our schedules mastered to the very second. This is deliberate—it has to be.

They have tried to exhaust me, starve me, dish out punishments and chores... and when that hasn't worked, they have resorted to isolation.

Laughing, I lay back on my bed, staring at the pale ceiling. I should have seen this coming.

What's the best way to torture someone with mental illness? Particularly me—who, according to Dr. Smith—craves validation and attention. You take everything and everyone away from them.

I thought sleep deprivation and hunger were the cruelest forms of torture but I was wrong.

Making someone feel like they are forgotten... *worth nothing*... alone. Well, that's the whole underlying reason that I'm here. And they are playing that card.

Surprisingly, I don't feel panic though.

Maybe a few weeks ago I would have felt dread and fear. But knowing that there's always eyes on me, I'm not worried. Someone will notice my absence again. And they will come rescue me.

Right?

Okay—I'm not entirely convinced. But after seeing Grey last night, I know that he and Theo care enough to know when I haven't eaten. Somebody will come to my room soon...

The hours continue to tick by and I lose track of the bells. It's only when the sun starts to set outside and I hear footsteps passing by in the hallway that I realize free time must be over.

Do I get a shower tonight?

Denying someone of basic hygiene is also up there on the torture scale. I didn't get one yesterday, and there's a tiny bit of fear that perhaps no one *will* come rescue me if I smell like a landfill.

Thankfully, a guard does come to grab me for a shower, shoving me in line behind the other girls. A few give me small smiles while others ignore me completely.

We're ushered into the bathroom and I quickly make my way to a stall, desperate for hot water. Stripping out of my dirty clothes, I hiss slightly as the hot water scolds me, also reminding me of the numerous paper cuts on my fingers.

I start to scrub my hair when a guard stops in front of my stall, looking over the shoulder-height door at me.

"White—you have some belongings. Here," he grunts, shoving a plastic bag over the door.

I quickly try to cover myself with my hands, but the guard barely looks at me, walking away as the bag splashes into the water on the floor.

It takes a few seconds for me to process the interaction, before I lean down and examine the bag.

I've never been given a bag in the shower before, and as far as I know, nor have any of my shower companions.

Opening it up, I'm stunned to find there's only one item inside.

A razor.

But it's not a plastic one—it's a proper metal razor.

Confusion washes over me as the water cascades down my back, before slowly, it dawns on me.

They are giving me the tools to kill myself.

They want me to harm myself...

I don't know how to feel. For a brief second, that old desire of escape comes back—the time when I used to dream about joining Paige. I quickly push those thoughts aside.

I'm not that girl anymore. They aren't going to fuck with my head.

I realize that I've been perched down in the shower for too long, our timer about to go off so we can be taken back to our rooms. If I don't do anything, it's unlikely they will just let me take the razor back to the room. But I can't leave it here either. What if the next woman to shower finds it? I can't be responsible for that.

Quickly, I disassemble the razor, carefully plucking the blade out. As the showers turn off automatically, I panic, wondering where the fuck I'm supposed to hide a blade.

We're the unhinged according to Grey. Unpredictable, unstable, wild cards who have fought our entire lives to survive.

Already starting to regret my decision, I grab my towel, drying my body as fast as I can. I grab my change of clothes, taking a deep breath, before carefully placing the blade between my ass cheeks. It's either that or my vagina—and rightfully so, I'd rather cut my asshole instead of slicing off my clit.

Slow steps. Baby movements.

Somehow, I manage to get myself dressed, squatting down with my ass clenched tightly to shove the disassembled razor back into the bag, just in time before the guard swings open the stall door to check on me.

"Part of it fell down the drain," I say quickly, slapping my hand over the drain cover for dramatic effect. "But you can tell Mr. Whittingham that these aren't my belongings." I stand up, shoving the plastic bag into his chest.

The guard scowls at me, grabbing my elbow to pull me out of the stall. I quickly fall into line behind the other women as they head out of the bathroom, doing my best to walk normally.

Please don't fall out...

Oh, please don't fucking fall out.

I hold my breath until I'm back to my room, only exhaling when the door slams shut. Hastily, I waddle to my adjoining toilet, popping my leg onto the seat as I carefully remove the blade in some weird yoga position.

"Thank fuck," I breathe out in relief, holding the blade between my fingers.

I'm not an idiot though. I know that they will check the contents of the bag soon and notice that only the blade is missing. It likely means they will come search for it.

Shit! This means that I have contraband in my room.

That's also grounds for punishment, right?

Pacing around the room, I try to find a decent hiding place. Under the bed is too obvious—same with the desk. Swallowing it is out of the question too.

Kicking off my shoes, I use the blade to pull the inside of the sole up. I slide the blade inside, spitting on the torn section as I try to make it stick together again.

It's the best I can do, and as expected, the guards arrive a few minutes later.

I'm laying on my bed, pretending to look bored as they enter. Keeping my face blank is hard because my heart is pounding so loud and fast that I can barely breathe.

Mr. Whittingham walks into the room after the guards, looking displeased.

"Ms. White," he snarls down at me. "We're here to conduct an inspection."

"Oh?" I feign ignorance, sitting up. "Did you need me to move?"

His eyes narrow briefly on me before snapping his fingers at the guards. Immediately, the three of them spread out across the room, lifting and opening things. One of them rips the mattress off the metal frame, nearly flinging me with it as I scramble to my feet just in time.

I keep my eyes on Mr. Whittingham, fighting the urge to look at my neatly placed shoes by the desk. He watches me carefully, so I glance away, leaning against the wall.

My heart stops completely when one of the guards grabs my shoes, turning them upside down. He gives them a shake, shoving his hands inside.

Fuck.

Fuck me dead in the ground.

I pick a spot on the wall, training my eyes to stay on it. The seconds passing feel like hours, but they throw the shoes on the ground, moving onto the next item.

"There's nothing here," one of the guards tells Whittingham. "Clean."

I glance back casually to Mr. Whittingham. "Is it nearly dinner time?" I ask him.

We both know I'm not going to be eating, but maybe one of these guards are in Damon's pocket and they'll relay this to him. It's a small flare, a cry for help—but only if it lands on the right mark.

"Dinner has already finished," he replies back. "You'll have to wait until tomorrow. Speaking of, I've assigned you a new task in the morning. I'll see you bright and early."

My lips curl at his words. In translation—you won't be having breakfast either.

He stalks out of the room, followed by the guards. The door closes behind them and I wait until the sound of their footsteps fade away before I quickly pick up my shoe.

It actually worked.

I fix up the mattress and blanket on the bed, curling myself on top. Now, I just have to wait and see if my plan worked.

"Avery."

I jolt awake, registering the darkness around me. I don't even remember falling asleep.

My eyes scan the room, checking for shadows to make sure I heard correctly. I spot Damon standing in the doorway, leaning against the frame.

"Come with me," he says disinterested, disappearing into the hallway.

I don't need to be told twice, springing to my feet as I quickly catch up.

"Did you get my message?" I ask, walking beside him.

Damon glances out of the corner of his eye at me. "And what message would that be?"

I shrug, feeling embarrassed. "I tried to pass a message through the guards."

"Ahh," he says, turning the corner and heading to a locked door past the library. "Yes, *that* message."

I frown as we walk past the entrance of the hall and library, confused. "Are we not going inside?"

"We're not having a meeting tonight," he answers bluntly.

We stop in front of the locked door, my eyes spotting the access card that he pulls from his pocket. The access pad beeps when he puts the code in, tapping the card. There's a metallic unlocking sound, before Damon pulls the door open, gesturing for me to go inside.

I've never been down this way before, but I quickly realize by the numbers on the wall that these are rooms.

"Where are we?" I ask quietly.

He doesn't bother to lower his voice. "Westwood Wing."

Familiarity creeps into my mind. I look at all the aligning doors and numbers, eyes widening. "This is the male dormitory?"

"Obviously," he sighs, annoyed.

They are identical to the Eastwood Wing, except these rooms start with the number three. We walk to the very end, my eyes immediately finding the only open door in sight. I glance at the number on the wall beside the door—*room 301*.

It seems fitting that Damon's in room number one, but I don't ponder that thought too long. As I approach the open doorway, I spot a figure sitting on his bed, twirling a knife in his hand, legs folded underneath him.

He looks up at the same time, a fraction of surprise appearing on his face.

"Grey?" I blurt out.

Damon pushes past me into the room, not bothering to facilitate our spontaneous catch up. Grey looks at him expectedly, and I quickly realize, this is a shock to him as well.

"What's going on, Deadman?" Grey asks, putting the knife on top of the bed.

We both look at him—me with uncertainty and Grey with boredom, my nerves getting the better of me as I linger outside the door. I could be seen at any moment, so I step inside, resting my back against his wall.

"It's time to end this," Damon replies casually, kicking his feet up onto the desk as he takes a seat. "Once and for all."

Chapter 15

Avery

"End what?" I ask, eyes shifting to Grey.

A few weeks ago, I would have automatically assumed they meant my life. Yet, despite Damon's recent threats to my existence, I'm feeling at ease. Well, as much as possible given the circumstances.

"I cannot have you pair dancing around each other on edge. You both work for me, therefore, consider this my *blessing*."

What the hell does that even mean?

Grey and I have already made our peace—I said what I needed to say, and he has somewhat accepted the fact we need to co-exist. Despite the obvious fact that we are nothing more than acquaintances now, I thought there was nothing else we could work out.

Grey lifts an eyebrow at Damon. "Your blessing?"

"Whatever you wish to call it," he grunts, annoyed.

It's clear that Damon has never given a so-called blessing in his life. Then again, I've only ever known him to take, rather than give. Sure, he looks after people in his society—treats them to luxuries not ordinarily granted to us, but that comes with a price.

It's payment.

This is something different.

I stay quiet, gaze flickering between them as they have some silent conversation that I'm not privy to. Probably would have made more sense to discuss it before fetching me from my metal confinement, but who knows what goes on in that head of his.

"And what exactly has changed since our last discussion?" Grey asks casually. "I thought we both made our positions clear."

Damon looks at me, eyes scanning over my straightened figure. "We did. However, let me be clear—you are both being pains in my ass recently. To make this work, it needs to be under my terms."

"You can't dictate relationships—whatever they may be," I mumble.

"Yes, I can," he says sternly. "Therefore, I have some rules for you to follow."

I raise an eyebrow at him. "Let me just stop you right there. Whatever happens is between Grey and I. This doesn't involve you, no matter how much you think it does. We're not going to be monkeys in your circus—*pun intended*."

I swear I see Grey's lips twitch as he fights a smirk, but I'm too focused on Damon. I never know what reaction I'll get from him when I fight back, so when he just smiles, I'm immediately on guard.

"I don't give a fuck what *you* do, Avery. I cannot be more clear—you mean absolutely nothing to me. However, Grey is important. But for some reason, you have a hold on him that is creating a problem with my plans."

Grey shakes his head, laughing as he picks up the knife. He presses the sharp tip into his finger, drawing blood. "Careful, Deadman," he warns.

"Don't patronize me, Grey," Damon shoots back. "She has a hold on you, and you know it. Therefore, I need you both to sort this mess out. Fuck each other if you have to. But from here on out, I expect no more spectacles or else I'll be forced to show my hand."

My heart is racing like a speeding bullet. I had every intention of chasing Grey and getting his attention—even if it meant just being friends. But this... is this the push we need? Is it the *shove* that Grey needs?

From Damon of all people?

It feels like I've entered into an alternate universe or the Twilight Zone. Keeping my mouth shut, I wait for them to finish their conversation, worried I might blow the only chance I have.

"I have to go speak to Byrone. I'll give you an hour. Don't mess up my room," Damon scolds us, walking past me out the door. He slams it closed behind him, the familiar sound of the lock clicking into place.

He's locked us in here. Together.

Slowly, I turn my gaze to Grey on the bed, smiling at him sheepishly. "That was bizarre," I say awkwardly.

Grey scans my face, still rolling the blade between his fingers. "Classic Damon."

I hover in place, glancing around at Damon's room to distract myself from the inevitable conversation coming. If I give myself a few moments to collect my thoughts, I might save myself from word vomiting again.

It's very similar to my own room, except straight away, I notice one key difference. Lilydale is notorious for its hideous floral design—the bathroom, the outdoor gardening, even my own room is covered in roses. Damon's room is still covered in faintly painted flowers, however his hosts the stereotypical lily that I had expected to see when I first arrived at Lilydale. The only other time I've seen a lily here is when I was first invited to the society's meeting—the blood stained lily on my bed as a welcome present.

Design aside, Damon also has more belongings and furniture stashed around his room. A laptop is on the desk, along with a suitcase in the corner. Even from here, I can see his bathroom is filled with stuff—products, belongings. My room feels like a prison... but his feels like a college dorm.

Am I surprised? Of course not.

"So, we have an hour," Grey says, breaking my train of thought.

I snap my gaze back to him, nodding slowly. "I guess so. I'm sorry though—I had no idea you were here. I didn't know where I was going. Damon just came and told me to follow."

Grey nods in understanding. "It's fine. I should have known when he vanished earlier. I assumed he was just off running errands."

"He was," I confirm with a small smile. "I was the task."

"How have you been?" Grey asks softly, ignoring my comment. "I didn't see you today."

I try not to read too much into his use of singular presence, just giving a shrug in return. "They locked me in my room. Probably just another ploy to make me crack."

Grey's expression darkens. "Have you eaten?"

"Of course not," I laugh sarcastically. "But at least I was allowed to shower today. That's a plus."

He pauses. "They have been denying you showers?"

"Only a few times..." I trail off, face scrunching up at their latest tactic.

Grey notices, stilling. "What is it?"

"It's nothing," I sigh. "Just Whittingham trying to test limits."

"Tell me."

It's a demand, softly spoken but still housing enough power to bring an entire room to their knees—including me.

I stare at him apologetically. "The guards passed me a razor in the showers tonight. I think they were trying to coax me to end my own miserable existence."

I say it jokingly, trying to lighten the mood, but Grey stands up quickly, crossing the room to me.

"He did *what?*"

The words are like a venomous stab, making me flinch. But it's a relief to know that it's not aimed at me this time.

Leaning down, I slip off my shoe, pulling back the sole. I trust him with this. If anyone knows what to do with a weapon, it's him.

Picking up the blade, I hold it up between us, watching his eye twitch as he scans the blade with narrowed eyes.

"That motherfucking cunt," he hisses, quickly grabbing the blade from my fingers.

"Yeah..." I answer, slipping my shoe back on. "They know I took it though. They did a search in my room."

Grey lowers his hand, closing his fist around the metal. "But you hid it," he points out, awe in his tone.

I nod. "I told them it fell down the drain hole, but I figured they wouldn't believe me. I'm not sure what to do with it."

"I'll look after it," he answers softly. "Hold on, I think Damon has some snacks stashed around here."

He lingers in front of me for a brief second, before pulling himself away to start looking through the desk drawers. There's a whole stack of candy bars inside, my stomach growling in excitement at the sight of food.

"Will he mind?" I ask wearily, leaning over to take a closer look.

Grey shakes his head. "It's our shared stash. I have some in my room too."

"You amaze me," I laugh quietly. "At least now I know why you always have chocolate—well, kinda."

He smiles to himself, pulling out a candy bar and handing it to me. "I think he has a bag of chips somewhere too. If you want something else, I could get it from the kitchen."

"We can't get out of here," I point out, nodding to the locked door.

Grey snorts, raising an eyebrow. "Can't I?"

I tilt my head in disbelief, before quickly admitting defeat. *They can do anything...*

"The candy bar is okay," I tell him happily, ripping the wrapper open. "It will be enough until lunch tomorrow."

"Lunch?" he asks slowly. "Don't you mean breakfast?"

I shake my head. "Whittingham has assigned me to a task again in the morning. I definitely won't be eating breakfast. Possibly not lunch either, if I'm being honest."

Grey slams the desk drawer closed, making me jump.

"Fuck this," he growls angrily. "I've had enough of him."

"Hey," I whisper, reaching for his arm. "I can handle it. Don't stress."

Suddenly, he moves toward me, pushing me against the wall. I let out a silent gasp, staring up at him.

"You shouldn't have to handle it," Grey growls. "He's fucking with you. Torturing you, starving you, trying to make you kill yourself. I'm going to kill him myself."

My lips part in disbelief at his sudden shift in mood. "He's not worth it," I say, trying to calm him down. "Let him try his hardest. I'm not going to break. Your secrets are safe with me."

"You think this is just about *Cirque des Morts*?" Grey asks. "It's more than that, little killer. He's targeting you to get back at us. We don't let shit like that slide."

Can he hear my heart pounding? It's all I can hear...

"Don't do something stupid just for me," I answer. "It's not worth it. You'll be removed from Lilydale and put into prison. You'll never get a chance to get out."

The anger in his face washes away as he stares at me incredulously. "You genuinely believe that, don't you?"

I frown. "Of course I do. It's the truth, isn't it? It's what was going to happen to me."

Something sinister flares up in his eyes, his gray irises darkening. "When I find out who framed you, I'll make their nightmares seem like a happy place. I promise you that, Avery."

My stomach turns in knots, the chocolate forgotten in my hand by my side. He has me caged in, his body flush against mine.

Danger resonates from him, bouncing around the room. I'm not scared though—not even a little bit. It's intoxicating, my body lighting up at his words.

This is the protective Grey I've missed. The one who made me feel like I was worth something, who would kill every single person in this place if they dared touch me.

The one I've been begging to come back.

"I don't want you to leave me," I whisper. "They might take you away."

Grey tilts his head slowly, eyes locked with mine. He looks at me knowingly.

"They haven't taken me away yet, have they?"

My eyebrows furrow together. "What do you mean?" I ask, confused.

A smile tugs on his lips, amused.

"Who do you think killed Hallman, little killer? He didn't take his own life. No—I ended it. I ended that sad, pathetic excuse of a man because he touched you. He tried to hurt what's mine."

Chapter 16

Avery

I hear the words but they don't instantly connect. Silence falls between us while Grey waits for the puzzle pieces to fall into place.

"You?" I stammer. "You killed Sam?"

Grey smiles, unfazed. "Of course I did. Now do you understand? We didn't frame you. I *killed* for you. So, yes—I guess Damon is right. You *do* have a hold on me."

I blink a few times, the candy bar slipping from my grasp. It hits the floor with a soft thud, but neither of us pay it any mind.

"But you were so mad at me," I murmur quietly in disbelief. "You told me we were done and that you didn't love me anymore. You told me to let you go."

He nods slowly. "I know. You hurt me badly. I want you all to myself and that was taken away from me. And on top of that, you let Ashwood *mark* you."

Grey's eyes drift down to the tattoo on my wrist, hiding the burns that taunted me for so long. I resist the urge to move it out of sight, but I know it wouldn't help the situation.

"I'm so lucky," I murmur. "I came to Lilydale expecting this to be the end of my life. And when I met you and Theo, I realized it might be the start of it. I should have been upfront and honest with you about it, but I've never been good with confrontation. I'm always worried that if I speak up, people will leave me. And then you did." I pause, forcing myself to hold eye contact with him. "It was my absolute worst fear come to life. But even when I was taken away by the police officers, you were all I thought about."

His face scrunches up with unreadable emotion, still boxing me against the wall.

"I don't like sharing," he says quietly. "It's ingrained in me not to want it. It destroyed my father." He spits the word out like it's dirty. My eyes trail down to the red scar on his neck, sorrow and pain filling me. It all makes sense now.

Even though we were never officially together, I can understand why he acted the way he did. It's my responsibility to own up to this. Everything he feels is valid—and because it was caused by me, it's my job to accept that.

"You're right," I murmur softly, looking back up at him again. "You're absolutely right. It's my fault for not thinking about this more clearly. I was caught up in my own feelings because of the file situation. I never wanted you to know all those things about me. I didn't want you to think less of me."

Grey's face softens, surprising me. "Little killer, I already knew all that about you. I just wanted to hear it from you. I wanted you to open up to me, to trust me."

"You what?" I ask with a gasp.

He smiles at me, a fraction of guilt on his face. "We read everyone's file before they start. We have the system hacked. That's what drew me to you."

I don't know how to feel about his confession. By comparison, I should be mad like I was at Dr. Smith, but I can't bring myself to feel the same way. It's a sickening feeling of relief, but also embarrassment.

And disbelief.

He knew everything about me... and still wanted me.

Me.

Flaws and all.

Murder charges, trauma, suicide attempt... everything.

"So, Damon read it too?" I ask wearily, looking down.

Grey hums in agreement. "I figured you'd be a good candidate to keep an eye on for the society. But as soon as I saw you in class, I knew you were going to be so much more to me."

"Until I fucked it up."

He laughs, letting out a sigh. "Maybe I fucked up too. Maybe that's the string that ties us together."

I look up in surprise, conflicted. "Then you'd be tied to every single person here."

"But you're the only one I want to be balls deep in, Avery. The only one I'd kill for."

"You'd kill for Damon," I point out confidently.

He nods. "Yes, but that's because of the bigger picture. I'd kill just to make you smile."

I can't help but smile at him. Perhaps I'm insane after all. Normal people get confessions of love. I get confessions of murder.

"But where do we go from here?" I ask nervously.

Grey frowns, leaning down to bring our bodies and faces closer together. "Here's your chance to be honest with both of us. Are you still going to be with Ashwood?"

My chest aches painfully. Swallowing hard, I nod slowly. "I can't give him up, Grey. I don't want to. And I don't want to give you up either."

He says nothing in return, that little voice of panic inside telling me to lie, to say what I know he wants to hear so he doesn't leave me. But I ignore it, trying to accept the fact that he will walk away again. But at least this time, I will have been honest with him. You can't have a relationship built on lies and distrust.

"I see," Grey mutters, deep in thought.

I reach between us, placing my hand on his chest. "Just tell me what I have to do to keep you. I'll do anything else. Anything."

Grey lifts his hand up, closing his fingers around my wrist. I can already feel my heart shattering, waiting for his rejection.

As he grabs my hand firmly, I get ready for him to break our connection, but surprisingly, he lifts our hands higher, placing my palm over his beating heart.

"This cold, black thing beats for you, Avery."

Hope starts to bloom in my chest, my finger tips pressing into his sternum as I desperately cling to his touch. "Really?"

He gives a singular nod. "I don't know how to make it work... yet. I want to kill him. I've thought about it every single day since I saw you together."

My mouth feels dry as confliction sends me into mental whiplash.

"But," he sighs. "I'll *try* my best not to kill him. That's the best I can offer right now. Besides, it's more protection for you, I guess."

I stare at him wide-eyed, fighting back tears. A war of emotion battles inside me, but this is a win. It's a huge win and I'll take whatever I can get.

"Grey," my voice breaks. I fling my arms around his neck, burying my face into his chest. He drops his arms and curls them around my back, and I notice how he visibly relaxes in my hold too.

"I'm not saying it will be easy," he mumbles into my hair. "And I'll be speaking to *him*. But he gets credit for looking out for you."

I nod against him, pulling back to look at him. He still looks pained at the idea, but at the same time, I feel that connection between us growing again.

He's back.

"Theo knows about us," I tell him slowly, checking for his reaction. "He wasn't mad."

I don't know why I'm telling him this. Maybe to inspire him... or comfort him. Or protect Theo.

"That you know of," Grey answers bluntly. "Have you relayed the specifics?"

I recoil slightly. "Well, no... he was trying to figure out what was going on when I got back from the police station."

"I suggest you start there," he says sharply. "Perhaps give him the same courtesy of knowing the full situation."

"I will," I murmur, nodding softly.

Grey's eyes flash before he takes a step back. I gaze at him perplexed, worried that I've said something to upset him.

"Before you do," he replies firmly. "I need to even the score."

"Even the score?" I repeat in confusion.

He grabs my waist with one hand, scooping me forward. Twisting us around, he lets go, my body falling onto Damon's mattress.

My body bounces, hands catching myself as I peer up at him, stunned.

Grey drops to his knees, pushing my legs apart. His fingers run over my inner thighs, examining the skin. "Right here," he murmurs, pushing his thumb into the top of my right adductor.

I glance down at my leg, too choked up to speak. I watch as he picks up the knife from the bed, running the sharp tip gently down my thigh.

"He marked you in his own way," Grey murmurs. "Now, I'm going to mark you in mine."

His eyes flicker up to mine, and although he doesn't say anything, I know he's silently waiting for the go ahead. I nod, his lips tugging into a smirk as he turns his attention back to my thigh.

Pressing the blade into my skin, a burning pain crashes through me. It's almost exactly like how it was with Theo—a bearable pain, extinguishing the emotional turmoil that haunts me. And like the tattoo... this means something. To me, and to the man between my legs slicing into my pale skin.

I feel blood roll down my thigh, dripping onto Damon's bed. I have no sympathy for his belongings though. This is what he wanted, right? He left us in his room with his blessing, so I guess it can be expected that we might make a mess.

A little hiss falls from my lips before I can stop it. I half-expect Grey to stop, but he doesn't. Instead, he slips his other hand under the legs of my shorts, pressing his thumb against my clit through my underwear. Fire rages through me at the feel of him, fueled by the knife cutting me open. As I bleed, it feels like all of my built up sadness is flowing out, leaving only the longing I have for him.

Grey pauses the knife's movements, turning his attention to my underwear as he pulls them aside under my shorts. Circling my clit, he groans under his breath, eyes flaring up at me.

"You're wet for me already."

I bite my bottom lip, giving him a little nod. "I might have a hold on you, Grey. But I promise that you have a hold on me too."

Something flashes in his eyes, the knife quickly slicing one final time before he flings it sideways across the room. It lands with such force that the tip digs into the wall, holding the knife horizontally in place.

Grey launches up from the floor, slamming his lips into mine. He kisses me hard, bruising my lips, but I couldn't care less. He sucks the air from my body, only pulling back when I start to tense up from needing a breath that I haven't bothered to take because I just want him.

Sliding back to the floor, he leans down, running his tongue up my thigh. The cut stings against his tongue, and when he pulls back, his lips are coated in specks of blood.

I watch breathlessly as he grabs the razor blade, slicing his palm in one swift movement. I make a choking sound in concern, but he squeezes his hand into a fist, holding it above my leg. Blood drips downs onto my thigh, mingling with my own.

Grey runs his fingers over my skin, mixing the red together. Leaning back, he smiles down at his work of art. Curiosity gets the better of me, and I hunch forward, looking down to see.

MINE.

Our eyes meet at the same time, his face proud. I swallow, feeling a wave of emotions.

I'm his.

Lifting the blade to his mouth, he runs his tongue over the metal without breaking our locked eyes. My chest heaves as I breathe deeply, and I reach down, running my fingers over his mark to feel it.

He watches intensely as I bring my index finger covered in our blood to my face, inspecting it before dropping it to my lips, slipping it inside. The metallic taste bursts on my tongue, but I barely get a chance to finish what I started before Grey is on top of me. My back slams into the mattress as he pushes me down, covering my mouth with his.

"You're fucking *mine,* Avery," he growls into my mouth. "This lifetime and the next one too."

Chapter 17
Grey

Avery's soft pink lips part, her eyes wide as she stares up at me in utter disbelief. It's as if she's still trying to grasp the reality that I'm here with her, our bodies pressed together.

"Yours?" she breathes out, a hint of desperation to her tone.

Fuck, I've missed her. I've missed the way she craves my touch, the way she silently begs for my approval.

I'm trying hard to hold onto my control, but it's diffi-cult. The feeling of our bodies together is blinding, like we're made to be as one.

Her torso shifts underneath me as she attempts to push herself even closer. There's no room, not a single inch of space, but it's still not enough for me either. The animal in-side of me wants to destroy her in all the best ways possible.

Black hair splays out around her, and I stop for a moment, taking her all in. These past few days were the longest of my life, and now, I need to direct that built-up frustration somewhere.

There's still many conversations to be had—with Avery, with Damon... and with *Ashwood*. But right now, the only thing that matters is beneath me, wiggling against my growing cock.

I reach out, wrapping my fingers around her neck. My black-painted nails match the color of her hair perfectly and I let out a little smirk.

Avery doesn't seem fazed at all with my hand around her throat. Despite tightening my fingers around her delicate skin, her eyes still dance up at me, sparkling with the same lust and longing that I have ripping me apart.

"I'm sick of being angry at you," I growl in a low voice, squeezing her neck. "I don't want to do it anymore."

She nods. "Then don't," she croaks out, and the sound of her broken, breathless voice sends me spiraling.

Sitting up, I hastily pull my shirt over my head, throwing it onto the floor. I shove her own shirt up, grabbing her tits through the gray bra. Avery moans, immediately arching her back and pressing her chest into my hands further.

I pull the cups down, freeing her tits before tugging on her pink nipples with my fingers.

More moans.

The sound is everything to me, but it's not enough. I need to hear her scream.

I want her to scream so loud that her vocal chords are hoarse and husky tomorrow. If she has to be in that cunt's office, I want him to connect the dots—realizing that I've fucked her harder than he's ever fucked anyone in his entire life with his pin-dick.

How *dare* he try to keep her away from me?

I'm going to take that shiny letter opener on his desk, spit on it, and ram it into his eye socket if he tries to punish her again.

Leaning down, I cover her nipple with my mouth, swishing my tongue around the taut peak. When Avery whimpers, I bite it, her gasp sending an electric shock straight down to my hard cock.

It's unbearable, and the only solution is to be buried inside her tight little cunt right this very second. Standing up, I kick my pants off, gripping my shaft in my fist.

Avery looks up from the bed, cheeks flushed as she quickly pulls her displaced shirt and bra off.

"*Slowly* slide your shorts off," I demand, stroking my length.

I see her face redden again, but she complies, lifting her hips as she pushes her shorts and underwear over her thighs and down her legs.

As she goes to sit up, I stop her. "Spread your legs," I order. Steadily, to her credit, she parts her knees, showing me her wet cunt.

My breath hitches at the sight of her, eyes darkening as I stare at her closely.

"Touch yourself—like how I touch you."

For a split second, she looks stunned, hand slowly trailing down her stomach to the apex of her thighs. Her index and middle finger part her pussy, dipping in to find her clit.

As she connects, her expression drops, mouth opening with pleasure as she runs her fingers in a lazy circle.

She looks fucking perfect.

It makes me want to rip her into tiny pieces just so I can put her back together again.

I drop to my knees by the edge of the bed to get a closer look. Her knees shake as she forces herself to keep them open.

She better not close them on me.

"Finger fuck your pretty pussy for me, little killer," I groan, fisting my cock. "I want to see how wet you are for me."

Avery nods, biting her lip as she dips lower, sinking her fingers into her body. This close to her, I can smell her arousal, the sweet scent calling my name.

She's wet because of me. Right now... she is *with* me.

I struggle to grasp the fact that someone else makes her wet too, but I remind myself that this is for me right now. Her cunt glistens, beckoning me, and when she lets out a moan again, I snap.

Wrapping my arms around her knees, I rip her toward me, burying my face into her cunt. My tongue laps at her clit while her wet fingers lay forgotten on her thighs.

The mark on her thigh has stopped bleeding, but blood is smeared over her skin, making the words look like they have a neon glow. I run my tongue over the letters, tracing them as I slide my fingers into her eager body.

Avery rests her hand on the top of my head, pulling my hair into her fist. I growl against her thigh, the vibrations making her shiver.

I fuck her with my fingers rapidly, watching the expression on her face as she cries out with pleasure.

"Say my name," I grunt, feeling her cunt tighten around my fingers as her orgasm approaches. "Look at me and scream my fucking name."

Her eyes find mine, and when she sees me staring back at her, a loud cry falls from her lips, my name ripping from her throat. She spasms around my fingers but I don't ease up with my pace, the palm of my hand slapping against her skin.

As her moans start to fade, I pounce from the ground, covering her with my body. I don't give her a moment to catch her breath, slamming my cock into her still-pulsating cunt.

"Fuck!" she yells, throwing her head back. I groan—from her cursing and the feel of her squeezing my length.

My balls slap against her ass as I pound her mercilessly, Damon's bed rocking. I slap my hand on the wall behind the head of the bed to steady myself as Avery slides up the sheets from the force of our hips meeting.

"*Who. Do. You. Belong. To?*" I ask her between thrusts.

"You," she breathes out. "You, Grey."

"Damn fucking right," I growl in response, impaling her deep.

Avery reaches for my arms, digging her nails in as she tries to seek out some stability. I fuck her harder in retaliation, the bolts securing the bed to the floor snapping before the sound of metal on concrete screeches around the room.

I bunch up her hair in my fist, pulling her forward slightly for a kiss. She parts her lips automatically for my tongue, moaning into my mouth.

I spot something reflective on the bed by her leg, my hand letting go of her hair to pick up the razor blade. While fucking her perfect body, I drag the blade down the center of my chest, making a small cut. Blood rolls down between my pecs, dripping onto my stomach. I grab Avery's hand, positioning it over my chest.

Still fucking her, I press her finger into the cut, feeling the skin rip as the tip of her finger tears it. The pain is magical—burning, aching, fiery. It's everything that I need. I need her to hurt me as much as I hurt her.

"This is what you do to me," I breathe out, growling as her finger presses into my flesh harder. "You tear me apart from the inside out in the best fucking ways possible. You make me kill for you, you make me want to die for you. I'll burn this whole place down to ashes and paint you with them like the muse you are."

A tear slips down her cheek, but the faint smile on her face indicates that it's not pain causing it.

"I love you so much," she whispers.

Letting go of her hand, I reach for her clit, running my bloodied fingers over it. "Prove it. Come for me, *my little killer.*"

Avery's gray eyes widen momentarily, before squeezing shut, the unmistakable tensing getting stronger. Her cunt squeezes around me, screams falling from her lips.

I fuck her through her climax, wiping blood over her pelvic bone. The sight of her covered in our mixed blood awakens something in me, an animalistic throaty growl ripping loudly from me as I thrust into her hard, falling over the edge as I spill inside her.

Not pulling out yet, I cup the nape of her neck, bringing her head up to kiss her swollen lips. I grip her face with my other hand, still buried in her.

"I meant what I said," I whisper to her between kisses. "I'll kill Whittingham. You tell me if he pulls any bullshit on you tomorrow."

Avery nods, brushing her forehead against mine. "Okay."

Reluctantly, I pull back, separating us. I know Damon will be back soon, and it's getting late. If I don't let her get some sleep, it will make things harder for her.

I don't want to let her go though. The thought of her going back to her room alone makes me want to rip heads off shoulders.

Reaching for her underwear and shorts, I slide them back over her legs, placing soft kisses along the inside of her thigh. After helping her with her shirt and bra, I pull my own clothes back on, noticing the red stains tarnishing the gray material.

Avery stands up from the bed, looking around. "Shit. Damon's bed," she mumbles in a panic.

My eyes look over the broken bolts, the sheets covered in sweat and blood. Shrugging, I give her a small smirk. "Don't worry about it."

"Is he going to be mad?" she asks hesitantly.

"No," I say confidently. "Now, eat something."

She looks at the fallen, forgotten candy bar, cheeks red before she makes her way to the drawer to grab a new snack.

Pulling the knife out of the wall, I twirl it around, watching her carefully. Her expression changes instantly when the chocolate reaches her mouth, a look of pure happiness.

It's everything.

The access pad outside the room beeps a few minutes later, the door swinging open to reveal Damon. He looks at me casually, then to Avery, before glancing unbothered at the bed.

"She needs to go back to her room now," he says to me, dropping a manila envelope on his desk.

I give a stern nod, holding my hand out for her. She takes it, squeezing my lacerated palm before giving Damon a quick smile of appreciation. It's surreal to witness, but I understand. No doubt he'll have some words for me when I get back, but to her, what he did means something.

I know there are reasons behind it, but still, it's the first time in days I've been able to think clearly. I'm thankful too, no matter what the price is.

Chapter 18

Damon

After Grey leaves to escort Avery back to her room, I head down the corridor to find Connor. He's stationed at the door for the night shift, and gives me a respectful nod as I approach.

"Fetch some new bedding and change my room," I order him.

Connor nods, rushing off to take care of it. Blood doesn't faze me in the slightest, but I have no compulsion to clean up Grey's mess.

I'm not surprised in the slightest to have found my room in that post-coitus condition, but I'm glad to see that they have *made* up. It was a slight detour in the road, but now we can get back on track.

I hate that I've had to accept that she makes him stronger. No one should ever have their emotions and strength controlled by *someone else*. But alas, this was just another situation that needed taking care of.

After reflecting on it, I decided that I can utilize Avery after all. Sadly, it just involves having her around in a more engulfing capacity. Preferably, I'd rather as little contact as possible, but winning is winning. It doesn't matter what you have to do to get there.

Sitting at my desk, I flick open the file from Byrone detailing the new patient's information. I had planned to meet him today, however it appears Christopher has decided to play difficult, sheltering him from me.

Never fear—tomorrow is a new day.

When footsteps head toward my room, I raise an eyebrow in surprise. Grey struts back into the room a few seconds later, an airy, carefree composure about him.

"I wasn't expecting you back so soon," I tell him lazily, scanning the file.

He sits on the bed, stretching out. "Avery needs rest. Besides, I have a suspicion she will be woken up early by Arthur. Apparently, he's assigned her to another task."

There's a darkness to his tone, distracting me from the file. Swinging the chair around, it's confirmed by the look on his face.

"What now?" I ask annoyed.

Grey's face tightens. "He's fucking with us, Deadman. He knows she's with us and is pressuring her for information."

I fold my arms. "And do you think she'll give it to him?" I question, wondering if it's too soon to regret my decision.

"No," he answers confidently. "Which is why he has resorted to other methods."

"The chores," I shoot back. "We were already aware of this."

Grey snarls. "It's beyond that. He's torturing her, cutting her off from everyone, trying to get her to kill herself."

That's actually a surprise. I know Arthur has a mean streak, but I wouldn't have thought it would go that far. Bastard is really ramping up his game.

"I doubt she'll do it," I tell him carefully, knowing it's a sensitive subject for him. "Would you like me to pay him a visit?"

A smirk tugs on the corner of his lips. "I think I'll do it actually. It's on my list tomorrow, as well as locating Ashwood."

I roll my eyes, turning back to the file. "Just don't draw attention. I don't have the patience to clean up two dead bodies."

Grey laughs. "I'm sure it will be fine. Now, are you going to go into some more detail about this... *blessing*?"

"You already know the answer to it. I need you to stay focused, and this is the best way for that to happen. Also, I've been thinking about what you said initially. Perhaps you were correct in how we can mold Avery."

"I see..." he says, pausing. "You want to use her against Arthur."

Closing the file, I swing back around, throwing it onto the bed next to him. "Yes. He wants to use her to get to us. So, we will use her to stop that. But if she becomes a liability again, there's no second chances. You need to sort this mess out."

"You're referring to Ashwood," he points out with a snarl at his name. "I'm working on it."

"Good," I say firmly, nodding to the file. "New patient details. Rian Thatcher. Interesting history, transferred from the county jail."

Grey picks up the file, flicking it open. "Thoughts?"

"Lilydale obviously picked him for a reason. I'm hoping to gain more insight into that once I'm able to get to him."

"Do you want me to distract Christopher for you?" Grey asks, reading the information.

I lean back in the chair, crossing my arms. "I believe Avery has an appointment tomorrow. That will give us a free window. Thatcher's schedule is in there. Locate him and bring him to me."

"Done," he says casually, still scanning the file. "Have you given any further thought as to what you want to do with Capello?"

"We need to question her. Markel's notes only detailed what we already assumed. I'll get Jillian to do it. Perhaps she'll be more willing to talk if it's another female."

Grey closes the file. "I need to find the asshole who framed Avery. You promised me a venting system—that's the way to do it."

I snort, giving him an amused look. "You didn't just vent before?" I ask, glancing over the bed. "Was it not enough blood for you?"

I'm teasing him, and he knows it. But his eyes darken, confirming the fact that he needs to really *hurt* someone.

"I'm serious, Deadman."

"I know," I murmur, strumming my fingers on my arm. "I'll sort it out."

The next morning, I tell Grey I'll be waiting in the library. He runs off happily on the hunt for the infamous Rian. I've already confirmed with the guards that Avery has been escorted to Arthur's office this morning, and as soon as her psychiatrist session starts with Christopher, we make our move.

It doesn't take long until Grey returns with a brunette in tow. He looks confused, but not at all worried.

Standing at the far end of the library, I wait until they reach me, not bothering with pleasantries.

"Hello, Rian. We haven't met yet but if you haven't heard of me, you will soon."

He glances at me with pale brown eyes, face as dead as I am inside. "Rightio. I assume this is some lecture about politics or some shit."

"You could say that," I murmur low. "You'll be answering to us. I have no doubt Whittingham has given you some poor excuse for a lecture at his *orientation*."

"I'm going to wager that you're Damon," Rian answers in a bored tone. "Yeah, I've been told about you."

Leaning back against the desk, I tap my fingers on the wooden edge. "By Whittingham?"

A smile appears on his face, his eyes focusing on me. "By Dr. Smith, actually."

My eyes narrow, as do Grey's. Christopher is a slimy piece of work, but I've never known him to step outside of his *professional* demeanor when it comes to the patients here.

"And what did he have to say for himself?" I ask, curious.

Rian laughs under his breath. "He asked me to pass a message onto you actually."

Grey stiffens next to Rian, hand twitching into a fist. "Did he now?"

I raise my hand to silence him, amused. "And what was the message, Thatcher?"

"He said *nice try*. And something about being one step behind."

Anger rushes through my veins but I don't show it. I should have known that Christopher would try to send a message somehow. He knew that we would approach Rian, so my only question now is what has he said?

"So, you're well acquainted with the resident psychiatrist now," I laugh. "I'm sure he's told you some interesting stories."

Rian nods. "He has actually," he quips back. "But I'm not going to relay them to you."

Grey's eyes flash and I step forward, intervening before he does something harsh like slit Thatcher's throat open.

"Well, I'm only going to say this once," I start, towering over Rian. "You'll quickly learn that it's not what it seems here. I would be *very* careful and considerate of the sides you take. Perhaps it would do you some good to make your own inquiries before listening to a quack."

He steps back slightly, uncertainty crossing his face. "I'm not afraid of you. You can keep your high-school hierarchy bullshit to yourself."

I smile. "Make those inquiries. Or else you'll likely find yourself somewhere you don't want to be." I shoo with my hand, signaling for him to fuck off. Rian gives us both a quick look before briskly leaving the library.

"That fucking bastard," Grey snaps. "Let me go there right now and rip open his carotid artery."

"Avery's in session with him," I point out.

Grey snorts. "I'll fuck her in his blood. That doesn't worry me."

"Try to contain yourself a little longer," I tell him. "Thatcher will quickly learn. I'll send Leighton to have a chat with him. In the meantime, Jillian should have an update for us this evening."

"Do you want me to call a meeting?" Grey asks, pacing slowly across the library.

I nod. "And get someone to clean this library. It's putrid and God knows what's on the floor."

Grey laughs, lifting an eyebrow. "I know of a few things," he says suggestively.

I curl my lips in disgust. "Definitely get them to scrub the aisles before the next meeting. In the meantime, I have to go attend to something. I'll catch up with you later."

He waves me off as we exit the library, and I wait until he's out of sight before I head down the corridor. I spot a guard lingering outside of Dr. Smith's office and when I give him a nod, he turns and walks in the other direction.

The sound of muffled voices inside are indistinguishable. I count to three before I kick the door hard open with the bottom of my foot. It bounces off the wall, wood splintering as Christopher and Avery look up surprised from the floor.

I step inside, raising an eyebrow at the chessboard on the ground. "Games, really? Is that what they are paying you for?" I taunt, not waiting for his reply. "Avery, come with me."

To my surprise, she stands immediately, heading to the door. I guess giving her a little dick reward has gone a long way toward her compliance.

After she steps into the hallway, I turn to a glowering Christopher who is now on his feet. He looks almost offended that she would willingly come with me, and I resist the urge to laugh.

"I got your message," I tell him cheerfully. "And you can shove it right up your bleached asshole."

Chapter 19
Avery

Mr. Whittingham has this ridiculous talent to look completely together no matter what time of day or night it is. The sun has barely cracked over the horizon, my hair resembling a bird's nest, while he sips on coffee in a freshly steamed suit.

"You'll be in here all day," he tells me with an artificial smile. "Except for your appointment with Dr. Smith. Unfortunately, that neat stack of paperwork got knocked over."

I resist the urge to twitch, but keep my mouth shut, getting started again on the scattered papers.

A few hours later, I'm escorted to Dr. Smith's office, and I'm surprised to find the chessboard set up exactly how we last left it.

"Do you remember the rules?" he asks, summoning me to the ground.

"Not really," I admit with a sigh, crossing my legs underneath me. "Other than some bullshit about the queen having all the power."

Dr. Smith laughs, pointing out the different pieces and relaying some basic rules. He doesn't ask any questions about my feelings or about anything else outside of this room. I'm on edge, but try to stay focused on the game, enjoying a moment away from getting more papercuts, which have returned on my fingertips with a sting. But in comparison to the still aching mark on my thigh, hidden by my shorts, it's nothing. Still, if I had to choose my pain, I'd opt for Grey every time.

Somewhere midway through the session, the door flies open with a loud bang, startling me. I whip my head around, eyes widening at Damon's figure lingering in the doorframe.

He's never interrupted my sessions before, but the way he's staring at Dr. Smith, I don't think his beef is with me. Besides, last night changed things for us. Well, I like to think so.

Even though I was woken up early and dragged from my bed, I'm still buzzing with a feeling I haven't felt in ages. And it's still baffling that it's somewhat because of Demon Boy.

"Games, really? Is that what they are paying you for?" he says. "Avery, come with me."

I rise to my feet, heading over to him. I'm not about to rock the boat when he just did me the favor of a lifetime. Besides, what loyalty do I have to the staff here? All they have done is punish me, allow my information to be stolen, treated me like I'm a criminal... *even if I am.*

At least Grey and Theo see me for who I am. And I guess in a weird turn of events, so does Damon.

I hear Damon shoot back a curse at Dr. Smith before gesturing for me to follow him down the hallway. I walk beside

him, checking around for the guards which have mysteri-
ously vanished.

"I'm due back in Whittingham's office after my session," I
say.

Damon doesn't look at me, but I notice his eyebrow raises
at my words. "And what does he have you doing today?"

"Alphabetizing paperwork... again."

"Pathetic," he mumbles. "That's Teddy's job. No doubt
she's too busy blowing him under the desk to handle her
actual job."

A shutter of disgust rolls over me, making Damon laugh.

"Do they really?" I ask, not sure I want to know the answer.

He hums, confirming it before leading us into the giant
hall. It's empty at this time of day, except for a few lingering
staff members getting the food trays ready for lunch.

I look around, noticing how no one pays any attention to
us. It's almost as if we are ghosts, just haunting and passing
by peacefully.

"What are we doing here?" I ask as Damon leads us
through a set of double doors to the kitchen.

Staff in white coats are bustling around, the smell of food
lingering in the air. A few curious eyes look over as we enter,
but no one says anything.

"Getting some food for you," he answers casually, walking
up to an older man with fading brown hair and green eyes.
"Tony, organize some food for her."

Tony pauses, knife in hand at a chopping board. He briskly looks at me with disinterest, nodding at Damon. "Alright. What does she want?"

Damon rolls his eyes, throwing his hand toward me. "Ask her yourself. She's obviously right here."

My eyes widen slightly as Tony slams the knife down, turning his body to face me. "What do ya want? I can spare about ten minutes to cook something up before we need to get lunch well and truly underway."

"Uh," I mumble stupidly. I wasn't prepared for this. I'm so hungry that I'd probably settle for the dry, plain pasta at this point. "Honestly, I'm happy with anything easy."

Tony groans, snapping his eyes to Damon. "I don't have time for this, Damon. I can't be fucking around on the clock. Whittingham will have my balls if lunch is late."

"Just make her a sandwich or something," Damon scoffs. "Whatever you have on hand."

Tony nods, disappearing into a nearby walk-in freezer. My mind is still turning, cooks rushing past us to attend to pots of boiling water and cutting up vegetables.

I spot an empty countertop not being used and I gesture to it. "Can I wait there?" I ask Damon.

He looks behind me to the stainless steel countertop, nodding.

We head out of the way of the staff as someone runs past with more steaming food. I push myself off the ground, sitting on the countertop with my legs dangling off the side.

Damon leans against the wall near me, folding his arms as he observes the staff.

"Is this how you guys get your food?" I ask, trying to make conversation.

He glances over at me. "For the society meetings? Yes."

I nod. "And your snack stash."

His lips twitch into a smile. "I thought I was missing some. I assume Grey made himself busy in my drawers."

"Yeah," I laugh awkwardly. "Sorry... and, uh, sorry about your bed."

I don't know why I mention it. I get word vomit when I'm nervous, and I'm not an idiot. He absolutely saw the state of his room. I know Grey said he wouldn't care, but still... an apology seems appropriate.

"I had the sheets changed," he murmurs, unfazed.

Nodding again, I look up as Tony approaches with a plate. My mouth waters at the sight of a large sandwich, piled high with various fresh ingredients—ones we never see at meal times.

"Here," he says, shoving it toward me. "Drinks are in the fridge."

He dashes off before we can respond and I look at Damon, picking up the sandwich with two hands. "Drinks?"

"Soda, alcohol. The usual. I'll grab one."

It's bizarre that he refers to it as the usual since we're never offered anything except water and milk. I watch as he heads to the other side of the kitchen, taking the opportunity to bite into the sandwich. It's easily one of the best meals I've had since coming here—second only to the society feasts.

When Damon returns, he holds out a can of Coke to me.

"I haven't had Coke in ages," I mumble with excitement, grabbing the cold can from his grip.

He doesn't respond, leaning back against the wall. I can only assume he's not thrilled about being on Avery-sitting duty, so I keep quiet, eating quickly.

I demolish the whole sandwich and the can of soda, leaving the plate on the countertop next to me.

Damon glances over at the empty plate, a bored expression on his face. "Are you full?"

"Yeah, I'm good," I tell him, sparing a sympathetic look to the busy staff. "We should get out of here. They seem stressed."

"They'll live," he shoots back, kicking off the wall.

We leave the kitchen and I give Tony a little wave to show my appreciation. He pauses slightly, looking almost confused, but quickly turns away, continuing with his tasks.

"Am I heading back to Mr. Whittingham's office?" I ask Damon as we cross the hall to the doors.

Damon looks at me, a smirk on his face. "Absolutely not. Unless you want to, of course."

"No," I answer quickly, shaking my head. "Anything but that."

He snorts. "Don't care much for his company?"

My face scrunches up in frustration. "He's not my first choice, that's for sure. Or my second. Hell, probably wouldn't even rank him anything above last."

"So, I'm a step above him?" Damon taunts, leading us toward the courtyard.

"Definitely more than a step," I mutter. "You're growing on me a little."

He laughs and we head past the empty rooms. I look inside, instinctively searching for Theo.

Theo...

I haven't seen him for days because of all this bullshit. I told him I wouldn't avoid him and now I've been forced to do that.

Is he mad at me?

Sick of me?

My eyebrows furrow with anxiety and worry. It's not unnoticed by Damon, who stops in front of the door to the stairwell.

I stop walking, remembering the last time I was here. Theo had smashed the access pad and swept me away underground to escape the bomb that had been dropped in the hall.

The keypad has been replaced, the shiny black metal untouched, not even a single finger mark smear on it.

"What now?" Damon asks, annoyed.

Looking at him in confusion, I quickly shrug. "It's just been a crazy few weeks. I'm just thinking of shit. It's okay."

Damon raises an eyebrow at me. "You need to learn to get a handle on your emotions. You have no control whatsoever. It's pathetic."

I scowl at him. "Every time I start to almost like you, you say shit like that."

"Lucky for me, I don't care about being liked."

"Why?" I blurt out. "Why would you not want to be liked?"

Damon looks at me, unfamiliar disbelief on his face. He's glaring at me like it's the stupidest question he's ever heard. "This is exactly the emotional bullshit I'm referring to. When will you learn that likeableness gets you nowhere? Power is everything, Avery. I'm not here to make friends. We're not going to sit in the library and braid each other's hair and share secrets."

"But we do share secrets," I point out sarcastically.

"No, we don't," he answers coolly. "I provide information as required. You should be mindful that you are lucky to be included. Sadly, that was out of my control."

I snort. "Something out of your control. Shit—Hell is freezing over."

I realize instantly that I'm going too far. Damon's arm slams onto the wall next to my head as he leans in, eyes darkening.

"We *are* in Hell. The only difference is I took over from the Devil. However, I believe in rewarding loyalty. Grey has been loyal to me since the day he arrived. Thus... I tolerate you."

My jaw clenches. "I know," I tell him quietly. "If we're being honest, I tolerate you for the same reason."

His eyebrow twitches, but I offer a quick smile, trying not to stir the beast.

"But regardless, I'm thankful for your... *tolerance*," I add.

Damon straightens up, scanning me curiously. "I'm glad to hear because there are many secrets about this place you don't know. It's best you do as you're told and follow orders."

"And that includes looking after Grey," I murmur. "Because you need him."

He nods. "Exactly." Pausing, he smirks, looking away. "You might think I'm the villain, Avery. And you'd be correct. But that's because we're made to be. There's nothing wrong with that."

I stare at him in confusion. What is he talking about?

Damon reaches into his pocket, extracting a staff card. He holds it up to my face between his fingers, tilting his head to the side.

"You remember how to get to the morgue, correct?"

Chapter 20
Grey

There he is.

Immediately, I'm ready to kill him. Before my feet have even taken three steps, I've already planned at least seven different ways to permanently delete him.

Shame there's an audience though.

I push past other patients as I cross the hall, eyes locked in on my target. He doesn't even glance up as I approach, though I notice his body tensing up. He can sense me, but he's not at all worried or fearful. And that fucking pisses me off.

"Ashwood," I growl, resting my hands on the table across from him.

Theo fucking Ashwood finally glances up, eyes narrowing on me. He barely moves at all, just peering up at me with his head tilted down.

"What?" he snaps back.

I twitch, the weight of the razor blade in my pocket heavy as I resist the urge to whip it out and give him a matching scar to my own neck.

"We need to talk," I say through clenched teeth.

People around us look over, doing their best to hide their curiosity but it's so obvious. A few people quickly move away, while others nudge their companions and point to us.

They think shit is about to go down.

Even the guards against the wall have taken notice, hands on their tasers and guns. The thought makes me laugh. I know Theo's reputation precedes him—I've witnessed his encounters before when people have tried to approach him. He's dangerous, unpredictable. But guess what?

So the fuck am I.

I'm worse, actually. Because I have something to lose, something I just got back.

And I have to be amicable with this fucker right here.

"I'm not the talking type," Ashwood responds sarcastically. "Perhaps find another person to converse with."

I straighten up, laughing. There's a clear radius around us of people who immediately scatter or panic.

Out of the corner of my eye, I spot a guard taking a step toward us, ready to intervene. I glare at him with a smirk, not familiar with him.

He doesn't know better yet. Obviously a new hire who thinks he has a cock made of gold. But even gold melts when met with fire.

I shake my head at him, watching as another guard rushes over to whisper something in his ear. He looks bewildered for a second, stilling.

"Listen here, asshole," I say, returning my attention to Ashwood. "This is about Avery."

Even the mere mention of her name rocks me. It's like a poetic tsunami—large waves drowning me but bringing such peace. Apparently, it has the same effect on Ashwood, because he looks up properly, his sneer dropping.

"Is she okay?" he asks sincerely.

I hate that he cares. At the same time, it also buys him a few more seconds of his precious life.

"She's fine," I tell him casually, looking at my black nails. "More than fine last night, actually."

Ashwood leans back from the table, folding his arms. "Is this your poor attempt at making me jealous?"

"Not at all," I taunt. "Just reiterating that she's alive and well."

"I should hope so," he replies. "Because if anything happens to her while in your care, I'll dig your grave myself."

My eyes snap to his angrily. "She's safer with me than with you," I spit out.

He rolls his eyes. "Is that a fact? Because it seems to me you're not doing a good enough job since she's been taken away again these past few days."

I slam my hands on the edge of the table, gasps echoing around the room as people start to get frightened. I need to rein it in. The whole point of this conversation was so I could try to be civil for Avery's sake. But fuck me, this asshole isn't making it easy.

"You know very well that Arthur Whittingham does whatever the fuck he wants," I hiss under my breath.

Ashwood leans forward, raising an eyebrow. "And yet when she returned from prison, you were nowhere to be seen. Who was there for her? Me. Not you and your little group of friends."

My jaw twitches. "That might have something to do with the fact that you took her from me."

"I didn't do shit," he fires back. "Avery is a grown-ass woman. She can make her own decisions and be with whomever she wants."

Well, at least we are back on track now.

"And here we are," I sneer. "So, get your ass up and follow me. We have a few things to discuss."

I watch with frustration as he looks away, picking up a faded brown napkin from his food tray and dabs his mouth slowly. Taking his time, he finally stands, shoving his hands in his pockets.

"Lead the way then, Hawthorne. I don't have all day."

Some might say I'm a masochist.

And I guess they would be correct.

Of all the places I could have picked for this discussion, I chose here.

The fucking morgue.

Well, at least they won't have to take his body far when I gut him.

Ashwood glances lazily around the room, not at all fazed by it. He doesn't even look surprised. Then again, everyone knows that Damon and I go where ever the fuck we want in this place.

But if he's shocked that I know about the incident in the morgue with Avery, he doesn't show it.

"Are you going to speak or are we just going to stand awkwardly until the guards drag us back upstairs?" he grunts.

I lean against the mortuary cabinet, slapping my hand against the metal door. "I just thought I'd bring you somewhere that you are familiar with. You know, to help make you comfortable."

He rolls his eyes, leaning against the pure stainless steel instrument cabinet on the other side of the room. "Is there an actual point to this rendezvous? You said you wanted to chat about Avery."

Frustration threatens to send me over the edge. This asshole is refusing to bite.

I need to fight. I need to argue.

I need to spill blood.

But he won't fucking bite at all.

"You fucked Avery in this cabinet," I point out. "Why?"

Ashwood raises an eyebrow. "Why did I have sex with Avery? Or are you questioning whether I have kinks that you might be interested in pursuing?"

"She's mine."

"We've already covered that, Hawthorne. Get on with the point."

Taking a breath, I remind myself that this is for Avery. And that Damon had promptly warned me not to murder anyone today.

"I don't like you," I spit out. "But I love Avery. And for some reason, she *likes* you."

He doesn't say anything in response, but locks eyes with me, acknowledging that he's listening.

"For the sake of her, I'm willing to not rip out your organs one by one."

"How delightful," he mocks. "I could easily break your neck and make it look like an accident. But that's beside the point."

I kick the mortuary cabinet hard as I spring forward, stalking across the room toward him. We're around the same height, but I tower over his relaxed, slouched posture. "I'm going to be civil for Avery. At the end of the day, she deserves to be happy. But if you cross me, or if you hurt her, I'll end you."

A half-smile curls on his lips. "The feeling is mutual. Try not to toss her aside again."

My hands reach out and grab the neck of his shirt as I slam his back into the cabinet. He doesn't flinch at all, smirking at me.

"Did I hit a nerve?" he asks in a low voice. "You're so caught up in whatever little scheme you have running here. You're Damon's little bitch and everyone knows it."

"What the fuck is going on?"

The sound of her voice stills me. I glance over my shoulder at the door, spotting a horrified looking Avery. The black familiar staff card is in her hand, eyes wide as she glances between me and Ashwood.

"Hey, little killer," I grin, still holding onto the scruff of Ashwood's shirt. "Fancy seeing you here."

I knew she'd be here. I asked Damon to set it up.

It might be the only chance for the three of us to have some privacy to sort this out. Or, at the very least, she would stop me from killing her *friend*.

"Grey," she whispers, eyes dropping to my clenched fists. "Let go of Theo."

I scrunch up my nose, waiting a few seconds before dropping him carelessly. He straightens up behind me as I turn to face her.

"We're just having a little discussion," I tell her fondly. "About you."

Her eyes drift over to Theo with concern and it takes everything in me to fight the ugly green monster that's threatening to break loose.

A hand slaps onto my shoulder, making my face curl up in disgust.

"We're *civil*," Ashwood mutters. "Aren't we, *Grey*?"

I shrug his hand off my shoulder, taking a few steps away from him. Composing myself, I grin at Avery, nodding.

"Good friends now. See—I'm making an effort."

Avery looks at me wearily. "Really?" she asks in disbelief.

Ashwood laughs under his breath. "It's fine, Avery," he tells her calmly.

She visibly relaxes a little. "That's... good," she answers hesitantly.

Seeing her in person, color back in her cheeks, starts to send a wave of calm through me. I know she was dragged to that cunt's office again this morning, and when I didn't see her at breakfast, I knew we had to do something.

And the fact that she's here means the plan with Damon went smoothly.

Well, as smooth as things can go when it comes to Deadman. I have no doubt he caused some havoc on the way.

"You weren't at breakfast," I say softly.

Avery looks at me, nodding. "Whittingham strikes again."

"He's never punished like this before," Ashwood chimes in. "What's the deal?"

I take a deep breath. "Avery's the deal. He's trying to overpower everyone."

"Right," he replies slowly, contemplating my words. "I assume because of *you*."

The way he says it, I know he's referring to us as a whole, rather than just me. Still, I'm tempted to inflict harm again, so I do the only reasonable thing.

I walk away from him, over to Avery, pulling her into my chest for a hug. She relaxes against me as I breathe in her scent, letting her presence control my temper.

Also, it's an added bonus to get to rub it into Ashwood's face.

"It's not like that," Avery tells him, resting her cheek on my arm to look at him. "I'm okay though."

"Have you eaten?" I ask her.

She nods. "Damon and I swung by the kitchen."

My eyebrows raise as I rest my chin on her head. Thankfully, she can't see my expression. The plan was to get Avery away from Whittingham and back to me. I knew I would need to organize food based on Arthur's history, but that was all Damon. We never discussed that.

"Good," I reply, letting her go. "Now, there's only one thing left to do."

"Oh?" she asks, looking over at Ashwood. She looks like she wants to go to him and the thought kills me. But against my better judgment, I give her back a little nudge, pushing her in his direction.

Her feet shuffle along the ground on their own accord before she takes control, walking over to Ashwood to embrace him in a hug.

I watch them, his hands curling around her back as he holds her tight. Waves of emotion hit me—too many to singularly focus on. Anger, betrayal, hurt. A tiny voice inside mimics my father's voice screaming that she's a cheater. But I know better. I'm stronger than he was.

Slowly, I observe them, fighting back the jealousy. Avery glances over to me, a smile appearing on her face. It's the brightest one I've seen in a while from her... and it's aimed at *me*.

She's happy.

And I did that.

Conflict tears at me, but seeing her look at me with that usual loving gaze while holding him, starts to build those bricks that were knocked down.

She's still looking at me the same.

She's at peace.

And as much as I hate it, Ashwood is right. He was there for her. He's protected her on more than one occasion, especially when I couldn't.

I hate these unfamiliar feelings but I hold onto that look on her face right now, letting it ground me.

"The only thing left to do," I start, smiling at her. "Is to invite Theo to the meeting tonight."

Chapter 21

Avery

The three of us head back upstairs, joining the tail end of the crowd as guards start leading everyone away to classes.

People glance back at us, me flanked by Theo on one side and Grey on the other—disbelief, confusion and fucking dumbfounded expressions on their faces.

"Someone will come fetch you this evening," I hear Grey say to Theo as we're separated by the guards.

"See you later, Avery," he says to me, ignoring Grey, giving my hand a quick squeeze.

I watch as a dozen students head into a nearby classroom with Theo while Grey stays by my side quietly.

"Ready?" he asks, nodding his head toward Charmaine inside the room.

I nod, waiting as Theo disappears from sight. "Let's go."

Class goes oddly quick, mainly because Grey can't take his eyes off me the entire time. He winks at me, giving me boyish grins, and it feels like my worlds have started to collide in the best way possible.

I think I have emotional whiplash but it's worth it.

When the bell goes for free time, Grey launches himself from his chair, offering me his hand.

"I know you probably want to go see him, but I really need you to come to the library with me," he says.

The thought and consideration from him touches me and knowing I'll be able to see Theo tonight, puts me a little at ease. I nod, grabbing his hand as we leave the classroom last behind everyone else.

Entering the library, I'm immediately hit with the smell of lemons and bleach. A few familiar faces are hanging by the tables and I glance at the shelves, noticing the usual dust is gone.

"Hey... the library has been cleaned," I gawk in amusement.

Grey grins at me. "I organized it. They did a good job."

"Who did?" I laugh, knowing full well that the Lilydale staff wouldn't have bothered.

He nods his head toward a few people in the back. "Leighton and a couple of others. We decided to give it a clean for tonight. *Who knows what's on the floor?*"

My cheeks blush as he looks at me knowingly. I playfully slap his arm, laughing as we join the others.

"Satisfied?" Leighton asks Grey. "We even managed to do the carpet."

I gaze down, noticing how much brighter the floor looks. I spare a quick thought for whoever was tasked with that, particularly since the aisles have definitely seen some things...

"It's good," Grey nods. "Food will be set up at nine sharp. Make sure to add another chair to the table tonight. We'll have a newcomer attending."

They appear surprised but don't ask questions. Damon is nowhere to be seen, so, naturally Grey takes charge, dishing out orders for tonight's meeting. It's surreal seeing it in action after only ever seeing it already set up.

The group works together confirming plans, assigning roles, and by the time free time is finished, I'm actually excited.

Stepping out of the library, I'm mid-laugh at one of Grey's jokes when his face darkens. I pause, following his line of vision to find Mr. Whittingham waiting by the hall entrance doors.

"Ms. White," he drawls out with a sneer. "You failed to return to my office."

Grey steps closer to me, shadowing my body. "Fuck off, Arthur. She's not your slave."

"She's my student," Whittingham snaps back. "And how I choose to discipline them is none of your concern, Hawthorne."

I cringe at the word *student*, hating the way it rolls off his tongue. It's an insult to everyone here. We know what we are, but his words are a stark reminder that we are nothing more than dollar signs to him.

"You won't be *disciplining* her ever again," Grey warns. "This ends now."

Mr. Whittingham's gaze shoots over to me, anger flashing in his eyes. I can see the realization in his gaze, his stipulations and warnings having gone unnoticed.

"You can keep away from that crowd you seem to have grown attached to. Otherwise, I'll ensure they are promptly removed from Lilydale as well."

"We'll see about that," he snarls at Grey.

I reach up and grab Grey's arm when I notice him start to shake from rage. My movement catches the attention of Whittingham, who looks at my hand with a scowl. He doesn't say anything, turning around, and disappearing in the direction of his office.

"Fuck," I whisper, gazing up at Grey. "What do we do?"

He relaxes, the dark demeanor vanishing instantly. Smiling down at me, he turns around to face me. "Nothing. It's just an empty threat, babe. Don't let it bother you."

Clutching my hand, he pulls me into the hall as students sit down for dinner. I spot Damon at his usual table, immediately giving Grey a brisk nod when their eyes meet.

Despite his reassurances, I can't help but feel like it's not an empty threat.

Sure, Mr. Whittingham doesn't have the power when it comes to them. But they can't protect me twenty-four-seven.

And inside, I have the niggling suspicion that we've just started a war.

I walk into the library, hand-in-hand with Grey, my eyes immediately scanning the *Cirque des Morts* crowd for obsidian eyes. Frowning, I look at Grey when I don't find Theo.

"He'll be here," he mutters quietly to me, giving me a smile. "We're just a little early."

I return the smile, looking around until my eyes land on Damon in the corner. He's talking heatedly with Jillian, who looks uneasy.

The two of them glance over at us as we approach, their conversation dying off. Damon gives her a final nod before Jillian sighs, heading off to join a crowd of people near the food table.

"What was that about?" Grey asks warmly.

Damon's gaze flickers to me for a brief second before returning to his second-in-command. "Capello. It didn't go as planned."

"Vivian is vulnerable right now," I interject, feeling sorry for the girl.

Sure—she's made my life hell ever since I arrived. Her piece of shit boyfriend assaulted me, she stole my file and plastered it around the hall to expose me... but still, despite it, I feel a little bit sorry for her.

"That's called the consequence of her own actions," Damon answers. "Perhaps if people listened the first time, they wouldn't make stupid mistakes."

"I know," I say in agreement, nodding. "I don't forgive her for what she did. But we're all facing battles here. And that's exacerbated by her boyfriend's death now."

My eyes shoot heatedly over to Grey, who looks at me with innocence.

"What?" he mouths.

I shake my head. "You know what," I snipe back.

Damon watches our exchange closely. "You told her."

It's not a question, just a definitive observation. Grey nods casually at him.

"Oops," he offers unapologetically.

Damon shakes his head, suddenly pausing to look behind us. His face drops as his eyes darken slightly. I instinctively turn around to see what has his attention, face lighting up when I spot Theo entering the library with Jemison.

"Hey," I say brightly when he reaches us.

"Hey, you," he answers, giving me a brief smile before glaring at Damon.

My heart races nervously. Did Grey clear this with Damon beforehand? I have to assume so, but then again, I never see it coming what they do next.

"Ashwood," Damon greets lazily with a sneer. "I see that you are joining us this evening."

I quickly look at Grey for reassurance, noticing the smirk on his face.

Still can't fucking tell...

"You knew, right?" I ask Damon, unable to help myself.

His light green eyes flicker over to me. "Obviously."

I let out a sigh of relief—even though it might only be temporary. We still have the whole evening to deal with. I can already see the other members of the society looking at us curiously. While it's now been confirmed that Damon knew in advance, it's clear that they didn't.

"Is this some fancy tea party or something?" Theo murmurs lowly, eyes scanning over the set-up.

The usual curtains have blocked the aisles, and I still remember my confusion and bewilderment the first time I attended a meeting. I'm not sure what's going to be more awkward—the meeting itself or the afterparty.

"Funny," Damon spits out, giving Grey a knowing look. "Take a seat at the table. We're about to begin."

Grey leans down to whisper in my ear. "Sit next to me. Ashwood can sit on your right."

I nod, turning to Theo. "I'll take you over."

Grabbing Theo's hand, I lead him over to the long table, sitting down. He takes a seat next to me, glancing around with a blank expression.

"They really do have control, don't they?" he muses quietly so only I can hear.

I pivot my body to face him, lowering my voice. "Yeah. It's a bit crazy."

"Crazy is what we all do best," he says. "Explains a lot."

A smile appears on my face at his blasé attitude. If anyone is going to be unimpressed or unthreatened by the situation, it would be Theo.

"Everything here is confidential," I relay, stating the obvious. "I'm not sure why they wanted you to come, but let's just roll with it."

Theo looks at me, eyes flashing. "You, Avery. It's because of you."

"I..." Pausing, I shake my head. "I'm sure that's not the only reason."

"You're the reason, Avery. For all of us."

"What do you mean?" I breathe out.

He leans down, brushing his lips against my ear. "You're my only reason for anything. And I think you're theirs, as well."

Snapping back, I gaze at him shocked. "Definitely not. There's a lot that goes on behind the scenes. We've just unfortunately found ourselves in the midst of it."

Theo smirks at me. "Is that what you tell yourself?"

Before I can respond, Grey brushes against my left side as he sits down, reaching under the table to grip my thigh.

"What are you talking about?" he asks curiously, but with a hint of demand.

I swing my head to look at him. "You," I tease.

His eyes narrow in suspicion but he doesn't say anything as Damon takes his position at the head of the table.

"There's no time to fuck around with pleasantries today," he starts with a frustrated tone. "To address the elephant in the room, we have a new guest."

All eyes fall onto Theo, followed by me. I can practically hear their thoughts, wondering what the hell is going on. One minute I was banished because of my involvement with Theo, then I came back, fighting with Grey for all to see, and now I'm here again—with both of them. As usual though, no one questions Damon's decisions, eventually ripping their attention away from us back to the man at the end of the table.

"Whittingham is doubling down, as are the other *staff* members," he sneers. "We've also made contact with Hallman's replacement who is not cooperating."

"Not cooperating?" Byrone asks. "How so?"

Grey laughs. "Someone else got to him first."

My eyebrows furrow as I try to keep up with the information. I haven't run into the newcomer yet, and while I'm not surprised Damon has met him, I'm baffled as to why someone is already making enemies.

Even in my first week here, I knew immediately who held the power. From the moment I was cornered by Damon, it was obvious that it would be a death wish to defy him. I didn't even know back then what I know now about the society—he just exuded that authority and darkness.

"It's a work in progress," Damon interjects after Grey. "There's about to be some changes around the facility. I do not anticipate it going smoothly."

"Does that affect our plans?" Jillian asks. She looks exhausted, still uneasy and on edge. I have to wonder what happened during her interaction with Vivian to unnerve her.

"No," Damon answers firmly. "We just need to ensure we are two steps ahead. For now, we are going to temporarily pause the grouping system overhaul."

I raise an eyebrow, looking at Grey. I still don't know what the deal is with the system.

"What do you need us to do?" Leighton asks casually, resting his elbow on the table.

"Keep monitoring the cameras and feeds. We need the access points available at all times. Also, bring Rian Thatcher into line. I can't have him messing up any of our plans."

Grey squeezes my thigh under the table, tapping his fingers against my leg. "Also, in the meantime, it's likely that Whittingham is going to continue to try to overpower us. He's still hounding Avery for information and has resorted to extreme measures. If you notice her absence or any unusual behavior with the staff directed at her, report it to us immediately."

Theo snaps his head to his left to look at Grey. "What extreme measures?"

I give him a sheepish look, already sensing his anger. "I'll fill you in with more detail later."

"This is where you come in," Grey mutters at Theo, jaw clenched. "I need you to stay with Avery during free time and keep her out of sight of the staff."

"Easy done," he answers confidently. "And I assume you'll stay with her during class time."

Grey nods. "Jillian, we need you to set up a live stream on Damon's laptop pinpointing the Eastwood and Westwood corridors, as well as Whittingham's office. If possible, we also need a direct link to the rooms underground."

"The morgue?" I ask, baffled.

Next to me, Theo laughs under his breath. Grey narrows his eyes on us, fighting back curses.

"There's other rooms down there as well," he says dryly. "I'm sure Ashwood has seen them."

I blink slowly, trying to figure out what he means. I can't tell if it's a jab or a genuine statement.

Theo nods though. "I've been past them but never inside. It's usually closed off."

"Isn't everything closed off?" I mutter.

Damon scoffs. "Of course. But this is a conversation for another day. We'll meet again in a few days as I expect there will be more developments. Report back to us with any new updates. That is all."

Chairs scrape back on the carpet as people stand, but I remain seated, turning to Grey.

"I thought you said that they were empty threats," I ask with worry.

He grins at me. "I'm sure they are. But let's err on the side of caution for now. Wait here for a moment, I need to talk to Ashwood about something."

I frown, looking over at Theo, who just nods, standing to follow Grey.

They disappear into an aisle, the curtain swinging closed behind them. I realize I'm stuck alone at the table with Damon, who's sitting with his arms folded.

"That was a quick meeting," I mutter, making conversation.

He glances over at me. "Time is irrelevant. It's the topics that matter."

I nod. "I guess so," I say awkwardly. "Do you ever eat or participate in the afterparty?" Tilting my head, I motion toward the food.

Damon cocks an eyebrow at me in amusement. "Is that your way of making conversation or are you genuinely curious?"

"Both," I admit. "You put on these events to *reward* everyone but I never see you reap the benefits."

He smirks. "You're usually too busy in the aisles to take notice of what I do, Avery."

My cheeks flush and I turn away to look at the wall of black curtains. "That's true. You should unwind though. You seem stressed or something."

"I'm not stressed," he replies. "I'm focused. There's a difference."

"I'm just saying," I smile weakly at him. "Doesn't hurt to look after yourself as well."

Damon shakes his head slowly. "You don't win wars with weakness, Avery."

Before I can answer, Grey stalks out of the aisle, my eyes turning to find him. I watch sadly as I spot Theo heading out behind him, leaving through the library doors.

"Come with me," Grey says, holding out his hand.

I take it, brushing past Damon as I follow. "Where's Theo going?"

He doesn't answer me, instead pulling me into an aisle. It's empty except for us, and he drags me to the end, pushing my body against the wall.

Covering my mouth with his, I kiss him back for a few seconds, before breaking the kiss. "Grey..."

"Ssh," he says, silencing me. "Trust me."

Chapter 22

Avery

Grey drops to his knees in front of me, running his hands up the front of my legs. When he reaches the hem of my skirt, he fiddles with it, pleased.

"I'm glad you wore a skirt today," he murmurs, dipping his hands underneath to find my underwear.

The feel of his fingers on my body sends a rush of heat through me, but I'm still conflicted and torn.

Hooking the sides of my underwear, he drags them down my legs, tapping my calves to direct me to step out of them. I comply, resting my hands on his shoulders for balance.

"Where's Theo?" I ask again.

No one left the library with him, so I'm worried that a guard will find him or that he won't be able to get back into the locked rooms.

Grey pushes my legs apart, trailing his fingers up my inner thigh. Pausing over his engraving, he looks up at me.

"Do you remember what this says?" he asks, demand in his voice.

"Mine," I whisper.

He nods, satisfied with my answer. "Exactly."

I gasp quietly when he slides a finger inside of me, pumping it slowly in and out. I can barely focus, and my legs shake slightly when he adds another digit.

"Look at how wet you are," he breathes out. "Who made you wet?"

"You," I answer with a small whimper.

"Good," he says. "You better remember that."

Grey circles my clit with his thumb while curling his other fingers. I lean forward, gripping his shoulders tighter.

"I want you to look at me," he growls, and when I find his eyes, I gasp at how much darker they look now. The usual gray orbs look cloudy, like there's a beast behind them fighting to get out.

He removes his fingers, wiping my arousal over his mark. Suddenly, I feel something behind me. It startles me, but before I can process it or move, my pussy is filled with something hard.

It hits me instantly that I'm pushed against the glory hole, someone's cock buried inside of me. I look at Grey in panic, expecting him to explode, but he just nods at me.

"Feel that, little killer? It should be familiar. You've taken that dick before."

My eyes widen in shock, a moan spilling from my lips as I'm slammed into from behind. "Theo?" I ask with a breathy broken voice.

Grey nods sternly. "He's in your cunt right now. But remember who made you wet. Remember who made you drip down your legs."

"Fuck," I hiss, shoving my ass against the wall as the force of Theo's thrusts threatens to send me spiraling forward.

"Look. At. *Me*," Grey says darkly. "I want you to watch *me* as he takes you."

I lock eyes with him, a pained expression on my face as I fight the urge to automatically close them. When Theo slams into me and my eyes roll back, a hand grips my throat.

"Focus, little killer. Pay attention."

"I'm trying," I murmur weakly, digging my nails into his skin.

Grey growls, tapping his fingers rhythmically against my neck as he squeezes. "I'm not going to let you forget me."

"I would never forget you," I breathe out. "I couldn't. I wouldn't. Not now, not ever."

His eyes flash before he leans forward, pressing his lips to mine. I kiss him back, moving my hips in motion with Theo's movements.

It's powerful, soul-breaking. Even though there's a wall between us, they are both here—touching me.

And suddenly, it all makes sense.

Grey organized this.

The question is... why?

I know how hard this is for him. Having to share me is unnatural for him—torturous.

Then bringing Theo into the society, practically announcing our strange relationship to the world. It's expert level, one that we should have walked into slowly. But I guess slow has never been a setting that Grey has been good with.

Except with me...

All those times he waited patiently, ensuring that I was comfortable. And now *this*.

"You're still mine," Grey growls into my mouth. "Every single part of you."

"I'm yours," I reply. "And you're mine too."

He nods, resting his forehead against mine. "When you go to heaven one day, I'll drag you back down to hell to join me. Because I'm never leaving you, Avery."

My pussy clenches around Theo's cock, my arousal coating my inner thighs. "Promise?"

"Promise. Now, I want you to explode on your other boyfriend's cock while looking at me."

His hand reaches to the apex of my thighs, fingers rubbing my clit. Knowing that they are working together to throw me over the edge is too much.

My mouth opens, a scream starting to slip out until Grey presses his lips to mine, silencing me. I tremble around Theo's cock, the vibrations shooting through him as his movements suddenly get frantic. He slams into me a few more times, jarring me forward. There's a bang on the wall as his hand hits the barrier between us and I feel his orgasm fill me.

I don't stop kissing Grey, too drunk on the taste of him and the feel of Theo. It makes me feel like I'm on fire—ironic since that's how I ended up here.

I guess the reality is fires are powerful, but not necessarily evil. They keep us warm and alive, just as much as they can torture and kill us.

Burning with the aesthetic of them, I'd happily die a million times.

Slowly, I feel Theo slip out of me, back to the other side of the wall. I drop forward, landing on my knees with a bang. My tongue flails against Grey's, the feeling of wetness rolling down my thighs and onto the newly cleaned floor.

Throwing my arms around Grey's neck, I curl my hand around, trailing my thumb across his scar.

"We're not them, Grey," I mutter softly. "We'll never be our parents."

His eyes falter slightly, scanning my face. "I know," he whispers. "We're better than that."

I nod. "We make the rules. And in some weird turn of fucked-up events, our life here is better than our childhoods."

Grey smiles. "It's better because of you."

The curtain behind him opens, my body tensing for a second until I spot Theo. I gesture for him to come in, Grey not bothering to turn around to look.

"I'll give you a moment to talk," he says, kissing my forehead and standing up. "Then, you better come out and get some food or else."

I laugh softly, watching as he heads to the end of the aisle, pausing to give Theo a curt nod. When he's gone out of sight, I smile brightly up at Theo from my knees.

"That was very cheeky of you," I muse.

He laughs, sitting down on the floor in front of me. "It wasn't my idea. But it seemed stupid not to go along with it."

I shake my head with a smile, cheeks turning pink. "There were definitely some benefits for you."

"I think that was his way of *trying*," Theo says. "Don't be fooled though—there were still threats involved."

Rolling my eyes, I sigh. "Of course there was. Interesting way to *try* though."

Theo lifts an eyebrow at me, pressing his back against the bookshelf. "It makes sense though. He doesn't like to share, so he picked the most secluded way to do it. He didn't have to see me and judging from what I could hear through the wall, he's still a possessive shit."

"You're possessive too," I shoot back. "Leaving fingers on my bed."

He shrugs. "I gave you a flower. Girls like that shit."

"Oh, *that's* the part you are focusing on," I scold playfully. "*Here's the finger of your enemy... it's in a rose though.*"

"I'm nothing if not unique," he smiles.

I shuffle forward on my knees, positioning myself so I can take a seat next to him on the ground. He reaches for my hand at the same time as I offer it, clutching it in his hold.

"Are you really okay with this?" I ask wearily. "We haven't had a chance to discuss it."

Theo hums in agreement. "Yes, speaking of discussing things. What's the fucking deal with these punishments? Why didn't you tell me?"

I shrug. "I thought I could handle it. I still think I can. I just didn't want to worry anyone. Well, worry isn't the right word. I didn't want either of you to fly off the deep-end and murder anyone."

"I'm serious, Avery. Imagine how I felt when I told you that you wouldn't avoid me any longer, just to have you disappear again."

"That was outside of my control," I whisper sadly. "It's been killing me not being able to see you lately. I was so worried that you'd hate me."

He squeezes my hand. "I don't know what this shit is," he says, nodding in the direction of the society table outside the shelves. "But whatever it is, it's obviously something big. I assume it ties into the fact that you thought you had to avoid me."

I nod, confirming it. "When I returned from that night in prison, I was warned to keep away from all of you by Mr. Whittingham. He threatened me... and you. He said he'd send you all away if I didn't comply."

"You thought you were protecting us," he points out.

"Yeah," I sigh. "And he wanted me to spy on everyone. When I wouldn't give him the information he wanted, he started assigning me to tasks. Just mediocre shit like cleaning the facility, doing paperwork. But he basically tried to starve and exhaust me with it. That's when you noticed I wasn't at meals."

Theo stays quiet and I wonder what's going through his mind. I give his hand a little squeeze, showing my appreciation.

"I'm so happy you approached them to try to help me. That would have been hard."

"Not hard," Theo replies coolly. "Just annoying. But I knew that they had some sway that I didn't have. I'm not too proud to ask for help when it comes to you."

I turn my head to look at him. "And now you're dragged into this mess."

"I've been assigned with protecting you. Therefore, who gives a shit? When are you going to realize that we're a force not to be fucked with. I'm not afraid of any of them—the staff, these morons and their society. No one. If souls exist, Avery, I don't have one."

"That's bullshit and you know it," I scold. "If that were true, you wouldn't want to protect me. You wouldn't care for me."

Theo lifts an eyebrow. "You're the exception, Avery. If I feel anything, it's because you put it there."

"Well, I'm glad," I say smugly. "So, deal with it. But I guess... that leads us to the next topic."

"Hm?"

"Grey is obviously struggling with this and he's as possessive as you are. Are you really okay with this? I've already made it clear to Grey that I won't give you up, but you should know that I feel the same about him."

Theo stares at me for a few seconds before shrugging. "You're a grown woman. You don't owe anyone anything. Don't you think we've given enough of our lives to other people? Why should you follow other people's rules? You should do what makes you happy."

I growl under my breath. "You're avoiding the question."

"What do you want me to say?" he shoots back. "That I won't share you... that I'll make you choose. Fuck that. At the end of the day, the truth is we've been through enough."

"What do you mean? What have you been through?" I ask, immediately scolding myself for being nosey. It's not a judgmental question. There's no accusation in my tone—just pure curiosity.

He's here for a reason... just like the rest of us.

I want to know him better. I want to know his story.

Theo looks away, jaw clenching as he falls into a deep thought. "It doesn't matter."

"It matters to me," I say gently, squeezing his hand.

He stays quiet for a few seconds and I nearly cave in and offer to change the subject, but he lets out a breath, leaning his head back against the shelf.

"My sister died."

Clenching his hand, I shift closer to him, trying to offer silent support. I wait to see if he offers details, knowing that there's more to it.

"She committed suicide," he finally says in a dark, low voice. "Because she fell in love with two people."

"Oh," I mutter.

I'm completely caught off-guard, torn between feeling heartbroken for him, and realizing that perhaps this is the reason I've been trying to pull out of him. "I'm so sorry."

Theo looks over at me, resting his head on a faded green book. "Don't be. They tried to make her choose and it broke her. So, I slaughtered them without an ounce of remorse."

Chapter 23

Theo

Avery stares at me, stunned. I can see the waves of emotion swirling through her mind, while she fights to pick the correct one to navigate with.

"They deserved it," she says, a hint of uncertainty in her voice.

I laugh, looking up at the roof. Even now, she's making excuses again. That's the beautiful thing about her—even with the darkest souls, she tries to find light.

Unfortunately for her, she won't find it here.

There's no good in me. And I'm perfectly fine with that.

Ripping them apart was the single best accomplishment of my life. They took Madison from me, and in return, I watched the life drain from their eyes while they begged for mercy.

It's still a mystery how I ended up in Lilydale. I know all the fucking bullshit they try to spew about this place.

Rehabilitation center, my ass.

People talk. It's a natural instinct. They want to be liked, they want to be loved. They blurt out every piece of intimate detail, desperate for their flaws to be accepted. And Avery is no exception.

The moment I arrived in this place, people were talking about their backstories—painting themselves as victims. They all had an excuse—mental illness, self-defense. It was because of those pathetic human emotions that they were placed here.

I have none of that. I don't have a mental illness. These men didn't try to harm me. I wasn't defending myself or trying to protect anyone.

Simply put... they stole from me. And I made them pay.

I guess you could say if anything, I've had anger issues all my life. But rightfully so because people are fucking cunts.

I have no patience for any of them. I don't have time to give pity, hold hands while someone cries about life. We all have problems—take a spoonful of cement and harden the fuck up.

"Did they really deserve it?" I ask her darkly. "Put the personal attachment aside and ask yourself again."

Avery pauses, hesitating. "They bullied her..." she says slowly.

"They did," I acknowledge. "But at the end of the day, she made that decision. They didn't hold the gun to her head. They didn't pull the trigger. She did. So, I ask you again... am I innocent?"

"No," Avery answers, surprising me. "I guess not. But, put yourself in my shoes. My father abused me. He had his friends rape me, he used me like currency. I have scars all over my body, inside and out because of him. He did the same thing... he forced my mother to leave this place, making her take her own life. Did he deserve it?"

"Yes," I growl back. "He deserved to fucking die."

She nods. "So I'm not innocent either."

I smirk at her, completely amused by her comparison. She thinks we're the same. It's... *adorable.*

"We're not the same, Avery. Don't act stupid. You didn't mean to kill your father. While he absolutely deserved every bit of suffering, you didn't do it on purpose. I, on the other hand, willingly and proudly murdered those men. I'd do it again in a heartbeat."

"I thought you said you had killed a man—singular," she points out.

Laughing, I shoot her an incredulous look. "I did. Then *another.*"

Avery lets out a disappointed sigh, and for a moment, an unfamiliar feeling sweeps through me. She looks away, picking at the skin on her knee with the hand that's not holding onto me.

"I thought about it," she whispers. "I nearly bought a gun."

I stare at her in silence, watching as she rambles quietly. I know it's aimed at me, but there's a hollowness to her voice that makes her sound like she's in a trance.

"A gun?"

She nods. "Things got really bad after my fifteenth birthday. He stabbed me, and it was shortly after that when I was raped multiple times. It was so bad."

Rage—blinding rage—rears its head but before I can speak, she cuts me off, still muttering away like she can't stop it.

"I always wanted a family one day. My best friend and I used to dream about getting away from our shitty families. We'd always say that we'd break the generational curse, have our own families and give our children everything we never had."

My eyebrows furrow, wondering where she's going with this information. It's concerning me—it's like she's becoming a shell of her usual self right before my eyes.

The light has vanished from her face, despite it being there only a few minutes ago. Even though it's dark in the aisle, the light largely blocked out by the shelves and curtains, I notice her skin appears more pale—grayish even. The post-fucking flush that had tinted her skin pink is gone, and it scares me. It feels like she could sink into the floor and vanish at any second.

"You wanted love," I state confidently, watching as she nods slowly.

"Yeah. I'm not stupid. I knew from an early age that my home life wasn't normal. Looking at other kids at school, they were so happy. Their parents never missed a recital or school meeting. They bought them supplies and prom outfits. Hell, even the varsity kids had their families go to football games and shit. It was like I was standing inside a glass box, watching the world around me. I was trapped, but I could see the normal world passing by, while no one looked into the box and noticed that mine wasn't the same."

The thought of Avery feeling invisible makes me angrier. The whole system has failed her—from start to end. I ended up here because of my own doings, but she didn't. If one person—just one fucking person—had taken the time to stop and really look, they could have saved her. Someone could have intervened, rescued her—fuck, even put her into the foster care system. She would have been better off.

But that's the problem with people. They are so caught up with their own lives they forget to look around. Selfish, egotistical vultures, only looking out for themselves. Even the people who were meant to protect her—teachers, doctors, family members—they all turned a blind eye.

Now they are living their best lives and Avery is trapped in Lilydale, living the guilt and trauma over and over.

She looks over at me with a sad smile, unfazed by my silence. "When the doctors at the hospital said I'd never be able to have children because of the injuries, it ruined all my plans for the future. *They* took the only hope I had. So, I tried to buy a gun from this little store in town. I was going to wait until my father was too drunk to notice his surroundings and pull the trigger."

"What happened?" I ask curiously, already knowing the answer.

Avery shrugs. "I couldn't do it. I just didn't have it in me to go through with it. And so... it became my own fault that it kept happening."

"Avery," I growl, jolting to turn toward her. "It was not your fault."

"I had the opportunity to end it," she murmurs softly. There's not a single tear in her eyes—just sadness. I know she's numb recalling it all, blaming herself. "And I didn't."

I shake my head furiously. "But you got there in the end. He's being eaten by maggots now and he'll never hurt you again."

She laughs quietly, some light finally coming back into her eyes. Smiling, she shrugs again. "And now we're here. I'm still trapped, but at least it's better than the outside. For me, at least."

"I hate it here," I admit to her. "Well, I used to. Until you came along. Now it's my favorite place."

"Your favorite place is an asylum?" she mutters in amusement. "You must be as fucked up as I am."

"Worse," I reply with a smirk. "I'm so much worse, baby."

Her eyes widen in shock, her lips parting. "What?"

I just laugh in response, standing up. "Come on. I better take you back to the overlords before you get in trouble."

Holding out my hands, I help Avery to her feet, eyes lingering on her flustered face. A simple word has rocked her, malfunctioned her existence and everything she's ever known.

Well, it's not hard when all you've ever known is fucking disaster.

You know things are bad when someone is surprised and delighted by the bare minimum.

I wish I had the words to talk to her about her confession, her trauma. But I don't. I think tugging at that stitch is just going to undo all the glue she's used to try to keep it sealed tight.

She deserves to focus on the positives right now—even if there's very little available. But, at least there's some. That has to count for something, right?

We duck out of the curtain, Avery immediately finding Grey with her eyes. I don't know what she sees in that asshole, but it's her—she sees things the rest of us don't.

She's spent her entire life in a box, studying people, watching them... so she sees it.

Or maybe it's because she sees herself in him.

Lilydale might be a fucking prison full of unhinged psychopaths, but we all have one thing in common—trauma.

And bonding over trauma is a natural instinct for most. Not me though—there's no trauma, only regret. I regret not making them suffer more.

If I had maybe one, it's that I regret missing the bus home and having to wait an extra ten minutes.

Maybe if I had been quicker, I would have found Madison in time. I would have stopped her before she pulled the trigger. Like Avery, all she needed was love. She needed someone to tell her it would be okay—even if it was just from her younger brother.

It was that single event that led to everything changing.

One late bus.

Seven minutes too late.

A person shouldn't know what brain matter feels like smashed under your knees. A person shouldn't have to call their parents on vacation to tell them that their daughter is dead—her lilac walls splattered in blood.

Like Avery's, my parents couldn't hold their shit together either—not that I blame them.

I wouldn't want to stay a family either. And I certainly wouldn't want to lose both children in the space of a week.

Four days. That's how long it took.

That's how long it took me to splatter their own brain matter.

It took a little planning and patience.

I toyed with the idea of killing one first, so that the other knew I was coming for him next. But given the police involvement around my sister's demise, I knew I probably only had one chance to get what I wanted. And there was only one time I'd have them both together in the same room.

Madison's Funeral.

The part that disgusted me the most?

I was able to lure them away after the funeral with false information about Madison's Will.

That was the final straw for me, the confirmation that my decision was justified. They were more interested in thinking they were getting something, instead of grieving her like the rest of us.

I killed Richard first, laughing when his guts flew all over a horrified Joseph. They weren't so tough anymore when I had a gun pointing at them. Where was that bullying, that martyrdom they had tried to project onto Madison?

Dead as they were going to be.

Joseph had begged—like I knew he would. Sobbed like a baby, asking for mercy.

He watched as I sliced open Richard's chest, ripping out his silenced heart with my bare hands. And then I made Joseph take a bite, watched him struggle to tear the strong muscle with his shaking teeth.

It's funny what people will do—what limits they will push—when they want to survive.

Joseph thought it would save him.

He was very wrong.

I pieced the two men together for one last time, symbolically honoring Madison.

Richard met the same end as Madison. And Joseph became one with Richard.

And in the end... the three of them wound up together.

Just like it should have been in life.

Chapter 24

Avery

When I emerge from the aisle, I spot Grey and Damon standing by the table, muttering quietly to each other. As usual, Grey's attention switches to me instantly, the moment I step out from behind the curtain.

I feel Theo's presence behind me, following me as I cross the small distance to the two men. It's reassuring to know that Theo has my back, even if I'm heartbroken as to why.

And as for Grey...

Well, he's trying. And that counts for everything.

It's never an easy task to fight something that comes naturally to you, but he's willing to give it his best shot. I try not to ponder on the possibility that things could go south at any moment, living in the present.

"Hey," I smile at Grey, stopping next to him.

He looks at me with a perplexed look, scanning my face. "What's wrong?" he asks, eyes shifting over my shoulder to Theo.

"It's okay," I tell him gently, knowing that my shit poker face gives me away every time.

I'm relieved that things are good for once, but similar to Grey, you can't just get over your trauma instantly. It's like telling people that you are depressed and they ask *'have you tried being happy?'*.

Have you tried not loving two people?

Loving them both feels like breathing to me. I need it to live, to function. And in return, I'm breathing in them. They are the life force for me right now, the strength to face Whittingham's torture. Let him do his worst—because look who I have behind me.

"Alright, little killer," Grey smiles, dropping the subject.

"We're all good, right?" I ask knowingly.

He nods, eyes flickering to Theo once again. Theo must also nod back to him because Grey's jaw twitches slightly, but the smile never leaves his face.

I turn to Damon, his bored expression staring off at the corner like he's being forced to watch a real life rom-com.

"Are we all okay?" I ask again, this time at Damon.

He looks over at me, slight surprise on his face. "What does this have to do with me, Avery? I couldn't care less what happens between the three of you."

"I know," I reply softly. "But this is your kingdom, Damon. It affects you, right? I know that having Theo join tonight wasn't part of the original plan, and despite you probably agreeing for the sake of Grey, I just wanted you to know I appreciate it."

Damon's eyes narrow over me, but this time, it's not in annoyance. "It wasn't Grey's idea."

"True," Grey interjects. "Deadman is the mastermind behind the plan."

"Really?" I ask baffled. "Well... thanks, I guess."

"Whatever."

I hover awkwardly for a few seconds before turning away to look at Theo and Grey. "So, what now then?"

Grey nods his head toward the food table. "Grab some food. I also brought some snacks that you can take back to your room to hide."

"That's so sweet of you," I murmur. "But hopefully I won't be missing any more meals."

"They are still a lot better than the bland shit we get served," he grumbles. "Theo can take some too."

It's nice hearing him use Theo's first name again. I give him a bright smile, heading over to the table.

Mountains of food still remain untouched, resembling a buffet. I watch as Theo's eyes slowly linger across it, wondering if he's going to eat anything.

Reaching for a piece of pizza, I remember an earlier conversation, raising an eyebrow as he takes a bite.

"No pineapple on that pizza."

Theo's nose wrinkles in disgust. "For good reason. At least they have taste."

I shake my head with silent laughter, grabbing a slice as well. "I'm not surprised you're a meat man," I say, noting the heavy protein toppings. "Not surprising at all."

"Avery, I need to see you in my office."

I look up from my bed in surprise as Dr. Smith stands in my doorway.

Breakfast has not long ended and I have no professional appointments today, so I assumed I'd be locked up until lunchtime.

"Okay," I mutter hesitantly, climbing off the bed.

Slipping my shoes on, I follow him down the hallway, wondering why he doesn't have a guard with him. He buzzes us through the doors and as we approach his office, I notice the door is wide open.

I'm annoyed—is he leaving his office unattended where anyone could wander in and try to access files again?

As we reach the open doorway, it becomes apparent as to why it's wide open.

Sitting inside Dr. Smith's office in the usual guest chairs is Mr. Whittingham and... Alexander.

My brows crease together as I'm ushered inside by Dr. Smith, noting an extra chair has been set up where we normally play chess. I sit down, looking at the two men suspiciously.

What the hell is this about?

I don't speak yet, just watching them as Dr. Smith takes a seat at his table, humming happily to himself. Whittingham hasn't taken his eyes off me since I walked in, a serious expression on his face. However, his guest has barely acknowledged my presence at all.

"Thank you for joining us, Ms. White," Mr. Whittingham starts, a slightly aggressive tone to his voice.

"I didn't have a choice," I murmur.

Out of the corner of my eye, I swear I see Dr. Smith try to hide a smile, but I keep my gaze on the other two men.

"You remember Alexander?" Whittingham says, gesturing to his colleague.

I nod once. "Yes."

"Avery," Dr. Smith interjects. "They wanted to organize a meeting to discuss your return. I thought it was best to have me here for support."

Finally, I pull my attention away, looking at Dr. Smith. "I've been back for nearly two weeks. What do you mean my return?"

Mr. Whittingham clears his throat. "Your stipulations, if you will."

My blood freezes, eyes narrowing on the well-dressed men. "What about them?"

Alexander takes notice of me for the first time, his sharp eyes piercing into my face. "I'm told that you haven't been following Arthur's conditions."

"Stipulations," I point out. "And I have nothing to report—to either of you."

"Now, that's not true, is it?" Mr. Whittingham hisses, catching me off-guard. "Besides that, you were advised not to interact with certain students. However, as you know, I spotted you with them."

I feel anger flood through my system, my fists curling in my lap. "There's only so many *patients* here. How do you expect me to avoid them?"

He opens his mouth to speak but Alexander raises a hand to Mr. Whittingham's face. "I'm here to *collect*, Ms. White."

"I just told you—I don't have anything to report to you either."

Alexander straightens up in his spot, intimidation starting to emanate from him. "Any information is appreciated."

I fold my arms when I notice Dr. Smith staring at my fists, hiding my hands under my elbows. "I have nothing."

"This is bullshit," Whittingham hisses in frustration. "I told you not to accept her back," he adds the last part to Alexander.

"Now, now," Dr. Smith says calmly, eyes shifting between the two men. "Let's try to take a breath. Perhaps you could start by providing examples of what you need from Avery.

She's been through a lot. This conversation isn't beneficial to any party right now."

"Don't patronize me, Christopher," Alexander snarls. "You and I will be having a conversation next."

Dr. Smith raises an eyebrow, the calm demeanor vanishing before my eyes. "Let me guess—about the new psychiatrist you have coming on board?"

The other two men look surprised, making him smile.

"Yes," Dr. Smith laughs coolly. "I'm well aware. Apparently, all the other staff knew about the newcomer except me. People talk in the staff room."

A new psychiatrist?

"Glad we have that sorted then," Alexander says. "You can start the onboarding process."

"I don't need assistance."

"That's not up to you."

Mr. Whittingham catches my eye, and I just stare back, baffled. I don't feel privy to this conversation, but at least it deflects from me for a few minutes.

"You'll be under a new doctor, Ms. White. We'll have a new psychiatrist on board to share the workload with Dr. Smith. I think it would be in everyone's best interests to transfer you."

"Why?" I blurt out, looking at Dr. Smith. "He's my psychiatrist."

Dr. Smith gives me a tight smile, but Whitface just scoffs.

"It's *unfair* to Dr. Smith to have to manage one-hundred patients on his own. It's not feasible long term with the amount of sessions each patient requires. And unfortunately, it appears that your sessions with Dr. Smith have not been helpful to your *recovery*. Therefore, we will try you with the new psychiatrist."

"How the fuck would you know if they haven't helped?" I snap, unable to help myself.

Sure, I don't like the guy much. But if I'm being honest, he's definitely helped put things in perspective for me—stolen file aside.

"Clearly, since you are still insubordinate," Mr. Whittingham snaps back, looking more and more stressed. I don't know if it's my lack of cooperation, the argument between the staff, or the presence of Alexander. No matter the reason, it's unnerving to see him lose his cool. He's always an uptight asshole, reminding us of his superiority.

Maybe he needs a room here.

"That's enough," Alexander says, voice raised. "Arthur, control yourself."

"Yeah... *control yourself*," I mutter under my breath.

Whittingham looks like he wants to get up from his seat to throttle me, but he falls silent, leaning back into his chair.

Alexander looks at me, still annoyed like I'm scum beneath his expensive Italian leather shoes.

"Ms. White... don't be foolish. We are aware of the gang situation within Lilydale."

"Gang?" I sputter. "What the hell are you talking about?"

It's news to me that there's a gang. Unless...

"I believe they call themselves the Circus of the Dead."

Silence falls in the room. My eyes shoot between the three of them rapidly, none of them surprised. Well, neither am I.

It's never been a secret that there's a hierarchy from the inside. Damon has had some hold on Arthur since well before I arrived. But so what? We're a bunch of people meeting, taking control of the only world we know. It's not like the Lilydale staff are jumping around, begging to help us.

"Not sure what you are referring to," I finally answer. "I haven't heard of it."

Mr. Whittingham's face twitches from beside Alexander, and against my better control, a smirk appears on my face for a split second before I quickly remove it.

"Get to the point, gentlemen," Dr. Smith sighs.

"Gladly," Alexander sneers. "I want that information, Ms. White."

I shrug. "I don't have any."

The three of them stare at me with different expressions. Mr. Whittingham looks pissed off—like I took a shit in his morning cereal. Alexander appears annoyed, sick of going around in circles. And Dr. Smith... well, he almost looks amused.

"Ms. White. Are you aware I could have you removed from Lilydale immediately?" Alexander starts, a threat in his tone.

Nodding, I hold his gaze. "Yep."

"And you also understand that while I am not a member of day-to-day staff at Lilydale, I have the authority to make decisions in regards to your admission."

"Still yes."

"Great," he says happily, surprising me. "Arthur, call the guards. Have them escort Ms. White to solitary isolation. I think a week should do it."

My demeanor drops, mouth opening in shock. "What?!"

Alexander looks at me, eyes narrowing. "Play stupid games, win stupid prizes, Ms. White."

"Wait a minute," Dr. Smith loudly chimes in. "That's not necessary."

"Do not question my decisions, Christopher, or else you will be out of a job. I easily found a psychiatrist to step into the new role. I can easily find a replacement for you as well."

Mr. Whittingham walks past us, opening the office door. I hear him motioning for someone, my heart racing. I turn to Dr. Smith, eyes pleading with him. He looks back at me with sorrowful eyes, defeated, shaking his head.

"You can't let them take me," I shout to him as a guard enters the room. "I haven't done anything!"

The guard grabs my arms, pulling me toward the door. I struggle in his grip, trying to break loose.

My feet drag along the ground as he pulls me into the corridor, the three men watching from the doorway.

I let out a scream of frustration, throwing my elbows back. I manage to clip the guard in the ribs, resulting in him slamming me chest-first into the wall to get a better grip on me.

"Get your fucking hands off me!" I screech, hearing footsteps behind me.

"What's going on here?"

I stop struggling at the familiar voice, turning my head to find Damon standing in the hallway. He's staring at the five of us casually, hands in his pockets. There's not another guard in sight escorting him, and when his eyes land on the three men by the door, his lips upturn into a smirk.

"Family reunion without me? I'm hurt," Damon says sarcastically, touching his chest.

"Get back to your room," Whittingham sneers at him.

"I don't think I will," he replies, unfazed. "Get your hands off Avery," he adds, staring daggers at the guard.

To my surprise, I'm let go, slumping against the wall. I quickly turn around, watching them all with wide eyes as I try to catch my breath.

The guard stands next to me, still close by at the ready, but he's watching Damon. I recognize him from other interactions—Connor, I think.

"Don't listen to him," Whittingham huffs to the guard. "Take her to solitary confinement."

Damon's eyes dart over to me against the wall before returning to Whittingham, smirking. "He doesn't answer to you, Arthur. I told you to remember your place."

He scoffs, turning to Alexander. "Do *something*."

My mouth falls open at the strange turn of events. Dr. Smith just leans against the doorframe, seemingly happy not to get involved—and also *relieved* to see Damon step in.

"Damon—" Alexander starts, a look of fury on his face.

"Oh, fuck off, Father. Save whatever pathetic bullshit you are about to say for someone who cares."

Chapter 25
Damon

The hallway erupts into spontaneous reactions. It's bliss-ful—I love causing chaos. Even Lilydale's most powerful men are no match for their emotions—falling like dominoes when I crush their minds.

Pathetic.

Which is exactly why *they* will never be *in control*.

Avery lets out a sharp gasp like the naïve little lamb she is. But at least she is showing growth. I'm starting to see what Grey sees in her—psychologically speaking, of course. Weeks ago she would never have resisted, cursed authori-ty figures. I could hear her screaming at them before they emerged into the hallway. Then, to see her physically swing at Connor, well, that was just downright amusing. I've seen that side of her before. It's a dark side resting underneath all those people pleasing tendencies. But it appears those emotions are ripping out of her psyche even faster than we could have predicted.

She's reckless, unpredictable. But not uncontrollable.

We have her exactly where we want her. She's loyal to us, fighting to protect *Cirque des Morts*.

It's also abhorrent. She still doesn't have a handle on those emotions, but I think we can work with it. She has potential.

Maybe Grey was right—we can mold her after all. It's more than I can say for the rest of them.

Arthur scoffs in frustration while my dear old father growls under his breath, spitting out my name again like it's poison on his tongue.

"Don't push me, Damon."

I lift an eyebrow in amusement. "If you want to go toe-to-toe anytime, all you have to do is ask. But may I remind you that I've been kicking your ass since I was thirteen. How's the old back, anyway? Still giving you grief?"

"Watch your tongue," he snaps back. "Stop playing these childish games."

"Nothing childish about them," I shrug. "But if it makes you feel more powerful than whatever helps you sleep at night."

I switch my gaze to Connor, giving him a small nod. He tips his head down, understanding my silent command with ease.

Walking forward, I grab Avery's arm, pulling her toward me. Like clockwork, she moves to me, body relaxing visibly.

"I'll be taking Avery now. But it was a *displeasure* seeing you again, Father."

As we start heading down the hallway, I hear the commotion as they try to stop us before Connor interjects. I *almost* feel bad for him—he'll lose his job now. But I'm sure he'll have no problem finding another one. The world is full of desperate employees looking for staff to abuse.

Avery keeps pace easily despite our difference in height, her cheeks flushed with anxiety and panic. But to her credit, she stays strong.

Neither of us look back at the chaos down by Christopher's office, and frankly, none of them will dare try to stop us now. That would mean physical restraints—and I'm certain none of them want their expensive suits damaged. They don't have the balls to do their own dirty work. I'm sure they probably say the same about me.

I know what everyone says about me.

I have an army. I have Grey so my hands don't get dirty.

My father knows very well that if push comes to shove, I'll fight back—and win. It's why he stopped trying to physically punish me the moment I outgrew him in size and height.

The first time he ever laid hands on me, I had him on the ground within fifteen seconds.

The second time he tried, I broke three of his fingers.

And the third and last time... I dug the tip of my knife into his stomach, promising him I'd cut out his kidneys to sell on the black market.

After that, he never tried to touch me again. And when he knew he was no match for me, he locked me up.

Bypassing the library doors, I take us straight to the entrance to the Westwood Wing. As soon as we're safely in the secure corridor, Avery lets out a long held breath.

"What the fuck just happened?" she whispers, and I'm not entirely sure if she's just mumbling to herself.

"We can't leave you alone for five minutes apparently," I shoot back.

Avery swings her head to look at me, still keeping pace. "I didn't have much of a choice, Damon. I had no idea what I was walking into."

"That's unfortunate," I say sarcastically, stopping in front of a door.

Knocking four times on the door of room 307, I slap my card on the access pad, punching in the code. It buzzes, the sound of metal unlocking.

Swinging open the door, my eyes fall to Grey, on his bed, staring at the roof. He's scarfing down a candy bar, tapping his foot to the sound of music coming from a laptop on the desk.

"Hey, little killer," he grins, ignoring me as his eyes find Avery immediately.

"Grey," she murmurs, brushing past me as she walks inside. "Jesus fuck. You should hear what just happened."

I let out a laugh, pulling the door closed behind me. It clicks, locking back into place. But unlike most of the other rooms here, Grey's room, like mine, has a hardwired pad by the door. It's set to deactivate the lock from the inside, allowing us to get out whenever we please.

I've had them set up for years, with only a few chosen people lucky to have one. Jillian and Byrone have one too, of course, particularly since my little hacker helped set them up. I know if I didn't allow her to have one, she'd go without, even though she could bring Lilydale's entire system down almost completely on her own. But with hard work comes reward—I'm not entirely ruthless. Besides, it gives Jillian and Byrone the power to see each other outside of free time. If sex helps keep them focused for me, then who am I to stand in the way of that?

"Huh? What happened?" Grey says, sitting up and looking at me.

Leaning against the wall by the desk, I throw him a little smirk. "My father is here. Apparently, Arthur thought it was appropriate to drag Avery into a meeting with them."

His eyes darken immediately, shooting back to Avery as if he's examining her body for evidence of harm.

"It's fine," I hear her say to him in a calming voice. "No one hurt me."

Hm. Apparently, Avery can read Grey too. I shouldn't be surprised considering how close they are to each other. Hell, Grey can sense Avery's whereabouts at any given time.

"They were trying to drag her off to solitary confinement," I interject, watching as rage washes over his face.

"Those cunts! Are they still out there?" he snaps, heading to the door.

Before I can stop him, Avery jumps in front of the doorway, resting her hands on his chest. "We're not going to do that. It's just going to cause unnecessary problems."

"They were trying to take you."

"I know," she murmurs softly. "But they didn't. Damon stopped them."

She looks over his shoulder at me, giving me a small smile. It throws me off a little. Her appreciation shines through her expression, and I just shrug, looking away.

I don't know why I stopped them if I'm being honest. It's not the first time I've seen people dragged away screaming.

I tell myself it's because it would throw Grey into a spiral. He'd probably kick down every door until he found her, drawing attention to us.

But still... there was something a tad unsettling about the way she was screaming.

It's nothing though. Just a stark reminder that we all need to be on guard.

I've known for some time what the plan is, and now judging by today's theatrics, I was correct. But it also means Arthur is getting ready to make his move. It was just lucky that Jillian alerted me that we had a *visitor* from the live camera footage.

"Thanks, Deadman," Grey says firmly, giving me a nod.

"Don't mention it. No, really—don't," I scoff.

Avery laughs, making both of us look at her in surprise. She notices, cheeks flushing.

"Sorry. I didn't mean to laugh. It's just... a little fucked up."

I know what she's referring to. And I assume she has questions. She doesn't need answers though—however, I do.

"How exactly do you know my father?" I ask her sternly.

Avery locks eyes with me, and I get ready to send her my best warning glare, but it's not needed. She immediately starts talking, one hand still resting on Grey like she's trying to ground him.

"Alexander came to visit me the night I was arrested. He was there with my social worker," she says confidently. "He didn't say who he was, but my social worker, Margaret, mentioned he was on the Lilydale board."

"He is," I confirm, watching her nod.

"He said that he was there because of my admission, indicating that the board was trying to decide what to do with me."

Grey snaps his head toward me, eyes flashing. He's starting to piece things together, the cogs turning in his mind. I shoot him a glance, gesturing for him to be patient.

"And what did the board say?" I ask her, annoyed that this conversation hasn't been relayed to me yet.

Avery frowns. "They said they weren't going to press charges and that they would accept me back into the facility. With stipulations, of course."

"Of course," I repeat, rolling my eyes. "Just like Arthur did upon your return."

She nods. "Margie made it out like it was a good thing."

Grey scoffs, shaking his head. "It was a *murder* investigation. Lilydale didn't have the power to press charges. It would have been up to the police."

"That would make sense," Avery mutters slowly, face scrunched up in thought. "It did seem odd that I was arrested, and then Alexander said it was a suicide. It happened too quickly for a thorough investigation to occur."

"Money speaks power," I answer. "They wouldn't have wanted the bad publicity."

Avery nods again, this time faster. "He said something about the facility's reputation."

"Of course he did," I laugh. "That's all they care about."

"Obviously," Avery sneers, but it's not toward me. We all know what the staff think about Lilydale—this is just a giant publicity scheme to generate money.

Grey turns to look at me, patience finally snapping. "You made a deal."

"I did," I agree.

Avery looks at me, baffled. "What deal?"

"I made a deal with my father," I tell her, before looking at Grey. "In exchange for your freedom back to Lilydale."

She gasps. "I *knew* you had something to do with it."

"And are you going to share those details now?" Grey asks.

"The deal was that Avery returned to the facility, Christopher's workload was reduced, and in exchange, I gave my father something he wanted."

Grey nods, apparently satisfied with that answer. It's not the full story, but it's enough to appease him for the time being. Avery, on the other hand, stares at me with a hardened expression.

"You wanted Dr. Smith's workload reduced? Why?"

My face twitches in annoyance. She shouldn't be asking questions that she has no business knowing about. But... for the sake of being *nice* I give her a response.

"I told you that there were secrets you weren't aware of. All you need to know is that we need to take back as much power as possible from the staff. Christopher was trying to meddle in things. After all, he gave you that fake key."

Avery grimaces at the memory. "I know. But still... I'm not sure I entirely believe that Dr. Smith is the bad guy here."

"Why do you say that, babe?" Grey asks, perplexed.

I resist the urge to roll my eyes. I have no doubt that Christopher puts on his best charming act for her. But deep down, he's an asshole who wants to see me knocked off my throne.

"In that meeting," Avery starts, looking at me. "Before Damon turned up, they were pretty harsh to him. It was almost like he was trying to defend me."

"It's his charm, Avery. Don't let it fool you," I scoff in disgust.

"He tried to argue that I shouldn't go into solitary confinement," she argues weakly.

Grey looks at me, trying to gauge my reaction. I just narrow my eyes, annoyed that the two of them can't seem to read any situation that doesn't involve each other.

"It's an act, Avery. Stop letting people pull the wool over your eyes."

Avery crosses her arms, looking away. "Doesn't matter anyway. I've been reassigned to the new psych whenever they start. They said Dr. Smith wasn't doing a good enough job to fix me."

"You don't need fixing, little killer," Grey murmurs, brushing some hair off her shoulder. "Your little deranged self is perfect."

A small smile appears on her face, but it's obvious she's still mourning the loss of *Christopher.* It makes me want to throw up.

"There's another reason why they were harsh to him," I say smugly. Avery looks up, eyes widening in surprise.

"Oh?"

"It's because he's my cousin, Avery. He's Alexander's nephew. So, if that doesn't convince you that people aren't who they seem, then I don't know what will."

Chapter 26

Avery

As soon as the bell goes for free time, the three of us sneak out of the boys' dorms to join the rest of gen pop. I'm surprised they didn't come look for us during class, but given Grey's occasional absence, I'm assuming they don't care enough to bother.

The crowd of patients file into the hall, waiting. Damon pushes his way through the crowd, climbing onto a table to grab their attention.

"Listen up. When I call your number, leave the hall. Do not cause any problems or I'll unleash hell on you."

Standing by Grey at the back of the hall, I watch as Damon holds up various numbers with his fingers, people leaving in intervals.

"Are you going to tell me about the numbers one day?" I mutter to Grey.

He laughs, leaning against the wall, carefree. "I hope not, little killer. But if I need to tell you, I will."

I grumble under my breath, admitting defeat. When Damon holds up the number three, I go to move, but Grey stops me, grabbing onto my arm.

"Your number has changed," he says.

"Since when?" I ask, confused.

He looks at me, flashing me a smile. "Since now. You're group one, effective immediately."

I throw my hands up in exasperation, sliding back against the wall. "I can't keep up with you guys."

"No one can," Grey laughs, leaning down to whisper in my ear. "And you should be thankful I have the stamina of a fucking God."

My cheeks flush red, and I look around at the remaining crowd of people, trying to distract myself. Immediately, I spot Theo, lurking on the other side of the room, glaring daggers at everyone around him.

"What's Theo's number?" I ask curiously.

Grey follows my line of vision. "Theo is in group five."

"Makes sense," I mumble, sarcastically.

Over the tops of heads, Theo spots me, eyes softening. I give him a smile, tilting my head toward the doors. He nods, and I look at Grey.

"So, I'm hanging with Theo now?"

Grey nods, giving me a tight smile. "Yep. Deadman and I have some things to take care of, so go have your fun—not too much though."

When Damon holds up the number five, I watch as Theo pushes through the crowd, making a beeline for us.

Grey leans down again to my ear. "You can go with him. No need to wait for your number."

"Stay out of trouble," I laugh, giving him a quick kiss good-bye and a smile of appreciation.

"Never," he whispers, eyes flashing wildly.

I watch as the two of them have some weird exchange, giving each other a small, stern nod before I leave the hall with Theo.

We head down the hallway, hand-in-hand, toward the empty rooms. People scatter out of our way, pressing against the wall while they stare at our locked palms in horror. I have to hold back a laugh, imagining their thoughts.

She's with that psychopath.

And what's even more funny... is that it could mean both Theo *and* Grey.

Our little studio room is exactly as I remember—a void, empty of life. We sit down on the floor and Theo reaches into his pocket, pulling out his tattooing kit. My heart races in excitement, my hips shifting as I get comfortable.

Theo looks over at me, doing a double take before his eyebrow twitches.

"What happened to your thigh?" he asks casually.

"Huh?" I look down, noticing that my shorts have ridden up, exposing Grey's hand drawn artwork. "Oh..."

I'm not sure how to explain that, mind tumbling and turning as I try to find words. Theo just laughs under his breath, shaking his head.

"He's a possessive little shit."

"Well," I start, lifting my arm to show off the tattoo. "He felt it was only fair since you got there first."

Theo smirks to himself, sterilizing the needle. "Did he now? And if I tattoo you again today, is he going to make you bleed more?"

"Probably," I answer honestly, not at all worried. "*Are you* tattooing me today?"

"Yes," he says, gesturing for me to move closer. "Give me your arm."

I slide along the cold ground until our knees are touching, face-to-face. Holding up my arm, Theo scans over the previous ink, nodding happily.

"It healed well."

"You seem surprised."

He sneers. "Considering what Whittingham put you through, I'm definitely surprised."

"Fair call," I mutter, wondering if the staff have noticed the fresh ink. They would have to be blind to have missed it, but then again, nothing we do seems to surprise them.

I fill Theo in on the earlier events while he gets everything ready, watching as his face contorts in anger. He dips the tip of the needle into the small bottle of jet-black ink, twisting it to shake a few loose droplets before positioning my arm onto his knee. I rest my arm against him, watching as he pierces my skin.

I don't flinch at all, unfazed by the burn. Theo takes notice too, shaking his head with a laugh.

"Pain tolerance has gotten better."

"It was never an issue," I argue. "You just exceed the level of normal."

He smirks, focusing on my skin. "I'm not going to argue with that."

More patterns appear over my arm as he expands on his previous work. I stay still, talking to him about things, and filling him in on the meeting from hell.

Surprisingly, he doesn't say much, but I can tell by the anger in his eyes that he's holding back—probably so he doesn't accidentally hurt me with the needle.

"What's solitary confinement like?" I ask him, knowing he's been in there before.

"It's fine for me," he says coolly. "But for everyone else, it's probably hell."

I nod. "You like being alone."

"It's peaceful. I don't have to deal with people."

"How does it differ from our rooms?" I ask, wondering just how much more lonely it could get.

Theo pauses for a moment, lifting the needle. He wipes a stray bit of ink with his finger, leaning back.

"It's small, probably half the size of our rooms. There's no adjoining toilet though—it's next to the bed, which is on the floor, no base. Essentially just a thin mat with no blankets or pillow."

"Ew," I murmur, disgusted at the thought of sleeping next to a toilet.

Theo rubs his thumb in circles over a patch of unmarked skin. "It's also dark. There's no windows, just one tiny light on the wall. It flickers non-stop."

"They can't do that surely."

"Yet they do. And meals are only once a day. The only way to know what time it is comes from the pipes. It's behind the men's showers—so it's deathly quiet until the pipes start banging in the walls at shower time."

I stare at him in horror. "That sounds terrible."

"You wouldn't have liked it," Theo answers simply, twisting my arm to examine the drying ink. "It's fucked up that they were trying to take you there. I don't know what their fucking problem is."

Nodding, my eyes scan over the pretty, weaving lines on my skin. "I would have survived."

"What do you think?" he asks, ignoring me. We both know I probably wouldn't have survived. I'm thankful that Damon stepped in when he did, even if I now know things that haunt me.

I'm not sure what to think about everything. My tumultuous relationship with Dr. Smith has taken another turn—just as I was starting to like him again, I find out he's related to Damon.

Not to mention Alexander. I can't even begin to process that.

Damon wasn't kidding when he said this place was full of secrets. What else were the Lilydale staff hiding from us?

"I love it," I tell Theo happily, resting my arm in my lap. "Are you going to do your skin now?"

Theo nods, grabbing a fresh needle and starting the sterilizing process again. "We are."

"We?" I laugh.

He smiles, pushing the ink toward me. "I can't let that fucker get one up on me."

"What?"

Theo hands me the needle before gesturing to his body. "Pick your spot."

My eyes trail over his body, not because I'm trying to find a spot, but because he's drawn my attention to it. His muscular, toned physique might be hidden under the depressing gray uniform, but my body knows what lies beneath.

When my gaze accidentally stumbles and pauses over his hips, Theo takes that as a sign, pulling his shirt off.

My mouth dries as I stare at his torso, noticing more ink. Like Grey, he has some down the side of his ribs, but I'm pulled away from it when he pushes the waistband of his shorts down a few inches.

"What are you doing?" I mumble quickly, looking behind me to the open door. "People will see us."

"We're not having sex," he says with a small laugh. "You wanted *here*."

I shake my head in confusion. "I'm lost."

"Write your name on me."

My head snaps up, then down at his hips—then back up again to stare at him wide-eyed. "You want me to write my goddamn name on your hips?"

"Yes," he answers without hesitation. "You better get started. It would be a bit awkward having just 'Av' written there."

I snort. "If I can manage the 'e', at least you'll almost have my nickname."

Theo's eyebrows furrow as he looks at me curiously. "Ave is your nickname?"

"It was Aves," I murmur softly, dipping the needle into the ink. "Paige used to call me that."

"A friend?"

I nod. "She was my best friend. Her family were assholes too."

Theo stays still as I approach him with the needle, my nails brushing over his hip bone. I look at the untainted skin, wondering if I should really ruin it with my name.

He twitches underneath me, jolting slightly from my touch. I drop a little lower, just under the bone. "Here?"

"Perfect spot," he agrees. "What happened to Paige?"

"Her brother murdered her," I tell him dryly, pressing the needle into his skin like he showed me before. "She was like a sister to me."

Theo reaches out to stroke my forearm, making me pause out of fear of bumping the needle. "I'm sorry."

"It's okay," I say sincerely. "She's free now."

"What was she like?"

I look up at him, gazing in admiration. No one has ever asked me about Paige—no one really cared about my friends.

Smiling, I continue piercing the first letter of name into his lower hip. "She was awesome. Loved country music and made me listen to it all the time, even though I was a pop-punk girl. If there was ever a problem to be solved, even if it was unsolvable, she would damn near drive herself crazy trying to fix it. Deathly allergic to nuts though. I nearly yeeted her from existence with my shampoo once."

"What the fuck?" Theo laughs, caught off-guard.

"I ran out of shampoo and my father refused to buy me more. By the two week mark, I was pretty desperate with greasy hair so I stole a bottle. And I figured if I was going to steal one, I should at least treat myself instead of the usual dirt cheap brand we used. So, I picked out some fancy blue one. Unfortunately, it had nut oil in it and when Paige hugged me, she went into anaphylactic shock. Luckily, we were at school and they had spare EpiPens."

Theo stares at me, bewildered. "I didn't even know that was possible."

"Me either. Paige thought it was funny though..." I trail off, focusing on the next letter. "I have a question for you though."

"Fire away."

My lips twitch into a smile. "The day you broke into my room to leave the little present."

"You're referring to Hallman's finger?"

"Yep. How did you get in there? The door was locked. I mean, we obviously know Grey and Damon can go wherever they want, but my access pad wasn't smashed to smithereens."

Theo snorts, knowing I'm referring to the day we snuck down to the morgue. "I borrowed a staff card and got the access code."

"Borrowed?"

"Bribed."

"Try again, Theo."

He laughs. "Threatened."

"There we go."

I'm nearly finished with my name when I hear footsteps heading toward the room. Pausing, I glance at Theo first, worried. He doesn't appear to share the same sentiment, just gazing at the doorway casually.

"Why the hell am I not surprised?" Grey murmurs, leaning against the doorframe. His eyes trail over my posture, bent over with my face in Theo's lap.

"I can do you next if you want," I laugh.

He pretends to sigh, walking into the room. "Maybe next time, little killer. Then again the scar on my palm is a nice warmup."

Taking my eyes off Theo's skin for a moment, I peer at Grey over my shoulder as he takes a seat on the ground. "You did that yourself," I point out, amused.

"True," he says happily. "But I'd still love for you to mark me."

"What the hell is with your obsession with me stabbing you?" I tease, shaking my head as I finish the tattoo. "There—all done."

Theo looks down, nodding. "Nicely done, Aves."

I freeze, locking eyes with him as he gives me a knowing look. But behind his expression, there's also the question as he waits for the confirmation that it's okay.

My face breaks into a smile. It's been too long since I've heard someone call me that. It makes me think of better times—or gives me the hope that good times are still a possibility.

"Shit, there's the bell," Grey grumbles, picking up Theo's shirt like it's contaminated and tossing it to him.

"Thanks," Theo says, standing up as he pulls it on.

I get to my feet, brushing off my shorts and noticing little black dots of ink staining the material. "Fuck."

"Don't worry about it," Grey says, brushing my hair back to place a soft kiss on my neck. "Did you want me to come see you tonight?"

"If you like," I smile. "But don't go out of your way. I'm also happy to sleep."

He grins at me, leading the three of us back toward the hall. "I'll be there, little killer. Just try to stop me."

Chapter 27

Avery

The next morning I'm woken up by a new guard—a quiet, older man in his late forties, who looks like he'd rather be anywhere but here. He barely speaks to me, not even man-handling me like the other guards usually do.

It's not *too* early thankfully, and surprisingly, I'm not taken to Mr. Whittingham's office.

"Good morning, Ms. White!"

I blink three times at Dr. Markel before I finally repeat the words back at him. Of course he's this chirpy in the morn-ings—when is he not?

"You've been assigned to my room this morning. It's not too strenuous, just some light cleaning and organizing."

"Fab."

"And you'll share the task with another patient. I don't like leaving it all to one person—it can be a little overwhelming."

"Right..."

Humming happily, he leads me through the side door in his office. I'm surprised to see his other room for the first time. In the corner is an old wooden desk, filed with paper-work and files. There's no sign of technology in sight, except for an old fax machine that's gathering dust in the adjacent corner.

Along the side wall is a medicine cabinet with the key dangling out, and immediately, my face twitches.

Maybe he takes the key with him when he's not in the rooms...

Seriously though—what is with these medical professionals? Did they hire from a catalog or something?

There's ruffling from underneath Dr. Markel's desk and when a head pops up to look at us, my mouth falls open.

"Vivian?"

My former nemesis glares back at me, rising to her feet. "What?!"

Dr. Markel is unfazed at our awkward exchange, walking over to put a hand on Vivian's shoulder. "Ms. Capello, you'll be working with Ms. White this morning. If you want to continue the filing, I'll have her start on the cleaning."

Sharp green eyes glare back at me and I quickly realize maybe I was too hasty at referring to our poor relationship as former. She's still hurt—not that I blame her—but on the plus side, she's not crying like last time I saw her.

Remembering, my eyes shift to her wrist and I'm happy to find the bandage is gone. There's a faint pink scar traveling up her veins and when she notices me staring, turns it away.

"Whatever. She can clean."

"Splendid!" Dr. Markel exclaims, picking up a bucket from the floor and holding it out to me. "Ms. White, you'll find gloves in there. Please be careful of the bleach. You can start in the office here if you like. Just give everything a little wipey-down. Not with the bleach though... just the spray in here. Once you're finished, you can clean the examination room with some hot water and a dash of bleach. Just wear the gloves."

I glare at him. "I didn't purposely do that—never mind," I grumble, grabbing the yellow spray bottle out along with an old cloth.

There's a knock from the corridor, Dr. Markel jumping in excitement. "I'm just going to close this door while I see this patient. Give me a shout if you need."

He disappears, closing the rickety wooden door behind him. Surprisingly, it blocks out all the noise from the examination room.

Tension fills the air immediately, and I turn, giving Vivian a tight smile as I try to pacify our shit morning.

"I'm glad to see you're doing better," I say softly. "I hope you're okay."

"Don't pretend like you care," she whispers angrily, grabbing a file and shoving some papers back inside.

As she jams them back in, I notice her cheeks become flustered. She's a shell of her former self—not the mean bully I knew when I started.

Before Sam's death she would have spat insults at me or clawed my face again. Now, she looks like she's struggling to hold it together.

I know that she leaked my file... I know that she hurt me... I know that her boyfriend assaulted me. But still... *I pity her.*

"I shouldn't care," I answer, spraying the front of the medicine cabinet. "You did some horrible shit to me."

I hear her pause behind me. Shit—is she going to attack me? Why on earth did I think it was a good idea to turn my back to her?

"Yeah," she finally replies. "I know."

Slowly, I turn around, watching as she leans against the wall behind the desk. Her mask drops, leaving her face blank. The green in her eyes appear more faded than usual, skin pale, washed out against her blonde hair.

"I'm not going to ask you why," I say. "I can already assume. But it doesn't matter. It's in the past now."

Vivian looks at me expressionless. "You indirectly did bad shit to me too, Avery. I lost someone because of you."

"I'm sorry, Vivian, but I'm not going to give you my condolences. If that makes me a bitch, then whatever. But your boyfriend was an absolute asshole. I just hope he was nicer to you than he was to everyone else."

"We all have battles. Sam had his."

I roll my eyes, unable to help it. "There's a difference between fighting to survive, and fighting just to make others suffer. Like fuck, Vivian—he tried to assault me. Your boyfriend was actually talking about raping me."

"I know," she sighs sadly. "And he paid the price for it."

My eyes shift to her wrist again, nodding my head toward it. "You deserve better. You still have a chance to redeem yourself. Don't do shit like that."

Vivian shifts uncomfortably but doesn't move her wrist out of sight. "It was a moment of weakness. I'm fine now."

"Good," I tell her. "Because one day we're going to get out of here."

"Doubtful," she mutters, turning back to the paperwork.

I don't respond, letting us fall into silence as I start wiping the medicine cabinet. Eventually, Dr. Markel opens the door to check on us, seemingly thrilled to find us still working.

"How are you ladies going?"

"Fine," we both say in unison, not glancing over.

"Fantastic! I'll come back soon," he replies, humming *Mary Had A Little Lamb* as he hobbles away.

I walk into the hall for breakfast, frowning when I notice Theo isn't at our usual table. Instinctively, I start searching for Grey, mouth falling open when I spot him sitting next to Theo at the other end of the hall.

My feet carry me to the table, still gaping at them like a goldfish.

"Morning, babe!" Grey greets with a grin, smacking the seat next to him. "You're just in time for breakfast."

My eyes dart over to Theo who, except for his company, looks exactly like he normally does at meal times. He glances up at me, shrugging.

"I was summoned to sit at the *Assholes-R-Us* table."

I snort, quickly covering my mouth as I gaze over to Damon, a disgruntled look on his face.

"Grey put the puppy dog eyes on," he scowls.

"That's so sweet," I taunt, giving Grey a smile. "You wanted my company."

"Yep," he answers without hesitation. "And it's a package deal now."

Laughing, I nod toward the line of food. "I'll go grab something to eat and come back."

I opt for some toast, fruit, and gray-ish looking eggs, motioning for the men to separate when I get back to the table so I can sit between Grey and Theo.

Munching on a slice of apple, I watch as Vivian heads past us to the food. "We had shared duty this morning," I tell the guys, nodding towards her.

"Capello?" Damon asks, starting sounding interested.

"And what did she have to say?" Grey interjects, cutting his best friend off.

I shrug. "Not much. She seems really chill now. Just keeping to herself."

"Fuck her," Grey scowls under his breath, reaching for my thigh under the table. "I'm not done with her yet."

"Leave her be," I order softly. "She's paid her dues."

Damon puts his fork down, folding his arms on the table. "Since when do you give out orders?"

"Since the whole mess started because of me," I retort. "You said you would consider my input about her actions. I say she's suffered enough now. Time to move on and focus on other matters."

He observes me carefully, picking up his fork. I pause, wondering if he's about to fling it at my face.

"I don't think she's suffered enough, but you're right, we have other matters to deal with," Damon replies, returning to his food.

I beam at Grey, excited at my little victory. His eyes flash, hand squeezing my thigh. I can see it in his eyes...

I want to fuck you so bad.

Remembering back to when I first stood up to Damon, Grey had told me how turned on he was. And by the way he's staring at me now, he'd throw me onto the table and eat me for breakfast if he could.

"I have an appointment with Dr. Smith after breakfast," he whispers excitedly.

Lifting an eyebrow, I put my hand over his. "Play nicely, please."

"Theo," Grey says, not looking away from me. "I need Avery at free time today."

Damon makes a sound of disgust. "Could you not discuss your sex life while I am eating my pancakes?"

My eyes fall to his plate in amusement. "I expected more from you, Damon. Something more savory or spicy—like eggs benedict or the souls of your enemies. Pancakes, really?"

"What the fuck is wrong with pancakes?" he snaps.

"Nothing," I mutter, shaking my head. "Nothing at all."

Theo puts his hand on my other leg, making me look down. My gaze shifts between the two hands, both squeezing my thighs.

I look up at him, puzzled when he smirks at me. "What?"

"Nothing at all," I repeat, feeling flustered.

Grey stills for a moment, deep in thought. Slowly, he looks over my head at Theo, raising an eyebrow. "Maybe you can join us."

My neck lets out a small crack as I whip my head to the side, eyes-wide at Grey. "What?"

He grins at me, lowering his voice.

"What's wrong, little killer? Scared of the two big bad men?"

Chapter 28
Avery

"Put your hands above your head on the bookshelf," Grey whispers heatedly, hands cupping my waist.

I swallow hard, turning to face the bookshelf. It feels like my whole body is shaking already, nerves burning to a crisp.

"That's it," he murmurs in approval, running his hands along the curves of my sides. When he reaches the waistband of my shorts, he hooks his fingers in, slowly dragging them down my legs to the floor.

Theo walks over, standing next to me, studying my face. I give him a shy smile, still utterly taken aback that I'm alone in the library with the two of them.

"You're shaking," Theo points out, brushing the hair off my shoulder.

I nod. "Maybe a little bit."

"It's a precursor for what's to come," Grey laughs softly, kissing the back of my thighs.

Theo smiles at me, leaning forward to kiss me. I relax, body slumping against the shelf as I let him take control.

Behind me, Grey removes my shoes, fingers drawing patterns over my naked lower half. He goes higher, grabbing the hem of my shirt, lifting it, until I have to break the kiss with Theo.

Suddenly, I realize I'm completely naked—the thought sending a wave of intensity through my body.

Hands push open my thighs as Grey cups my pussy from behind, his middle finger slipping inside me with ease. Little whimpers get caught in my throat as I kiss Theo, hips rocking gently as Grey finger-fucks me from his knees.

They are completely right—the shaking isn't going to stop any time soon.

Gentle kisses fall on my ass as Grey snakes one of his arms around, holding my lower abdomen firmly. Slowly, he lowers his hand, thumb brushing against my clit. I jolt forward, nails clawing at whatever I can on the bookshelf. I try to search for a sturdy grip, but all I can find are books. One slips from the shelf, landing next to Grey on the floor with a thud, making him chuckle.

Removing his finger, he grabs my hips, turning me around to face him. My back presses against the shelf, and I stare at them both with flushed cheeks.

"I think you are both overdressed," I breathe out, noting their gray uniforms.

Theo kisses me deeply, breaking our lips a few seconds later. "Undress Grey," he says quietly.

Grey rises from the ground as I turn back around to face him. There's nothing holding me back—I need to see them both.

I just need them.

Fisting the hem of his shirt, I lift it up hastily, Grey helping me remove it as we toss it to the side. My eyes linger over his torso, taking the time to appreciate the man in front of me. As they trail down to his shorts, I dip my hand inside first, gripping his cock.

"Fuck," Grey hisses, hand slamming onto the shelf next to him for support. "Keep touching me, little killer."

The encouragement awakens something in me. It's like I *need* to please him—to do what he says. I want him to feel all the pleasure that he gives me.

My hand pumps his length, thumb swiping over the head. I smear pre-cum around the swollen tip, dropping to my knees for a closer look.

There's no other way to describe it—I rip his shorts off, the sides tearing a little as I pull them from the bottom. Grey steps out of them, cock springing toward my face.

I gaze at it, mesmerized for a brief second, before I circle my thumb around the tip again.

A growl lingers in his throat, control on the verge of break-ing as he lets me take my time exploring. I lean forward, swiping my tongue along the tip with curiosity, pleased when he jolts with a shiver.

Theo cups my face from behind, voice low. "Open your mouth, Aves."

My stomach—and pussy—clenches, lips parting around Grey's tip. Slowly, Theo guides my head forward, making me take Grey's length inch by inch until I bottom out with a little gag.

"Fuck, fuck!" Grey hisses, staying still. "You're killing me, babe."

My gaze flickers up to him, staring at him through my lashes. His eyes darken, the stormy gray swirling as his breath catches.

Theo lowers one of his hands to my throat, gently holding the underside of my jaw. I wonder if he can feel Grey's cock through my skin.

"That's it," he says proudly. "Now, move your head back and forth."

His fingers grip my jaw, directing me as I pull back along Grey's cock. When I get to the tip, I quickly move forward again, engulfing him in my mouth.

Grey rips his eyes away from mine to look behind me, an unreadable expression as he stares at Theo. The faintest smile tugs at his lips before he glances back down at me.

"Theo's turn," he says, gripping the base of his cock as he removes himself from my mouth.

I shuffle on my knees, turning around to face Theo, watching as he pulls his shirt off for me. Immediately, I reach for his shorts, confidently pulling them off.

He's perfect too. They are both perfect.

Long, hard and glistening, I quickly wrap my fingers around Theo's length, giving a few curious pumps. Without wasting any more time, I cover the head of his cock with my lips, my cheeks hollowing as I suck.

Fingers thread through my hair, gathering it into a ponytail as Grey whispers words of encouragement to me.

"That's it, babe. Fuck him with your sweet mouth."

I moan against Theo's shaft, the vibrations making him groan.

I don't think Grey is the only one with an animal inside him, because at the sound of Theo's pleasure, I'm ready to burst out of my skin.

Grey picks up one of my hands, lifting it toward Theo. I watch, still applying pressure to the tip, as Grey guides it.

"Grab his balls," he says, pressing the palm of my hand against Theo. He lets go, but my hand stays, gently squeezing the sacks in my grip.

Theo groans louder, and I thrust my head forward, taking as much of him as possible. Pulling back, I bob back and forth, still fondling his underparts.

Suddenly, Theo steps back with a hiss, cock falling out of my mouth. He looks at me with dark eyes, breathing deeply.

"You're going to make me come if you keep doing that," he warns.

"I want to," I say, reaching for him, but he grabs my wrist, pulling me up from the ground.

Slamming his lips against mine, I mold into his body, our naked torsos flush against each other.

"I need to be inside you when that happens," he growls. "I want to know that you're walking around, dripping from both of us."

My eyes widen in surprise, but I don't have time to react as Grey wraps his arms around me, lifting me off the ground from behind.

Without even exchanging words between them, Theo grabs my legs, hooking them around his waist. Grey's hand cups one of my breasts, pinching the nipple softly as Theo lines himself up.

"Take her slowly," Grey says to him. "I want to feel her writhe against me."

Theo laughs quietly, nodding as he enters me, inch by torturous inch.

My back arches into Grey, and I gasp as my pussy is slowly stretched. Fingers tweak my nipple, tugging on the sensitive peak as my legs dangle down the back of Theo's thighs.

It feels like it takes forever to fill me, my hips jerking desperately as Grey holds me upright. Theo lets out a low groan, digging his hands into my upper thighs.

"Fuck, Aves. You're so fucking tight and wet."

I let out a moan, throwing my head back on Grey's shoulder. "Please fuck me."

"Begging won't get you anywhere," Theo replies smugly. "I want to feel you squeeze my cock."

He reaches down to my hips, stroking my clit while sheathed inside me. My body clenches down around him, arms circling behind Grey's neck as I fist his hair in frustration, aching for ecstasy.

Grey lets out a growl, hands grabbing my body roughly. "Come on, little killer. You can do better than that."

Drawing out slowly, Theo takes his sweet time, sliding his length in and out. I rip at Grey's hair, clenching it hard as I try to rock my hips against Theo.

"Harder," Grey growls again, a command in his voice.

I readjust my fist, tugging roughly at the strands. He groans, hand reaching down to my clit.

Gasping, I look down as both of them rub my pussy at the same time. It's like they are fighting over who can bring me the most pleasure—but at the same time working together as a team.

I'm on the brink of orgasm, but it's halted by Theo's agonizingly slow movements. I ache painfully, desperate for release, but they refuse to give in.

"I think she's getting frustrated," Grey taunts, sliding his wet fingers up my lower abdomen. "Do you want to come, *our little killer?*"

His words are like knives, slicing right through me. But there's no pain—only an awakening I didn't know I needed.

Our little killer.

"Please," I beg. "Faster."

Theo hums to himself, stopping completely. I nearly cry, on the edge of madness.

Cupping my neck from behind, Grey leans down to my ear, tugging on the lobe with his teeth. "I asked you a question—*Do. You. Need. To. Come?*"

"Yes," I cry out.

He looks over me at Theo, giving him a nod. "Then I guess we better give her what she needs."

Theo smiles at me, locking eyes. "I guess so," he answers, a sinister tone to his voice.

Suddenly, he pulls back, slamming into me with such force that Grey has to take a step back to steady himself. I let out a small bellow, head smashing into Grey's collarbone as Theo starts fucking me hard and fast.

Hands find my clit again but my eyes are squeezed shut, unable to focus on anything except the release I know is coming quickly.

I barely have time to take three breaths before my body explodes with my climax, clenching around Theo. He lets out a sharp growl, slamming our hips together half a dozen more times before my name falls from his lips with a groan.

As he lets go of my legs, I notice that my feet somewhat touch the ground, but I'm still not supporting my own weight.

Grey places me firmly on the ground, spinning me until I face the bookshelf. He runs his palms up my arms, guiding my hands to the shelf. I clutch it, eyes fluttering closed as he trails a hand down my back, pushing me forward so I'm bent over as he goes.

Standing behind me, he shocks me by slapping my ass hard. I quickly look over my shoulder at him, melting at the grin he gives in response.

"You're going to hold on and take me," he murmurs, bringing his hand down again to smack my other ass cheek.

I groan, looking back toward the books as I do my best to ready myself. I feel his cock press against my wet pussy, still slick with Theo's release.

Grey buries himself in me in one swift swoop, grabbing my hip. "You feel so fucking good. We're going to fill your tight, little cunt so much that it's all you'll feel for the rest of the day."

I let out a cry, digging my nails into the wooden shelf as he thrusts into me hard and fast. My eyes are tightly closed, barely noticing as Theo crawls under my body, wrapping his arms around my legs.

Opening my eyes, I look down at him, his back to me. Suddenly, he pulls me forward, my body changing angles as my lower abdomen smashes into his forehead.

Grey doesn't slow down at all, unfazed by the change in angle. Something warm lands on my clit, and I realize with a gasp that it's Theo's tongue.

"Fuck," I moan painfully, resting my head forward as the two of them hold my hips and legs upright.

Theo's mouth and tongue cover my clit, teasing it, as Grey fucks me from behind. It's easily the hottest thing I've ever seen before in my life—my vision becoming a mess of black spots and blurry lines.

A hand claws down my back, nails tearing the skin—not enough to make me bleed, but the right amount of pressure to leave red marks.

"Give me your orgasm, Avery," Grey demands huskily. "I want everything. You're mine."

"Ours," Theo shoots back hastily against my clit, pulling it between his teeth.

My legs start to shake violently, scratches appearing on the wooden shelf as my nails embed themselves in it.

"Who do you belong to?" Grey asks, the sound of our hips meeting together.

"You," I breathe out loudly with a cry. "Both of you."

They both growl appreciatively—*possessively*—ramping up their efforts as my climax builds. I can feel Theo's release dripping down my thighs as Grey fucks me harder, while a tongue swishes around my clit in perfect circles.

And then I fall.

Blissfully over the edge, down the cliffside, into the icy waters below.

I scream out both their names, vision completely black. I'm not sure if my eyes are still closed or if I'm on the brink of passing out, but either way, it feels like paradise.

Muffled noises reach my ears, the faint sound of Grey groaning as he spills his release in my body, joining Theo's. The pressure around my clit doesn't ease up, sending me spiraling into a level of pleasure that becomes almost painful, breaking me in the best ways possible.

Noises continue to fade, darkness seeping in, and when someone lets go of my legs, they buckle. Hands catch me, guiding me to the floor as I feel the familiar scratchy material underneath my back.

It takes a few seconds, but slowly, things come back into focus. Immediately, I find Grey and Theo on either side of me, amused expressions on their faces.

"Are you alright, babe?" Grey asks with a pleased laugh.

I nod, taking a deep breath. "I think so," I mutter back weakly.

"If anyone can handle two men, it's you," Theo teases.

"It might just take some getting used to," I laugh quietly, still trying to get a grip on my floating body.

Grey leans down, kissing me. "I hope you *do* get used to it. Because we're going to have so much fun breaking you in, little killer."

Chapter 29

Avery

The next morning I wake, sore all over, but feeling lighter than I have in weeks. It's short-lived though when I head to breakfast, noticing the guard by the door is on edge.

Immediately when I enter the hall, it's pure pandemonium. Everyone is on their feet, huddled in groups. The food at the end of the hall remains untouched, and to my left, I spot a few people crying.

What the fuck happened?

I don't pay proper attention as I try to make my way through the crowd, bumping into people. I accidentally collide with Siobhan's back, taking a step back when she turns around to snap at me.

"Watch where you're going!"

"Sorry," I mutter in confusion, eyes shifting to the girl next to her. I recognize her from my shower group—her strawberry blonde hair tied up in pigtails. She gives me a small, sympathetic smile. Of all the people I've met here, she's one of the most normal ones. I still remember how she was kind to me in the showers, helping me understand the routine.

"It's fine," she says softly, answering for Siobhan. "We're just a bit overwhelmed this morning."

"I'm not overwhelmed, Eliana!"

It's nice to finally put a name to the face, listening as Siobhan rambles to herself, cupping the sides of her head.

"What happened?" I ask Eliana, gazing around at the patients.

She opens her mouth to answer before she spots someone by the entrance, pausing in her tracks. I turn around to look, eyes narrowing as Mr. Whittingham strolls into the room, a guard on either side.

It's only when I notice a podium in the middle of the room that it dawns on me this must be something significant. He doesn't like making announcements unless they are important.

As he stands on the podium block, I observe the tightness in his jaw—the way his face is scrunched up in frustration.

"Morning all," he addresses through the microphone. The room falls silent, except for the sobs of a few people.

I frown—really worried now.

A burning sensation tickles my face and I instinctively look to the wall, finding Grey. He's standing next to Damon, and when he notices that I've finally spotted him, he gives me a small nod.

"As some of you are already aware, the facility staff have been notified of the passing of another fellow student," Mr. Whittingham says crisply.

My heart jolts in my chest, scanning Grey's and Damon's faces for their reaction. They hold blank expressions, and I look back to Whitface, trying to piece together who it is.

"Unfortunately, my staff found the body of Ms. Vivian Capello in her room this morning. Sadly, she took her own life."

I let out a small gasp, in disbelief. I don't believe it—Vivian seemed fine yesterday.

I guess it just goes to show that you never really know what someone is fighting. Maybe it's the ones who seem okay that we should be worried about.

Vivian tried to kill herself a few short weeks ago, but even she said it was a moment of weakness. Did she lie?

Was it because of our conversation? Did I push her over the edge?

"Our new psychiatrist has started today, so if anyone requires further support, both Dr. Smith and Dr. Elsher are happy to hold extra sessions today. In the meantime, classes are canceled for today and we are extending free time to allow you time to process the situation. Our hearts and prayers go out to Ms. Capello and her loved ones."

Stepping off the block, he pushes through the crowd to the door, vanishing just as quickly as the echo of his words.

As soon as the door closes behind him, the room erupts back into chaos, the sound deafening me.

"*Again. Again. Again. Not again. No! Again. Fuck!*" Siobhan mutters, shaking her head wildly.

I stare at her for a few seconds, remembering her brother's suicide, and that she's Vivian's room neighbor. If what they are saying is true and she did it in her room, it was right next door to Siobhan. My heart breaks for her.

Eliana gives me a sad smile, motioning that she's got Siobhan. I give her a small nod, weaving through the room until I get to Grey and Damon.

"What the fuck?" I breathe out.

Grey wraps his arm around me, pulling me against the wall with him. "I know."

My eyes shift to Damon, trying to gauge his reaction to the news. I can't tell if he already knew or if he's in the midst of processing it.

"Do we know what happened?" I ask them.

Damon looks at me, green eyes locking with mine. "Not yet. It's surprising."

"It is," I agree in a somber tone. "She wasn't suicidal yesterday. It doesn't make any sense."

"I agree," Damon replies, looking away to scan the crowd. *Really?*

I half-expect them to tell me that these things happen at Lilydale. It's certainly not the first time—even disregarding Sam's assisted death. I know there was another loss before I started.

It's why I started.

"Does the society know anything about it?" I ask quietly.

This time, I'm not accusing them of anything. They are usually the first people to know what happens around here. Surely they would have seen activity on the camera feeds or been notified from the guards.

The society knows everything.

"I need to go chat to Jillian," Damon says, turning to Grey. "We'll have a few extra hours to look into this, but I've noticed there's a handful of new guards on duty."

Grey nods firmly. "Arthur is trying to keep control."

"Does that mean we won't be able to move around freely?" I chime in. "We need to look into this. Something doesn't sit well with me."

Damon glances over at me. "I agree with Avery. It's suspicious. We certainly didn't do anything, but that doesn't mean no one else did."

"Did Vivian have any enemies?" I ask hesitantly. "Why would anyone target her? She's just been keeping to herself."

"I don't know, babe," Grey answers. "But we'll find out. If we're not around at free time, stay close to Theo. I'll come find you when I can."

I nod, grimacing. "I have a psych session with the new doctor after breakfast."

Damon smirks slightly at me. "Sorry."

"No, you're not," I shoot back. "Though maybe it wasn't a bad idea to reduce poor Dr. Smith's workload—especially now."

"Please," Damon sneers. "Christopher lives for chaos like this. He'll be mad that he has to share."

Grey grabs my hand, giving it a squeeze. "Let's go grab some breakfast before the bell rings. We'll keep you updated."

"Alright," I mutter, giving Damon a small smile before we head to the food. I notice him duck through the crowd, probably looking for Jillian and Byrone.

We'll get to the bottom of this, Vivian. I promise.

"Avery White."

I glance over the desk at the new psychiatrist, taking in his appearance. He's the complete opposite to Dr. Smith—in his mid-fifties, bald, dark blue eyes, and dressed in smart casual wear.

I've gotten so used to seeing the staff dressed in suits that Dr. Elsher's black button-down shirt and dark jeans have thrown me off.

"That's me," I murmur, shifting in my chair.

He glances over the manila file on his desk, scanning the papers briefly before flicking it closed. "Why don't you tell me a bit about yourself?"

I shrug. "Not much to say really. It's all in the file."

"Fair enough," he says, exasperated. "Let me guess—you usually prefer silent appointments."

My eyebrows furrow. "Dr. Smith and I had a decent relationship and expectation with sessions. Aren't you going to ask me a bunch of questions about my feelings and shit?"

"I fear there's little point," Dr. Elsher shoots back. "I can already tell that you're not very cooperative."

Blinking at him in surprise, I decide that I already hate him. It's clear he doesn't give a shit about being here, let alone about us patients.

Folding my arms, I lean back in this chair. "Is that what Whittingham told you?" I ask heatedly. "That I'm not cooperative? A trouble-maker? Incurable?"

Dr. Elsher looks up lazily, unfazed. "Ms. White, I'm not under any false pretenses here. Lilydale Foundation Center is full of troubled youths—you're not special in that regard."

"I never said I was," I snap back angrily.

"Regardless, it's no secret that sessions here will be difficult to conduct. None of you are willingly seeking therapy for your issues. Due to the nature of your admission requirements and conditions, I'm certainly prepared for pushback, as it were."

My eyes narrow. "If you have that kind of attitude toward the patients, why bother working here at all?"

It crosses my mind for a brief second that perhaps there's a reason he was chosen. Obviously there would be—Alexander seems to do everything for a reason, just like Damon. I can't help but wonder if he's known to the Lilydale board or was just the best candidate that applied.

If he's the best... then I'll fuck a cactus because this guy is horrible. At least Dr. Smith pretends to give a shit... makes an effort somewhat.

"My employment is none of your business," he says casually, turning his chair to the side, gazing out the window. "However, when you decide you want *actual* help, let me know."

He falls silent, leaving me to gape at him. He's easily one of the worst staff members I've met in this place, which is no easy feat.

"The whole purpose of this facility," I start through clenched teeth. "Is to help rehabilitate us. Of course the patients here have mental health challenges. I'm sure you've read their files, and if you're a professional, you'll know that there's going to be pushback for reasons out of their control."

Dr. Elsher glances over his shoulder at me. "You speak on behalf of the collective, not yourself. I'm not going to waste my time being lectured by someone who struggles to grasp life in a rational fashion."

"What the fuck does that mean?" I spit out, nails digging into the chair.

He lifts an eyebrow. "I *have* read all the files, Ms. White—yours included. Admitted here due to murder charges pertaining to your father. Your mother committed suicide when you were a teenager. You've suffered several different types of abuse and have been formally diagnosed with post-traumatic stress disorder and borderline personality disorder. However, despite taking up a place in this facility, which as you pointed out serves as a rehabilitation center, you have no desire to actually change."

I take a few seconds to compose myself. "You've sat here and spoken to me for all of five minutes. You don't know anything about me."

"But I have *the file*," he taunts, tapping his fingers on the folder. "I know everything about you."

"No, you don't," I argue back, keeping my voice level. "You know my mental illnesses and my history. Absolutely none of that depicts who I am as a person. At the moment, you only have a biased perspective from Mr. Whittingham—who, I might add, has just spent his days torturing me. Other than that, all you can do is draw inferences from the information in that file."

Dr. Elsher smiles at me—but it's not a warm one. "From the moment you entered this room, I could tell what type of person you are. I don't need outside information to see that. However, unfortunately, your history and mental illnesses do make the person you are."

"No they fucking don't," I say. "I *have* mental illness. I'm *not mental illness*. I'm worth more than what you paint me as psychologically."

"Ms. White?"

"What?"

"Be sure to close the door on the way out. I'll have the guard escort you to your room for the remainder of the session."

"What the hell are you rambling on about?"

I stop pacing, swinging around to face the doorway. I was so caught up in my thoughts that I didn't hear the door open or notice Damon standing there until he spoke.

"The new psychiatrist," I spit out. "He's a fucking asshole."

Damon steps into the room, looking around casually. "So I've heard. You're not the first to share these thoughts."

"Do you know him?" I ask, somewhat aggressively.

He peers down at me with a blank expression. "William Elsher? No—I don't. He's not a relative, if that's what you're asking."

Somehow, this information calms me down a little bit. "Good. Because I think he might be an even bigger asshole than you," I mutter.

Damon smiles at me, obviously amused at my thoughts of him. "Seems impossible, but thank you."

Taking a breath, I relax, sitting on the edge of my bed. "Anyway, what did we find out?"

"Not much yet. Jillian is checking the feed. I need to go investigate something else, but unfortunately Grey is with Leighton sorting something out. I need you to come with me."

I nod, standing back up. "Now?"

"Yes, free time has just started. Time to head downstairs."

Chapter 30

Damon

I hear Avery's nervous breathing as we head down the stair-well to the underground rooms.

I haven't told her exactly where we are going or why, but she's followed without complaint.

As we enter the underground corridors, I take a peek at the black camera in the corner, confirming that the red light is turned off.

"Where are we going?" Avery asks quietly, walking beside me.

"We're going to the morgue," I reply bluntly.

Her gaze burns the side of my face, but I ignore her. I don't have time to answer her annoying questions.

While Jillian has deactivated the cameras underground completely for the moment, it's still only a matter of time before the staff realize I'm missing.

Judging by the new guards on duty, Arthur is planning to make a move, and he'll be watching closely. I don't anticipate the guards will be around long. They will either leave, be fired, or they will start working for me, but Arthur's counting on that short window to upstage us.

I would normally send someone else to do a task like this, but after this morning's news, I have everyone assigned with other tasks. Also, if my suspicions are correct, I need to confirm them for myself.

We reach the morgue entrance and Avery pauses beside me, glancing at the doors in thought. I roll my eyes, pushing them open.

It's freezing cold in here, but immediately I notice that the examination table is untouched.

Avery sticks close by, eyes darting around in confusion. "What are we looking for?" she asks.

"Capello," I answer, opening the first mortuary cabinet door. "Help me check the trays."

She hovers awkwardly for a moment before walking to the other end, putting her hand on the handle. I can sense her hesitating, and I'm ready to snap at her to hurry up, but she opens the first door.

Relief filters through her face when she finds it empty, grabbing the next handle. With each empty cabinet, she gets more confident, checking quickly, until the two of us meet in the middle.

"There's no one here," she says perturbed.

"Exactly," I breathe out, starting to feel a little worried.

It's not a usual emotion for me, and it makes me feel a little physically sick.

"If it only happened this morning, wouldn't she be here?" Avery asks.

I nod, pleased that she's able to connect the dots. She's smarter than I gave her credit for. "Yes, she would."

Her eyebrows furrow as she leans against the closed cabinet. "What's going on, Damon?"

"I don't believe Capello killed herself," I tell her, looking over at her slumped figure. "I don't think she's dead at all."

Avery blinks at me, her gray eyes scanning my face curiously. "What do you mean?"

I straighten up, resting my hands in my pockets. "I told you this place has secrets. I think they are about to be cracked wide open."

"I—"

Her next sentence gets cut off by the sound of a door opening and closing down the corridor, footsteps heading in our direction.

That fucking bastard. I knew he'd be onto it quickly.

At least I have the confirmation I needed. We can make a plan now and go from there.

I start to head toward the door to get ready to meet the guards when Avery flies forward, grabbing my arm.

"What are you doing?" she whispers heatedly. "We need to hide."

"There's no point hiding," I scoff. "They know we're down here. It's just a shame we didn't get more time."

Avery's eyes dart to the mortuary cabinet, and I raise an eyebrow, sensing her train of thought.

"I'm not getting inside the damn box, Avery."

Amused, I watch as she runs across the room, opening an adjoining door. Her small gasp nearly makes me laugh as she comes face to face with the storage room, random caskets perched up on racks.

What the fuck did she think would be in there?

I can see her body tensing, trying to come up with a solution.

She turns around, running back to me as the footsteps grow louder. "Come on," she hisses, pulling me with all her strength toward the storage room.

I'm surprised by her power, finally stopping her when we're in the doorway of the storage room.

"What the hell do you think you're doing?" I ask her.

Her eyes light up, as if she's mastered the greatest plan in the world. "Get into a casket," she says, watching as my eyebrows shoot up. "I'll let them find me. They will think that they have caught whoever is down here and you can keep looking when we are gone."

"That's preposterous. Arthur will know I'm here."

"But they will be distracted by me for a while. It will buy you time."

"Avery," I growl in frustration. "You do realize that if you're caught, they will put you into solitary confinement."

Her face drops slightly, but she just nods solemnly. "I know. But this is important. We need to protect you, especially if shit is going down."

"I don't need protecting."

It's like a lightbulb goes off in her head, lips parting. "*You have to protect the king.*"

Well, now she's just fucking rambling like a lunatic. I have no idea what she's even going on about. However, *we do* need more time down here. It might be our only chance.

Begrudgingly, I grab her wrist, pulling her into the storage room and closing the door behind us. "Get into a casket," I order. "Quickly."

"I need to distract them," she argues.

Rolling my eyes, I reach down and open up a mahogany case, pushing her into the box. "Get the fuck in."

Quickly, I switch off the overhead light. I don't have enough time to open another one, and frankly, I need to make sure she stays quiet.

I hear her squeak feebly as I climb into the casket with her, closing the lid as she rolls onto her side to make space for me.

"What are you doing?" she whispers.

"Shut up," I growl back quietly, listening for sounds.

Outside the storage room, footsteps echo around the acoustic sounding morgue. My chest is pushed against Avery's, the feel of her rapidly beating heart vibrating through her shirt.

The door next to our casket creaks open, the sound of the light switch flicking on as someone looks around the room. Avery holds her breath, laying completely still. It's then I realize she's holding onto my shirt, the thin material bunched in her tiny fists.

The light switches off again, the door closing with a click. I strain my ears, following the trail of footsteps as they pace the morgue.

Eventually, they leave, fading off into the corridor.

Avery lets out a sigh of relief, her breath shaking. "What do we do now?" she whispers so quietly that it's barely audible.

"We wait for a bit," I mutter. "It should take them about fifteen minutes at most to check this side of the facility."

"Okay..."

The two of us lay in silence, her heart slowing down as the minutes tick by.

Letting out a frustrated sigh, I reach up, grabbing her wrists. "Can you let go of my shirt?"

"Shit, sorry," she says embarrassed, unclenching her fists.

The casket is tight, and a funny feeling passes through me when her fingers brush against my chest. I feel her struggle, trying to make room, but with the little space we have in here, her hands have nowhere to go.

"Just rest them," I snap at her under my breath when she tries to hold them upright between us.

"Right, sorry."

Avery places her palms flat against my chest, surprising me. "I didn't mean on me."

"Well, I don't know what you want then!"

"Shut up," I hiss at her, covering her mouth with my hand. "You are the worst hider ever. They have to walk back down this way to get to the stairwell. Do you want them to find us or not?"

She mumbles sorry against my hand. I let out a sigh, removing it and resting it above her head.

More minutes tick by, her squirming body rubbing against me. I'm on the verge of snapping at her again, when she brushes against my dick.

"Avery," I growl. "Stop moving."

"My back is cramping up," she mutters. "It's an old injury. The scar tissue just hurts now and then. It's okay—we should be able to leave shortly."

"Oh, for fuck sake."

Wrapping an arm around her back, I move us both, laying her flat on the bottom of the casket. Holding myself above her, I put my weight on my forearms and knees, allowing her to stretch out.

"You don't have to do that," she says softly.

"I'm aware," I retort back. "But Grey won't let me hear the end of it if I don't return you in one piece."

Avery laughs quietly to herself. "I think you'd be fine. He cares about you more than anyone else in the world."

I squint through the dark, trying to find her face. "You're infuriating. You know that, right?"

"Yeah, I do. But I can't help it. It's just a wonderful personality trait at this point."

"You have a death wish," I point out. "That infuriating attitude nearly got you killed."

"By you?" Avery asks thoughtfully. "Surprised you haven't yet, to be honest."

Letting out a small scoff, I keep my hands on either side of her head as I balance. "You're not in the clear yet."

"I thought you were going to kill me the day I slapped you," she admits.

I smile to myself. I *was* very tempted to kill her that day. But at the same time, I was amused that someone had the balls to hit me.

"Like I said, it's still a possibility," I tell her. "I did tell you I'd nail your casket shut. I already have the casket here."

Avery laughs softly. "You're not so bad, Damon. Still a demon... but you're not the person I thought you were."

"I'm exactly who you thought," I point out.

"No," she disagrees. "You're not. I'm sorry for being such a pain in your ass."

Dropping to one of my forearms, I reposition myself. "Don't get all touchy-feeling on me. I don't do emotions."

She shuffles, making room for my arm. "I don't blame you. Emotions lead to trouble. I wish I could turn mine off."

Her words cause me to freeze, disturbing something in me. She repeated what I always say—but coming from her, it's... *weird.*

I can't imagine Avery not having emotions. Sure, she needs a handle on them. But there's something about hers that always surprises me.

They make her... *Avery.*

Grey was right. She's got everything bottled up, and once she gets a grip on them, they will unleash, destroying everything in their path. But I'm starting to realize it's not in a negative way.

She's everything I hate—annoying, unpredictable, overly trusting. But also caring, thoughtful, receptive. Most people here respect me out of fear. They are loyal to reap the benefits.

Not her though.

While I had forced her to stay on task, she did it because she wanted to.

Even now, she opted to try to *protect me*—without me asking for it. Not that I would ever ask someone to protect me—I am more than capable of protecting myself. But she wanted to do it for no reason other than she wanted to.

Peculiar feelings stir inside me, making me shift uncomfortably. Avery notices, grabbing my forearm gently.

"Are you okay?"

"I'm fine," I snap back.

I wait for her to recoil, but she doesn't. "Are you sure?" she asks concerned. "Here, let me move."

She goes to move her body but I grab her waist to keep her put. "I said I'm fine."

"Don't be ridiculous," she scolds. "It's not comfortable in that position. My back feels better now. Lie down."

"Back off, Avery."

She pulls my arm, trying to tug me toward the floor of the casket. "God damnit, Damon. Stop being a stubborn ass—"

I don't know what possesses me to do it. I don't even think about it in advance.

Her arguing, her defiance, her caring, the way she grabs my arm—it snaps something inside of me.

And before I can stop myself or realize it's happening, I do the unthinkable.

I kiss her.

Chapter 31
Grey

"You're being very strange this evening, little killer."

Avery glances over at me as we walk down the deserted corridor, exhaustion written all over her face. Part of me waits for her to deny it, to tell me she's fine.

"I know."

My brows crease together as we cross the entrance threshold to Arthur's office. It's late—well past midnight, so thankfully, he's not here. If he was, I'd probably gut him, chop his fingers off, and poke Avery with them until she tells me the issue.

She's been acting weird ever since free time. All I know is her and Damon went downstairs to look for Vivian's body and came up empty handed.

When we went back to our rooms for the evening, Damon instructed me to search Whittingham's office for clues. We just had to wait until he was gone for the day and the guards changed shifts for the night.

Even when I collected her from her room, she was staring at the ceiling from the bed, in a thought-filled daze.

The access pad beeps and flashes green, and I pull the door open, holding it for her. Avery steps into the office, eyes scanning the darkened room.

I grab her hand, leading her further inside, flicking on the light switch.

"What are we looking for exactly?" she asks, walking around the desk.

"Anything unusual," I reply, skimming through the discarded paperwork on the desk. Spotting the letter opener, I pick it up, jamming it into the lock of the desk drawers, breaking them. I don't give a shit if he knows we've been in here—I hope the thought terrifies him.

Though, if I'm being honest, he's probably expecting it. I don't think we'll find anything. I'm sure he's got whatever we are looking for hidden somewhere else. Perhaps we should check Teddy's desk on the way back out.

"That doesn't narrow it down," Avery mutters softly, lingering by a bookshelf as she checks the books.

"You're starting to worry me," I say. "What's going on?"

She pauses, falling silent. Slowly, she turns to look at me, face pained.

"Something happened today," she mentions, appearing uncomfortable. "And I don't want to keep it from you. But I also don't want to upset you."

Straightening up, my nerves start buzzing. I twirl the letter opener in my hand, leaning against the desk.

"Now you're worrying me. You can tell me anything, little killer. You know that."

I can see the way her body tenses up, stressed. She's running through words in her mind, trying to figure out the best way to say whatever is on her mind.

I'm growing impatient with waiting, the anxiety eating me alive. But I force myself to wait, to give her the opportunity to tell me on her own time.

"When Damon and I were in the morgue," she starts, voice shaking slightly. "The new guards nearly caught us. I pulled him into the storage room to hide."

"Right," I respond sharply, wondering where this is going.

Did Damon hurt her somehow? I thought he and I had an understanding now. I thought he was starting to tolerate her.

"We ended up hiding in a casket," she murmurs, face scrunched up. "They didn't find us, thankfully."

I'm already aware of this information. Damon mentioned they were nearly found. The back story is taking forever, so I push the tip of the letter opener into my palm to distract me.

"Yes, I know. What did he do?" I ask accusingly, getting angry.

Is she trying to protect our friendship? I love Damon like a brother but Avery is my everything—my life, my death, my destruction.

She glances up, locking eyes with me.

"When we were in the casket, we started arguing."

Still nothing unusual...

"Avery," I growl, frustrated. "What did he do?"

She pauses, the seconds ticking by. We stand in silence, watching each other until she finally breaks eye contact, looking at the wall.

"He kissed me, Grey."

My body freezes, an ice-cold chill rushing through me. Out of everything she could have said, that was the last thing I would have guessed.

I feel betrayed. Fucking deceived.

By Damon.

I almost want to throttle her too, except I can tell by her body language and pained expression that she's as shocked as I am.

We had finally gotten to a good place. I've been working hard to accept Theo into the mix—solely because he makes her happy.

But Damon? They don't like each other at the best of times.

So what fucking business does he have kissing *my girl*?

"Please, say something."

Her voice breaks me out of my thoughts, a worried look on her face. Tears are pooled in her eyes, the gray orbs shaking with fear.

The fear that I'm going to leave her again.

"I don't know what to say," I mutter darkly.

Avery nods slowly, tears slipping down her cheeks. She doesn't brush them away, instead taking small footsteps toward me.

I can sense her hesitation, but she perseveres, desperate to touch me.

Her hands rest on my chest but I don't see her. I can't see the room at all.

All I can see is Damon's lips on her, kissing what's mine.

It's almost unnatural to imagine, especially since I've never seen him kiss anyone before.

I know in the past he's participated in *fun* at society meetings—a means of release. But he's never kissed anyone though. It's not his thing. It's too personal, too emotional.

"I'm so sorry," Avery croaks out, the imaginary ripping from my mind as her face reappears in front of me.

"Did you kiss him back?" I ask, voice breaking.

She frowns, an agonizing expression staring back at me. "I don't know," she admits quietly. "It happened so quickly. I think I froze up at first. And then suddenly we were out of the casket."

"Right."

"Please," she begs painfully. "Please, don't hate me."

The words cut right through me, my chest tearing apart. "I don't hate you. I'm mad at him. How could he do this to me?"

Avery breaths a small sigh of relief, throwing her arms around me. I hug her back, inhaling her scent.

I'm going to fucking kill him.

"What the fuck are you doing here?" a voice snaps from the doorway.

We pull apart, eyes darting to the door. A guard stands there, hand on his taser and gun, eyes wide with flashing anger.

"Get out of here," I warn him, my gaze darkening at the new hire.

"You're out of bounds," he spits out, taking a few steps forward. "Back to your rooms—*now*."

And suddenly, I'm not seeing the guard anymore. I'm just seeing Damon's face, little bits of red filling my vision.

Avery hovers by my side quietly, assessing the situation. When neither of us respond, the guard closes the distance between us, charging at us with determination.

As soon as he's within reach, I fling my arm back, lunging forward with the letter opener. My aim is perfect—the tip of the blade jarring into the corner of his eye.

The guard lets out a hoarse scream, clutching his face as Avery gasps, stumbling back. I grab him by the scruff of his black vest, tossing him onto Whittingham's desk.

Retrieving the letter opener with a *pop*, I turn to Avery while the guard writhes in pain, blood dripping onto my hand.

"I want to make one thing clear," I say to her, putting it down. "You're *mine*. I've made exceptions for Theo, but Damon will need to explain himself."

I spot a stationery canister on the desk, picking up a Sharpie. I scribble the word '*Mine*' across the guard's cheek, dropping the marker on the ground as I reach into my back pocket. Pulling out my shiv—the one I fucked Avery with for the first time—I lift the guard up, his torso dangling above the desk, pressing the blade to his left ear.

"Your voice is the only one I want to hear," I snarl, pushing the sharp edge through the flesh. Blood spurts out, pooling onto the desk as the guard screams, begging me to stop.

Avery just stares, wide-eyed, frozen. I lift the severed ear, dropping it into Arthur's stationery canister.

"Your lips are the only ones I want to kiss."

I hear her gasp softly as I move the blade to the guard's mouth, dragging the sharp edge across as I thinly carve his lips off.

"Grey..."

Reaching over, I shove my finger into the corner of his eye, replacing the letter opener. "You're the only one I want to see," I growl, wiggling my finger around his sclera.

He bucks underneath me, like an electrified goldfish, arms and legs flailing as he weakly tries to push me off.

"I'd fuck his eye socket, but my cock is only for you," I finish, ripping my finger back out.

Avery's cheeks are flushed with confusion—horrified at seeing the real monster I am, while conflicted by my words of love.

And I mean every single one of them.

Lifting the knife, I hold it above the guard's chest, locking eyes with her. "My heart is only for you, little killer. I'll kill *anyone* that dares to touch you, hurt you."

Plunging the blade down, it enters his chest, straight into his heart. The guard stills, only the faintest of twitches as the last few beats of his fading life vibrate through the knife.

I grab his vest, tossing him off the desk like the trash he is. He lands between us, in a heap on the floor, bleeding out while making gurgling noises.

Avery's eyes dart to the knife in his chest, the pool of blood on the desk. Part of me wonders if she's going to run away screaming.

Slowly, she steps over his body, pulling me in for a hug. I know she's trying to calm me down, appease me. I'm covered in splattered blood, and when she leans back, I spot some on her.

Seeing her covered in someone else's blood, snaps something inside. It's not the usual calming effect that blood has on me, it's monstrous. It's the devil in me, acknowledging my two loves.

I pull her mouth to mine, hand firmly planted on the nape of her neck. Kissing her, I swing her around, slamming her onto the pool of blood on the desk.

Avery doesn't seem fazed, too focused on me as I kiss her heatedly, ravishing her face and neck.

Reaching down, I lift her skirt up, ripping her underwear off. The fabric tears instantly, dropping next to the face of the now dead guard.

I dip my blood-covered hand in my shorts, pulling my hard cock out. Without waiting, I slam into her body, sending little bits of blood flying all over the carpet.

Avery cries out at the force, hands digging into my shoulders and biceps as I smash our hips together.

She's mine.

I won't let anyone take her from me.

Pulling back from her lips, I look her directly in the eye, our faces covered in little droplets of blood. "We're bonded by this blood. Together, the King and Queen of the Unhinged."

Before she can respond, I cover her mouth again, reaching down to rub my fingers against her clit. Her hips buck into my hand, making me growl as she meets my thrusts.

I'm so close to exploding in her, filling her with *my* essence. Because she's mine.

Fucking mine.

When I feel her cunt spasm around me, her moans and cries falling into my mouth, I fuck her harder than I ever have before, letting the blood soak into her hair and shirt. And then I blissfully detonate, filling her tight little body.

Mine.

No one is going to take that away from me.

I'll kill every last person until we're the last two left. And then we'll burn the world down together.

Chapter 32

Damon

The candle in my room flickers, sending shadows into havoc, climbing up the walls.

I'm sipping on a glass of aged bourbon, the bottle on the bed next to me as I wait.

I've sent Grey to search through Arthur's office for information. He's probably due back any minute with his findings. It's around two in the morning—we probably only have five hours before Arthur returns. He'll know immediately that we've been in there, and I'm expecting backlash.

But I can barely focus on that.

I'm repentant, disgusted with myself.

I don't remember the last time I lost control. I'm supposed to be the master of it, the one who never falters. After all, I'm setting the example. The society needs me, now more than ever, and for a brief thirty seconds, I nearly ruined everything I have worked hard to build.

And I fucking did the unthinkable.

Not only did I enter into a period of mania, breaking my most absolute rule... I did it with fucking *Avery*.

I cannot stand her. Her docile act, her knack for getting into trouble. She has everyone wrapped around her little fingers... except for me.

I was tolerating her for the sake of Grey, but slowly, somewhere along the way, I think she got to me as well.

In retrospect, I should have seen it coming. From the first moment she argued back, to the time she slapped me, I should have recognized that I had her figured out wrong.

Avery isn't like the other women here. Underneath the layers of nauseating emotions, she's fearless. She has no regard for herself, and while that normally wouldn't bother me, today it did for some reason.

She's been treating me like I'm her *friend*.

I'm not her fucking friend. I'm her leader.

But the way she smiles and jokes with me, as if she's not afraid of repercussions, it's something I haven't dealt with in a long time.

I'm used to people bowing down, following orders, and respecting me out of fear, but never has anyone at Lilydale treated me like a friend.

Like they're my equal.

It's outrageous. I should have put a stop to it long ago, strangled her with my reins. I should have impaled her on my crown, choked her with my thorns. But I've been too distracted with *Cirque* business.

And now she's infecting me like a virus.

My door opens and I gaze up as Grey walks in, covered in blood. I shouldn't be surprised to see him like that, but I thought we had a window where they wouldn't be disturbed.

Unless it's Avery blood. That would solve all my problems right now.

"Damon," he greets coldly, and instantly, I know.

She told him.

"Grey," I mutter back, holding the glass to my lips as I take another sip. "Did you find anything?"

He leans against the wall, body tense and emanating danger. "No, I didn't."

"I see you had a run-in with someone," I point out, tilting the glass toward his blood-stained shirt.

"A new guard interrupted us," he replies casually. "He's no longer with us."

I nod. "Fair enough. Why don't you get on with it?" I direct, knowing he's biting his tongue.

Grey's eyes darken at my standoffish attitude, anger and tension bouncing between us.

"You kissed her."

"Don't remind me."

His eyes flash, staring at me wildly. "What the fuck is wrong with you?" he asks, and for once, I'm not sure if he's referring to the fact I lost control, or because I kissed Avery.

My eyes narrow on his, lowering the glass. "It was a mistake," I spit out angrily. "A simple moment of pathetic weakness. It won't happen again."

"It better not," he warns. "Because I'll knock you off your throne so fast, Deadman."

"I'd like to see you try," I snap back. "But that's beside the point." I take a pause, knowing there's only one thing left to do. I hate doing it, but for him, I'll give in.

"And what's that?"

"I'm sorry."

It's the sincerest apology I can muster. At the end of the day, he is the one I care the most about in this place, and I'm not too proud to realize that I've fucked up with him. He's my brother, my best friend... the one I need for the next steps in my plan.

Grey goes quiet for a moment, surveying me. Finally, he calms down, some of the anger leaving his face.

"Don't ever touch her again," he growls quietly. "You don't even like her."

Now it's my turn to fall silent. I want to agree with him more than anything. But truthfully, I'm not sure what I feel. It's all foreign to me, and I hate myself for it.

"Damon," he snaps. "*Do you like her?*"

"I don't know," I grumble. "I tolerate her. But perhaps she's growing on me. She's shown us great loyalty recently."

He gazes at me incredulously, lost for words. Shaking my head, I finish the contents of my drink, putting the glass down.

"Don't overthink it, Grey. It was a mistake. It's not going to happen again. Even if she does mean something, it's nothing compared to what she means to you. I have other things I need to focus on."

"I want to kill you," he admits with a growl. "But I won't."

"How noble of you," I taunt, taking a deep breath to steady myself. "So, nothing in Arthur's office?"

Grey's face softens, a small smile appearing on his face. "We couldn't see anything. I was then distracted. I would prepare for some fallout in the morning."

I rub my forehead. "Grey... is there a dead body in his office?"

"Yes," he replies coolly. "And his desk will need replacing. He won't be pleased."

"When is he ever?"

He stalks over, swiping the bottle of bourbon off the bed. Popping off the cap, he takes a swig, sitting down next to me. "I've put Avery to bed. We had to detour so she could take a shower. I think you should call a meeting tomorrow."

I nod in agreement. "We'll do it at free time. I don't think this can wait. Tell everyone in the morning."

Grey stands, taking the bottle with him. "I'll do that." He pauses at the door, looking over his shoulder. "And Deadman? That conversation isn't finished yet. Don't fuck with her. I'll let it go this time, but if you do it again, you'll have a different war on your hands."

I linger around the facility, watching everyone carefully.

So far, the day has started like normal. No one has said anything about the events of last night. I expected Arthur to come barreling through my door this morning, but there was no sign of him.

It's eerily quiet and peaceful, not what I was expecting at all.

Everyone is either in their rooms or in their professional appointments—a few people passing by with guards as I wait by the library entrance for Grey.

When he arrives, we head inside for some privacy, sitting at the back of the room.

"The society is ready," he says, kicking his feet up onto the table. "We'll meet here at the start of free time."

"Good," I reply, leaning back in my seat. "Bring Avery and Ashwood too."

Grey's eyes narrow slightly but he just nods. "I'll grab her at free time. I believe she's with Dr. Markel at the moment and then has an appointment with that new asshole."

Movement out of the corner of my eye catches my attention, and I watch, bemused as Ashwood strolls into the library. He makes a beeline for us, and judging by the look on his face, he followed us in.

"What can I do for you?" I ask as he stops at the edge of the table.

The two other men exchange a glance, more pleasant than usual. I can't help but note that apparently Avery also has the skill of bringing peace—impressive when you consider the fact that it's between two of the most psychotic men in here.

"I'm waiting here for Avery. I'm not letting her out of my sight," Ashwood says casually, taking a seat.

I raise an eyebrow. "Aren't you meant to be in a session?"

"Aren't *you*?" he shoots back.

Laughing, I close my eyes. Theo Ashwood and myself are cut from the same cloth—and I can respect that.

All of us are meant to be in session or locked away, but we fight the system, because we know that they are just wasting their time. We don't need salvation—we'd rather slit our own throats than be subjected to that psychobabble bullshit.

"She with Elsher?" Grey asks Ashwood, who nods in reply.

"I'll grab her from the guard when she's out," he answers. "I don't trust anyone."

"For good reason," I snipe back.

The library door swings open with a bang, cutting me off. The three of us look over, my eyebrows lifting in surprise as

Christopher storms toward us. Grey rises from his seat, ready to grab him, but I hold my hand up, wanting to hear him out.

"Christopher," I greet. "Shouldn't you be working?"

He glances over at Theo. "Someone didn't turn up for their session—yet again."

"You can save your breath. I'm not interested," he replies firmly. "You can wait for your next patient and play with your dick for all I care."

Christopher turns his attention to me, appearing more frazzled than usual. "What the fuck did you do, Damon?"

I look at him innocently. "*I* haven't done anything. But go on then—elaborate for us."

"Arthur is going insane," he spits out. "They found the mutilated body of a guard in his office this morning."

My eyes shift to Grey, who just shrugs, answering casually. "He pissed me off."

Looking back to Christopher, I wave my hand around lazily. "You have your answer. Off you go."

"You don't understand," he says through clenched teeth. "You've just set things in motion. It's happening—*today*."

I raise an eyebrow, leaning forward. "What is?"

Christopher scoffs. "Don't play stupid with me, Damon. You know exactly what Arthur's plan is. You think you're the only one who does? I've known all along. That's why I tried to stop it."

Grey looks at me, concern etched on his face. "Dead-man..."

"What do you mean you tried to stop it?" I ask, curiosity getting the better of me. I always suspected that Christopher may have had an idea of the real secrets of Lilydale, but a bigger part of me figured he was here just to piss me off.

Christopher runs a hand through his hair, shaking his head. "Avery's been on Arthur's list for a while. And whatever you fucking did has pushed him over the edge."

"Get to your fucking point," I snap, getting frustrated.

He takes a breath, eyes darting between the three of us. "I'm the one who framed Avery. I had someone plant the staff card in her pocket."

The three of us fly out of our seats. Before I can stop him, Grey has Christopher by the throat, slamming him into a bookshelf.

"*You* fucking framed her?" he yells.

I walk over, putting my hand on Grey's shoulder. We can't afford another homicide right now. "Hold on a minute," I say to Grey, fury underlining my voice. "I want to hear him out first."

Christopher falls to his feet as Grey lets go, fists curled. My cousin straightens up, looking directly at me.

"I was trying to get her out of Lilydale," he says sharply. "That way Arthur and your father couldn't get to her. I knew she was a target."

Theo storms over, shoving my shoulder to get my attention. "What the hell is he talking about?"

My mind spins endlessly in circles, trying to make sense of Christopher's confession. We knew it was a possibility, but I assumed with Avery being close to Grey, they would go for someone easier.

I run my hand over my face, stepping back. "Fuck."

"Someone better tell me what the fuck is going on right now," Theo snaps.

Grey breathes heavily, trying to calm himself. His fists are shaking, desperate to hit something. "We need to find Avery—now."

I turn to Theo, realizing I have no choice but to tell him. We need everyone on board, and right now, we need his help too.

"My family owns the facility, Ashwood. They have a very generous financial contract in place with the government—human testing on mentally ill youths for scientific research. It's how they get the bulk of their money."

Theo stares at me, wild-eyed. "And they are planning on conducting science experiments on Avery? On all of us?"

I nod, glancing over at Grey. "We've managed to stop it the past few months, but they will be getting desperate. Charitable donations aren't enough to cover the maintenance costs to run this place. That's why I invented *Cirque des Morts*—to stop them."

"Where's Avery?" he spits out, looking at Christopher. "Where the fuck is she right now?"

Christopher looks at us with a troubled glance. "She's with Dr. Elsher, I believe."

Grey shoves him out of the way, heading toward the library doors. Theo and I quickly follow, Christopher tailing us.

As we barrel into the corridor, I spot Jillian, darting toward us with a panicked expression.

"Damon!" she shouts, skidding to a halt in front of me. "We've lost access to the cameras. Everything has gone offline. They've taken back control."

My stomach drops. I swing my head to look at Grey, trepidation on both of our faces. "Find her—right fucking now."

Chapter 33

Avery

I wake up, a storming cloud lingering over my head that rivals the one outside.

Last night was surreal. There's no other words to describe it.

I saw a side of Grey that I've never seen before—but I guess always knew was there.

Is that what Sam saw before his life was cut short? Is that the beast that lurks below the playful, flirty man I've grown to love?

The reason question is—*why am I unfazed by it?*

I'm no stranger to death. I've taken a life before, even if it was by accident. But to physically witness someone being murdered—no, tortured—is a sight I'll never forget.

It's conflicting, terrifying... yet at the same time, he was protecting me... protecting us.

Normal people would run screaming in the other direction, but I think it's become apparent that I'm not normal. Maybe I was in the past, before my life was subject to hatred and harm. I don't know who I was back then, I don't even remember it.

The few fleeting memories I have of better times were solely experienced with my mother and Paige. Any other happy times have been here at Lilydale, with people like Grey.

My Grey.

My monster and protector.

I was so terrified that he was going to leave when I told him about Damon. I was scared that I was going to rip them apart, disintegrating a brotherly bond. But I couldn't keep this from him. I've worked so hard to regain his trust. In return, he's made a huge effort to include Theo—like in the library.

A relationship has to go both ways, and I owed him the truth.

I just never expected *that* reaction from him.

By the time he dropped me back to my room, he was his usual happy self again. If he wasn't covered in blood, you'd never know that he had just brutally ended a life.

He fucked me in blood.

I wish I knew where the term cold-blooded came from because it's certainly not relatable to humans, no matter what people joke. It's warm, thick... and staining.

My bloodied clothes are shoved under my mattress, the evidence of our late night adventure. I have to figure out how to get rid of them, but I'm sure Grey will know what to do.

There's a knock on my door as a guard pushes it open, looking at me lazily as he gestures for me to follow him.

It's time for my appointments, and I follow suit, the guard leading me to Dr. Markel's office.

"Good morning, Ms. White!" he says happily, bouncing around.

I'll never get over how someone can be so energetic and carefree in the mornings, so content with life despite their surroundings.

I pop myself up on the examination table, muffling a yawn. "Morning."

Dr. Markel gives me a quick look-over before ducking into his office. I hear the key turn in the medicine cabinet, before he returns with a clear plastic bag, a white pill inside. I spot my name on a label, fixed to the front of it.

"Here's your slow release painkiller," he says, plucking open the bag to dump it into my palm.

I quickly throw it back into my mouth, taking a cup of water from him. Swallowing, I chuck the empty cup into the bin in the corner, wondering if I still have blood in my hair. I supposed even if I did, it wouldn't be overly noticeable, my jet-black hair hiding all my secrets.

The doctor scribbles some notes on a piece of paper, shoving them into a manila folder with my name on it. "As usual, let me know if you have any issues with pain," he says, waving me off as he hums *'Ring Around the Rosie'* to himself.

"Ring around the rosie. A pocket full of posies. Ashes... Ashes... We all fall down..."

I give him a brief nod, meeting the guard in the hallway as we head down to Dr. Elsher's room. I'm not keen on seeing that quack again, but I have little choice.

His doorway is open when we arrive, his stern face looking up from his desk, uninterested, as I walk in.

"Ms. White," he sighs. "Are we going to make any progress today?"

"You tell me," I mumble, flinging myself into the chair across from his desk.

Dr. Elsher shakes his head, making a note in my file. "Uncooperative, as usual."

"Maybe you could try being less of an asshole," I suggest. "I don't really vibe well with that."

He ignores me, raising an eyebrow as he makes another note.

We sit in silence, my arms folded as I wait for him to speak. Finally, he looks up, putting his pen down.

"Frankly, Ms. White, I don't believe you have the capabilities for successful therapy."

"So, you're saying I'm incurable."

"I'm saying," he says a little louder. "That until you *want* to be helped, you're going to remain as you are."

My eyes narrow on him. "What's wrong with who I am?"

"Tell me—do you have any remorse for your father's death?" he asks, blindsiding me.

"Of course I do," I sputter. "I think that was made clear in my notes with Dr. Smith and from the court documents."

Dr. Elsher leans back in his chair. "Dr. Smith didn't make excessive notes about your sessions. Most of your initial sessions very little was discussed. It appears he only really targeted your mental health, not the actions that led you here."

I raise an eyebrow, annoyed. "*Obviously* I'm here because I accidentally killed my father while attempting to take my own life. The whole event is the reason for my mental health."

"Is it?" he snorts. "I'm going to assume because of your childhood you already had these mental illnesses. I'd say they very much contributed to your father's death."

I clench my teeth, trying my best to remain composed. "That's a very clever observation, Doctor. Of course it was linked—did you not just hear me? I was trying to kill myself."

"With a fire though?" he questions, scoffing at me. "What made you decide on that? Because surely a reasonable person would expect that a fire would have the possibility of inflicting harm upon others. Most people who commit suicide opt for different methods such as asphyxiation, exsanguination, or unloading a bullet into a main organ. Most of these methods would be far quicker, less painful, and without the risk of harming others."

I stare at him, angry at his audacity. He's known me for a short amount of time, and already he thinks he knows me better than I know myself.

He's trying to insinuate that I intentionally killed my father.

Nothing to do with the fact that my house—the same one I found my dead mother in, the same one I received all my abuse and torture—was the catalyst. I wanted to escape, I wanted to leave.

And most of all, I wanted to burn those memories to ash. If the house was gone, then no one would ever have to suffer abuse inside those walls again.

Once I was dead, my father would just find someone else to torment and hurt. He'd lure someone in, repeating the cycle like he did with my mother and I.

My father had no job, very little money. His biggest asset was that house, and I wanted to take that away from him so he couldn't use it as a weapon.

Those walls were painted with my screams, embedded into the gyprock like muscle memory. I deserved to have the final say in what happened with that house.

I knew I was going to suffer. I knew that the fire would burn me alive. But at the time, I didn't care. Whatever pain I suffer at the end, I was ready to accept, because it was no match for the mental torture I was living with. It would end eventually, returning me to the earth from which I came.

"Some people kill others before they kill themselves," I point out. "I didn't plan to do that."

Dr. Elsher lifts an eyebrow. "Why didn't you seek help? According to the court documents, there is no reference to you seeking help from any professionals."

"What professionals?" I argue. "I wasn't allowed to go to the doctor because we didn't have insurance. The few times I was taken to the emergency room, it was obvious that I was being abused. What sane person would pull shards of glass out of someone's back and assume it was there by accident? What sick and twisted person would look at my bleeding intimate parts, surmising that I'd had normal intercourse? They all had their chance to report it, but if they did, nothing was ever done. The people with authority had opportunities to pull me out of that house, but no one ever came."

"But did *you* seek help?" he asks again. "No—you left people to assume. In fact, one of the hospital reports indicated that you stated you fell and injured yourself."

I gawk at him, bewildered. "What about women in domestic violent relationships? They often lie too, terrified that their abuser will hurt them more for trying to tell the truth. Sometimes they get murdered trying to escape."

"I think the truth is you kept it to yourself because you thought you deserved it—so you accepted it."

For once, he's not completely far from the truth. I was so beaten down, my soul broken and crushed, that I did often believe I deserved the abuse. But I know now that I was wrong—no one deserves that.

"I was trained to believe that," I say quietly. "But I deserved better. I deserve to be happy and loved."

He looks at me with a bored expression. "While you might believe that now, you still don't want to heal yourself. From what I'm told, you're too focused on having others heal you. I assume that's why you are dating multiple people. Do you think you're too much for any one person to handle on their own?"

It's like a slap in the face. He might as well have gut punched me, painting a picture in my head that can't be unseen.

Is that why I want to love them both? Is that why I let Damon kiss me?

The more people that want me, the more I will believe that I'm worthy?

I didn't kiss Damon back at first, but I didn't stop him straight away either. And while the whole situation had shocked me, sending me into a moment of frozen confusion, I think I kissed him back for a split second.

Damon would be the ultimate validation. He hated me so much that I wanted him to like me. I told myself it was because of Grey—I wanted his best friend to like me. But now... I'm not so sure.

If I could make someone who hates me change their mind about me, it would start to undo all the words and damage my father did. It would prove that I was likable—loveable—after all.

I go to open my mouth to speak, trying to figure out words to respond, but my head starts to spin. I rub my temple, closing my eyes to get a grip on myself, but when I open them again, the room is still fuzzy.

There's two Dr. Elshers sitting at the desk, swaying from left to right. I can't see straight, things quickly losing focus.

Sounds start to muffle like underwater noises, and I faintly register a knock.

"Is she ready?" a voice asks.

Someone walks in front of me, kneeling down to look at me face-to-face.

"Ms. White, how are you feeling?" Mr. Whittingham asks coldly.

"It's... woozy," I slur. "What's happening?"

His blue eyes scan my face before he turns away, nodding to someone by the door.

"Take Ms. White to the lab. The doctors are waiting for her."

Book Three – Ravage

Pre-order book three RAVAGE

Here Lies War and Bloodshed

Stalk the Author

FB Readers Group - Steph Macca's Asylum for Pectoral Perves

https://www.facebook.com/groups/authorstephmacca

Instagram

https://www.instagram.com/authorstephmacca/

TikTok

https://www.tiktok.com/@authorstephmacca

Facebook

www.facebook.com/authorstephmacca/

Online Store

www.stephmacca.com

Other Books by Steph Macca

DANCE WITH MY DEMONS SERIES

(Unhinged, Echoes, Ravage)

ALL TOO WELL

THE LIES WE KEEP SERIES

(Vicious Games, Pretty Savages, Recklessly Damaged, Sweet Anarchy)

THE BLACK SPADES SERIES

(King of Spades, Queen of Fire, Aces and Ashes, The Hunter)

THE CHRONICLES OF MAXWELL DUET

(A Day of Ruin, A Day of Chaos)

MIDNIGHT PSYCHOS TRILOGY

(Ruthless Savages, Ruthless Redemption, Ruthless Reign)

WICKEDLY SWEET

SLEIGH

BEAUTIFUL DECEPTIONS & SWEET MISERIES

ANATOMY OF A KILLER

RAYNE